Rebecca's

Robert Hart, born in 1945, grew up with his family in the East End of London.

He became a teacher, dedicated to helping children be creative and self-fulfilled and earned a reputation as a pioneer of child-centred education.

After becoming a head teacher and then a Government Education Adviser, Robert and his wife founded their own education social enterprise company, Intuitive Media, which has encouraged hundreds of thousands of children around the world to make new friends, share their interests and learn together – winning a dozen major education awards including the BAFTA, for their pioneering work.

Hart's first novel is based on his East End childhood.

Dedication

This is for:

Carol, my sister (lost and then found) and Jacqueline (wherever you may be);

My children Peter, Caryl and Sam and their children – to answer some of their questions.

Acknowledgements

I would like to thank all the people who encouraged and helped me to tell this story:

Carole Fletcher – my wife, best friend, best critic, editor and my inspiration.

Barry Craig, Alan Black and Denis Nyman – dear friends from 1956.

My Aunt Lillian and all the Aunts and Uncles who have now passed away – for their stories, love and care over many years.

My cousins – for sharing a childhood.

Ken Marsden for his memories.

Ben Fletcher, Karen Pine, Helen Fletcher, Glyn & Chris Holt, Eileen Devonshire, Leslie Holstrom, Pat & Stuart Smith, Terri Golightly, Alice and Rick Lee-Overton, Holly Owen and Lynn Owen – for being critical friends.

Suzanne Tucker – for the cover photo and Shutterstock.com for their excellent service.

In fond and loving memory of Rebecca and Daniel Hart and their children, including Sylvia – for all the gifts they gave me.

Robert Hart

Rebecca's Secrets

What happens when a boy starts asking questions?

Rebecca's Secrets
Published by Lulu.com 2009
ISBN 978-1-4092-5593-2
Copyright © Robert Hart 2009
The moral right of the author has been asserted.

All rights reserved. No part of this book may be reproduced in any form or by any means without permission in writing from the publisher, except by a reviewer who may quote brief passages in a review.

This book is sold subject to the condition that it shall not by way of trade or otherwise, be lent, resold, hired out, or otherwise circulated without the publisher's prior consent in any form of binding or cover other than that in which it is published and without a similar condition including this condition being imposed on the subsequent purchaser.

A creation of Little Angel Press
QuerQuay, Britannia Crossing, Bridge Road,
Kingswear-on-Dart, Devon, TQ6 0DZ, United Kingdom.
www.littleangelpress.com
robert.hart@littleangelpress.com

Cover Image © Suzanne Tucker. Used under license from www.shutterstock.com

Set in Garamond
V.5.4

Rebecca's Secrets

Contents

PROLOGUE	11
PART 1: A CURIOUS BOY	13
Out of the Shadows	15
Rebecca's Secrets	17
The Silver Box	27
Rebecca's Lies	33
Running Away	39
Tell the Girls Their Daddy Loves Them	51
The King and Queen Were Drinking Gin	57
Deceiving Mrs. Green	61
Mrs. Levy Loses her Head	69
The Lone Ranger and the Bedspring War	73
Saturday Night	77
Fear of Dark and Vermin	89
Ring of Silence	93
The Tower Hill Mob	101
The Invasion of Eric Street	113
PART 2: LOST BABIES	121
In the Forest	123
Hannah's Secrets	137
Best and Borrowed Clothes	145
All Our Fathers	151
Sylvia's Secrets	161
Malinski's Alphabet	171
Getting an Education	182
Old William Walking	196
Sylvie's Last Letters	205
Into The Smog	215
Surprise in Wentworth Mews	221
The Blind Beggar	227
The Tunnel of Death	239
Granddad Comes Home Late	245
EPILOGUE	251

PROLOGUE

A few years ago, after visiting friends in Vancouver, my wife, Carole and I caught a ferry to Orcas – one of British Columbia's beautiful Gulf Islands. After a day's exploring we settled into our hotel and took dinner in the restaurant. I finished the meal with a wonderfully rich chocolate pudding.

Walking back to our room, I felt a little strange. My head was spinning. My vision was distorted at the periphery, like looking through a glass tube.

Carole asked, "What's wrong?" and I said, "Where are we?"

Over the next few minutes it became clear that something was wrong with my memory. I knew who Carole was, but I had no clear recollection of anything prior to the last few hours. I knew I lived in a village in another country but I didn't know the name of the village or even the country. I knew I had three children, but I couldn't remember their names. I couldn't count from one to five and I couldn't spell anything. My words came out wrong. I called the sea *birdsong* and car park was a *parrot camp*. We vacillated between fascination at the weird incongruence of my language and fear of the possibility of a permanent wipeout of my past life.

After two hours my memory and language returned. It was a huge relief, but the experience shook me.

Just imagine if you lost your past forever and forgot what made you, what drives and inspires you. Imagine losing all that personal history – your childhood and growing up, all the people who touched you, hurt you, helped you and loved you. Imagine losing everything and everyone that contributed to who you are.

We learned later it was a migraine attack – just a foggy interlude. But worried that the fog might return and obscure the past again, I decided to write down some of this life, so if I ever lose my memory again I'll know where to find it.

How do you begin to write a life? I soon realized the blindingly obvious – that you can't, because all memory is fiction. So I've let this story become a fiction containing a great deal of truth. It's about Tommy Angel, a boy like me growing up where I did in the East End of London in the Fifties, with a family like mine and friends like mine who had adventures just like we did. It's about a curious boy who started to ask questions and shine a light on the dark mysteries of his childhood.

- *Robert Hart, Kingswear-on-Dart, Devon, UK, 1st June 2009.*

Rebecca's Secrets

PART 1: A CURIOUS BOY

Out of the Shadows

On 1ˢᵗ January 1956. After weeks of snow, sleet and fog, the first sun of the New Year cut across Eric Street, burning light into the cold shadows. It crept inch by inch, probing one dark place, then the next.

I'd just turned eleven. I don't remember much about the previous year or the three years before that in the Home. That was another life, like a story about someone else.

Until this day I'd lived unaware. I didn't live my life – it lived me. But I did know I was different from other kids. There was something different about me and my family.

That morning I became curious.
That day I started asking questions.
That week I opened a box full of dark family secrets.
That year I found out who I was.

Rebecca's Secrets

"Missed me. Hit the lamppost!" I lied.

The ball hit my thigh and bounced straight back to Larry. I rubbed the stinging red patch on my leg and hobbled across the street to Viv.

It was freezing cold. The pavement was covered by two inches of hard-packed snow. Long icicles hung from the lampposts, smaller ones dripped from the railings.

Eric Street runs south from the Mile End Road – the main artery from the East End to the City of London. That's where I lived with my Gran, my Granddad (who I called Dad) and Uncle Vinny.

Viv and I huddled together by Mrs. Levy's railings.

Most of London's railings had been taken away and melted for guns for the war, but ours were still intact. Granddad said it was too dangerous to take them from Eric Street because all the drunks would come rolling home from the Wentworth on pay day, and fall down Kutchinski's airee.

Larry aimed at my legs again and I grabbed the railings and swung my feet into the air. The ball bounced off my bum.

"Hit the railings!" I lied again.

Larry scrabbled for the ball, slipped on the ice and landed on his back. Viv danced over him.

"Can't catch me – couldn't catch a flea."

She was only ten and small for her age, but she was tough and a lot faster than any of the boys.

Larry, still on his back aimed at Viv. He missed. The ball whizzed past her ears and straight at me. I punched it high in the air. We all gaped as it hung at the top of its flight, and watched it fall into Mrs. Levy's airee. It glanced off her basement windowsill, bounced off the airee wall and hit the lower windowpane dead centre. A crack zipped diagonally across the glass as the ball dropped to the airee floor.

All the terraced houses on the evens side of the street had bay-windowed sitting rooms at ground level and a basement with an open airee protected by the railings. Our footballs and tennis balls often fell into neighbours' airees. Usually we'd ask if we could get the ball and perhaps tidy their airees while we were down there. We knew who would say yes: Mrs. Bresslaw and Mrs. Kutchinski – who was always smiling and Errol's mum, Mrs. White.

Mrs. Kutchinski had the biggest grin in the East End. We'd clear the litter passers-by had dropped and she'd give us bread and dripping.

Mrs. Bresslaw liked us to water her basement window boxes. She gave us orange juice and potato latkes and handed out photos of her son Bernie who was on the telly. For some reason she called me "Poor Tommy" and while we'd stuff ourselves on her doorstep, she'd mumble "Poor lost babies. Poor lost babies." and shake her head. We thought she was mad, but she made good latkes.

Mrs. White gave us crispy spicy things that burned your mouth. Larry took one home for his dog Prince. The dog swallowed it whole and charged round the house yelping. We always said "Thanks, Mrs. White – we'll save them for later." and we gave them to kids we didn't like.

If a ball fell into a grumpy neighbour's airee, we didn't ask – we just climbed over for it. Sometimes we got caught, but we usually got away with apologies or lies – like today.

"Quick. Get the ball," Viv said, "before Old Levy finds out or we'll be for it! Do it quiet!"

I climbed over Mrs. Levy's railings, hung down as low as I could, pushed away from the wall and dropped the last two feet. There was just the quietest "pling" as my plimsoles hit the ground.

I heard a loud "whoosh" behind me as Mrs. Levy pushed the window up. It stuck about halfway. She parted the lace, bent down and stuck her head out.

"Sorry, Mrs. Levy," I said, "I did knock on your door three times, honest, Mrs. Levy, but there was no answer and I knew Mr. Levy was at the shop and I thought you must've had a bad night with your rheumatism and I didn't want to wake you up."

Mrs. Levy squeezed an arm out and waved a skinny finger at me. "You know God sees everything, Tommy Angel, and punishes dirty little boys who get into sin and mischief!"

I glanced at the cracked pane above her head and then at the sky and I held my breath and waited for the window to shatter or for God to strike me down. It was the first blue sky in ages, even bluer against the white of the snowy rooftops. The clouds were small and puffy, flying fast. It made me dizzy to look. I waited.

The last time I'd waited for God's punishment, I was five – in the Muller Home. I had the mumps and had to stay in the dorm on my own. I was bored and tore a page from Mosey Abraham's Big Picture Bible and made a paper plane from the Story of Ruth. Too late I realized what I'd done – desecrated God's Holy Word. I knew He would strike me dead on the spot. I curled up in a tight ball on my bed and waited for the lightning bolt, but nothing happened.

Nothing happened. There was no crash of glass, no thunder and no lightning. He didn't strike me down.

"Well, boy?" Mrs. Levy said, "Well?"

"Huh?" I stalled for time. I was thinking – I'm still here. No lightning. So... either God doesn't exist after all – or He isn't all-seeing-all-knowing-all-powerful like I'd been told, or perhaps He's having a lie-in this morning. Or perhaps cracked windows don't count as sins – only smashed ones. Perhaps He's seen me do it but He isn't angry and vengeful like He's supposed to be. Perhaps He doesn't mind boys having a bit of fun. Anyway Mrs. Levy was wrong – they all were. Perhaps God's a mate.

"Well, boy? What have you got to say for yourself?"

The back of Mrs. Levy's neck was pressed against the window frame and I thought any moment a triangle of broken glass would fall and slice off her head.

"Want us to clear some of this rubbish, Mrs. Levy?" I asked, waving my arm over a pile of soggy newspapers and rags.

"Cheeky bugger." She shook her head but reached back into her pinny and held out a three-penny bit.

"Go on then – might as well do something useful, but thruppence is all you get." She withdrew her head and reached up to close the window.

"Mrs. Levy. Be..." Before I could finish she slammed the window shut. "... careful!"

I was sure it would shatter. But it held.

I found the ball, stuffed it in my pocket and started throwing the old papers up to Viv and Larry. I wanted to do a good job for Mrs. Levy to make up for the cracked window and after ten minutes we'd cleared most of the rubbish. I lifted some sacking and a mouse ran out making me jump and drop the sack.

"Got anything?" Viv asked.

I lifted the sack again gingerly.

"Got a box."

"Bring it up."

Viv and Larry made a sled from a sack. We piled on the rubbish and dragged it across the road to the bomb site opposite Gran's house. We squatted in the snow and I opened the cardboard box.

"Cor. A gas mask!" Viv said.

We'd cleared out plenty of airees and sometimes we'd find treasures like this. Most of it we flogged for a few pence or swapped with other kids, but we hid the best stuff in Gran's air-raid shelter. We already had a gas mask, lots of bike parts, a scrapbook of hand-coloured photos of people with orange faces on green elephants in India, and some live rifle bullets in a biscuit tin.

"Wannit?" I said, offering it to Viv.

"Can I?" She asked, eyes wide.

"Go on." Larry said. "You can wear it when your brother farts."

We'd never seen Viv's older brother. He was always away at work, but thanks to Viv stories, his farts were legendary for their volume and fruitiness.

There was a notice glued under the box lid. It was stained and faded but I could read a bit.

"Here's instructions" I said, *"How to fit the respirator."*

"Done it!"

Viv had already pulled the mask over her face and buckled the straps behind her head. She looked like a space monster with two big round eyeballs and a snout like a tin of beans with holes in the end.

She said, "Hummmm umm ummmmm umm ummm."

Larry stuck out his bum and pretended to fart. Viv clutched her throat, dying from the fumes. Soon we were rolling in the snow and giggling uncontrollably, until we all lay flat and weak under the speeding sky.

"I've got an idea." I said, "Come with me."

We ran across the road to Gran's. I threw the ball down the airee. It landed on the huge pile of rubbish that came halfway up the basement window. Larry and Viv climbed down and pretended to search for the ball. Viv, pushed rubbish away with both arms like a deep sea diver doing breast stroke, saying "Hummmm ummmmm umm ummm um."

I jumped up the steps, pushed the street door open and shouted for Gran. I waited while she slowly negotiated the dark passage, puffing and grumbling. She walked with a stick and her knees were a long way apart so she rocked her whole weight slowly from side to side, like a big ship on a swollen sea.

First to break into the sharp sunlight was her paisley pinafore inflated by an ample belly and bosom. Then the light caught her nose, her glasses, her knitted brows, and her turned-down mouth. She squinted in the glare and shaded her eyes with her free hand.

"Now what do you want?" she asked, as if I had made her sail that stormy passage a dozen times already.

Her face was severe, with a fixed frown and a lower lip pushed up in the middle and down at the corners like Churchill's fight-them-on-the-beaches face. It was a mask of disapproval.

She was called Rebecca, but she wasn't like Rebecca in the bible who was beautiful and hospitable. No, she seemed to be always grumpy and critical and she was impossible to please – I had tried for years. Nothing was right. Whatever I did, she would say I was lazy, thoughtless and forgetful. Mostly she called me *meshugener* – crazy or *luftmensh* – a dreamy head-in-the-clouds.

It wasn't just me; she had a bad word for everyone in the family – usually in Yiddish. Her children were all ungrateful. Aunt Hannah was stuck up; Aunt Miriam was a *klogmuter* – a misery; Aunt Stella was conniving; Uncle Samuel was a *shmegegi* – a clown; Uncle Solomon was a *kolboynik* – a know-it-all and Vinny was *toig ahf kapores* – good-for-nothing.

The in-laws were all unworthy. Aunt Marlene was flighty. Aunt Nina was *draikop* – scatterbrained. Uncle Arthur was *grober* – an oaf and Aunt Hannah's Harry was *alter kaker* – an old fart.

The neighbours didn't escape her judgment. Mrs. Bresslaw was toffee-nosed because her boy was on the telly; Mrs. Kutchinski was filthy; Mrs. Levy was *yachneh* – a loud mouth gossip. Mrs. White merited extra malice because she was a foreigner and a *swartzer*, and her house was painted daft colours and she left rubbish around and gave the street a bad name. The rest of the street were *ganef* – rogues, rascals and thieves.

"Well... what do you want, *luftmensh*?"

As she glared down from the top step, I realized that she looked and sounded just like Gilbert Harding – that grumpy old man on *What's My Line*. He always looked like he was about to do a big burp. He did an advertisement *"I have indigestion but I don't suffer from it."*

"Have you got indigestion, Gran?"

"What?" Her frown deepened into a scowl – which was normally enough to shut me up. But not today. Today was different.

"Why do you always look so grumpy, Gran?"

I took a step back. God had let me off this morning for two little lies to Larry and Mrs. Levy's potential manslaughter, but Gran was more formidable than the Almighty, less forgiving, closer and quicker to anger. She raised her stick and shook it at me.

"I can't help what I look like. You were born with a smile on your face, Tommy Angel, and you don't have a care in the world. I was born into hardship and pain and my life has been filled with worry and heartache and that's what's written over my face and there's nothing I can do about it."

So, I thought, it's not all my fault then! Gran was born miserable – nothing to do with me. It was… a sickness, like indigestion. She was born grumpy and she got grumpier, so… no matter how I tried – and I did try – I would never-ever be able to do anything right. She told me off all the time, made me feel guilty, ashamed – whatever I said, whatever I did, but I couldn't possibly be bad *all* the time.

So, I thought, it can't be me – it must be her – it's just her way of being in the world. From that day, although she gave me plenty of headaches with her constant complaints, I never took her so seriously again and I mostly ignored her judgments. I decided God could be my judge, and, as I found out that morning, God was a mate. He didn't strike me dead down Mrs. Levy's airee, so He probably liked boys, and if I did anything *really* bad, He'd let me know.

"Our ball's down the airee, Gran." I said.

"So, now you want me to climb down and get it for you?" she shrugged and opened her hands, palms up looking to God for sympathy.

"No, course not, but we can't find it in the rubbish. What if we clear the rubbish out?"

"There's no rubbish down there. I don't keep rubbish. Its just things that'll come in handy – one day." She said.

Gran would win the prize for the most things-that'll-come-in-handy-one-day in the street. It wasn't just our stuff – people walking by would throw their rubbish on top of ours – newspapers, old comics, sweet wrappers and fag ends. The mountain of rubbish had been there for years and I thought there must be some treasures buried in that pile. I'd often ask if I could clear it, but she always said no.

I told her there were rats in the airee, but she didn't believe me.

"Honest, Gran, Ronny Needleman saw a rat when he came round the other day. He said it was brown, about a foot long, with a long tail."

"No," she said, "We don't have rats. I keep my house spotless. That boy Ronny exaggerates."

She was right – Ronny did exaggerate. In fact he told bloody great lies and boasted much of the time, but this time he was telling the truth.

"But Gran, I *know* there's rats. I can hear 'em."

I slept in the basement and I heard the rats at night, in the coal cupboard or scrabbling in the airee, scratching at the window. They made a different noise to mice.

"You're just imagining things like you always do. Half your life you live inside your head. There's nothing in that airee and I don't want you poking around down there. No. You leave it be."

She turned to Viv and Larry. "Get your ball and get out." She said flatly,

"But Gran!"

"Don't you 'But Gran' me. If I let you do it you'll only fall down, break your leg and I'll have to take you up the hospital and I'll be in trouble with the Welfare."

Now that wasn't fair. I was a good climber – best in the street. In the Muller I used to climb right to the very top of the tallest trees, way above everything. I was skinny and light and I could lie back on the thinnest branches and look up at the clouds, like I was in heaven and let the wind sway me side to side. I'd stay there for hours, missing meals and lessons, until the teachers noticed and sent a kid to look for me.

"But I'm a good climber."

"I said no, Tommy and that's it! Why don't you listen? I don't understand why do you want to go digging up this old stuff! I don't want boys digging!"

She turned away grumbling towards the dark passage. "That boy. Won't leave things alone. *Meshugener*! Always digging – asking questions. Why, God, did you give me a boy like Tommy Angel? I swear he'll be the death of me with his digging and questions.

She was right. I was always asking questions – mostly about her and Granddad. Although I lived with them my whole life, I knew nothing about them. I asked her what her life was like when she was young and where she went to school and what lessons she did. I asked about the war and what it was like when Granddad and my uncles went away to fight Rommel and she was left here alone with the Blitz. But she never answered and if I persisted, she would snap and shout at me, "That's the past. What does it matter?"

I wanted to know about the family. I asked what her parents were like and where her grandparents and great grandparents came from and what they did for a living and why we were called Angels. I asked about my aunts and uncles and my cousins and why they mostly lived far away and only came to visit on Saturdays, while Mrs Kutchinski's children and grandchildren all lived around Mile End, and why I lived with her and Granddad, and why I didn't have a mother and a father and live with them, like all my cousins and most of my friends did. But she never answered. She would just glare at me and shout, "Children! All they bring is heartache." and she'd turn her head away and if I persisted, she'd shout some more "Stop asking your bloody questions!" and sometimes Granddad would hear and come into the room and say,

"Steady on, Becky, the boy's only curious. It's only natural."

"Too bloody curious!" she'd say and she'd thunder out of the room.

Eventually I realized I never got answers and I noticed how after Gran blew her top, she would go quiet and look sad for the rest of the day, and I felt bad about that, so I stopped asking questions.

But today was a new day of a new year and the sun was shining and the sky was blue and God was on my side and I was in the mood for digging and asking questions – if not now, then later.

Viv and Larry had climbed out of the airee. "Gotta go", Viv said, "Mum'll kill me if I'm late for dinner." and she skipped off. Larry followed her.

"OK see you."

Larry gave me the thumbs up. The diver nodded, gestured OK and swam off towards home. I stood and watched them until Viv knocked on her street door and her Mum came out with a big smile, hooked Viv under her arms, lifted her off her feet and swung her inside and I watched Larry disappear from view down the end of Eric Street and round the corner into Ropey Street.

I know my Gran loved me, but she never bothered if I was late for dinner, or even if I didn't turn up. She never asked me where I was going when I played out, and sometimes I went on adventures for a whole day, sometimes over the other side of London and came back after dark and she never asked me where I'd been. I loved the freedom it gave me, but I felt it might sometimes be nice to go home to someone like Viv's Mum.

A few weeks later, on Monday, after tea I told Gran I was going out to play. She didn't say anything or look up from her knitting. I grabbed my gabardine raincoat and woolly scarf and ran across the road to find Viv and Larry. They were in a corner of the debris, sitting on an orange box under a tent made from a pair of doors. They'd lit a small fire, in front of their tent, in a grate we'd made from bricks and a discarded oven grille.

Viv was holding her head in the smoke to see if the gas mask worked. It didn't. She threw herself back coughing. It looked like she was choking to death. I reached out to rip the mask off but she pushed me away. Her coughing turned to laughter. She was OK.

Larry was fiddling with his mum's tranny, which he borrowed every Monday so we could listen to Journey into Space. While he was trying to find the Light Programme, I told them my plan. We would do Gran's airee on Tuesday morning after Granddad, Vinny and the lodgers had gone to work. Gran would be round Great Aunt Betty's, helping with her greengrocery on Hamlets Way. The whole house would be empty and she wouldn't find out who cleared the airee. If she asked we'd say it was the council vermin people.

"What do you think?" I asked

Viv said "Huuuum ummmm."

Larry said. "Shuttup. Nearly half-seven! Wait...I got it! Yea, OK, we'll do it tomorrow. Listen."

"The BBC presents Jet Morgan in Journey into Space."

The opening music induced instant fear. We huddled together in the dark. We didn't want to miss one single moment of the very last episode of *The World in Peril*.

It was gripping stuff. The Martians were planning to invade the Earth thirty years in the future in 1986. Their leader had been trying to recruit Jet Morgan and the crew of the Discovery to his side. He told them that men were poisoning the planet with smoke from the factories and it would destroy the Earth. He told them that one day all the people would be hypnotized by televiewers. I'd told Uncle Vinny about that and he said it was all nonsense, but we believed it was true. We liked Lemmy best because he was played by Alfie Bass who was in the Army Game with Mrs Bresslaw's son Bernie, so he was sort-of related. Last week Jet, Lemmy, Doc and Mitch were in deep trouble. Larry and Viv couldn't wait to find out what had happened, but only half my mind was listening to the radio – the other half was planning a dig.

The Silver Box

Tuesday morning, before Granddad, Vinny and the lodgers went to work and Gran left for Great Aunt Betty's, I ran round to Ropery Street and called for Larry.

He couldn't come out. He was in trouble for busting his mum's radio and dropping a plate of cornflakes. Larry was big boned and well muscled – not skinny like me. Everything about him was long – long face, long neck, long legs, long arms and big hands. His mum, Joan, said he was growing too fast. He tripped over his own legs. He was really good at breaking things. He could do it without trying.

Larry called his mum by her first name, so the rest of us could too. It was strange and felt disrespectful, but she didn't mind. Maybe it was because she was young, and they lived alone. They had no one else to talk to, so they used their proper names. She was a small woman and, even at eleven, Larry was taller by a foot. She had to look up to tell him off but she made up for her size by shouting very loudly and poking him in the chest.

"Larry, I've had just about enough (poke) of your soddin' clumsiness (poke). You can just stay in today (poke) and clean the whole (poke) bloody place (poke) to make up for it. I want to see it all (poke) done (poke) by the time I get in (poke) from work." She swept out slamming the street door behind her.

Two seconds later she opened the door again, grabbed Larry, hugged him and kissed him on the cheek. "Bye-bye, my Daaaarling Boy." she sang and slid out.

"Bye-bye, my Daaaarling Boy." I mimicked, and blew exaggerated kisses and laughed at Larry. But inside I was suffering a strange mixture of feelings. I was glad I didn't have a Mum who embarrassed me in front of my friends, but at the same time I wished I had someone who loved me enough to kiss me or even touch me.

"Aw shuddup!" Larry smudged Joan's lipstick into his cheek

"This'll take me all bloody day." He rubbed his wounded chest. He was very practical and capable, but he thought in straight lines.

"No it won't – five minutes. Come on."

I ran round the house moving the furniture, ornaments, pictures, everything, just a few inches from where they were. Larry looked puzzled, but shrugged and joined in. We shook the curtains, punched the cushions and ruffled the candlewick bedspreads. At last everything in Larry's house had been moved just a little.

As we ran off towards Eric Street trailing Larry's go-cart, he shouted, "Will it work?"

"Works on my Gran. I clean the house every week."

Before we started on the airee, I had to be sure Gran hadn't returned for something and Vinnie wasn't taking a sickie. I opened the street door and called, "Gran?" No answer. We tiptoed down the passage. I knocked on Gran and Granddad's bedroom door on the right. Most people in the street used the front room as a parlour, but because we had lodgers upstairs, Gran used the ground floor rooms as bedrooms. It smelled musty – like cinema seats. No, like Matron at the Muller.

The bay window was filled with a big feather bed with a mahogany headboard. Next to it, an upright piano, a row of family photos along the top and more nailed to the wall above – all Gran's living children with their spouses and all the grandchildren. Uncle Samuel and Aunt Nina and their five kids Lucy, Sam, Joey, Alice with baby Debbie propped up on a donkey on the beach at Southend – everyone laughing. Uncle Solomon, Aunt Marlene and their kids Connie and Sarah, looking proud, outside their new house in Brokesley Street. Aunt Hannah and Uncle Harry Diamond standing either side of Big Cousin Louie, who was named after dead Uncle Louis.

On the wall Aunt Miriam, looked miserable by Uncle Arthur who had a big cheeky grin, with Rita and Esther in front, all posing outside Great Aunt Betty's shop. Aunt Stella and Uncle Lionel with Jessica and Ellen looking bored having tea in their garden in Buckhurst Hill.

There was no photo of Vinny. Gran once told me, "I see him every day. I don't need a photo to remind me what a scruffy *toig ahf kapores* he is!" Vinny was the only living son who wasn't married – so he didn't count. Uncle Louis who died in the war was also missing and so was Poor Dead Katy. Dead people were kept downstairs.

I noticed a slightly cleaner rectangular patch on the wall between Aunt Miriam and Aunt Stella. Someone else was missing.

"Wow – a piano!" Larry said.

"Never been played." I said.

Lots of people in the street had pianos but no one could play. People sometimes dumped them on the debris when they needed the space. We would smash the beautifully polished and inlaid wooden cases and expose the strings and hit them with sticks to make Chinese music.

Gran's spare pink stays hung over a chair at the end of the bed. Larry picked them up, held them to his belly and danced the can-can.

"Come on, Laz!"

Half way down the passage, we crept up the stairs to the lodgers' rooms. On the way up I called, "Maurice, Ron, you there?" No answer.

On the top landing the lodgers had a kitchenette made of Formica units that fell off the back of Uncle Sammy's lorry. A door led to their front room. Larry peeped in. "No one here... Wow, look at this!"

They had a radiogram – a huge curvy mahogany thing as big as a sideboard, with a twin-speed automatic record changer in the middle that took a whole pile of 45s or 78s, a radio with big knobs and lots of dials and speakers built into each side.

"Lets see what they got." Larry rummaged through their 78s.

"Not now, Laz, we've got work to do."

The lodgers let me in their room to play music and it was a good place to hide from Gran who never went upstairs. I didn't want Larry breaking any of their records and risking my best hideout.

We ran downstairs to check Vinny's room. He sometimes took sickkies off work without telling anyone. "I'll do this, Laz. You do the scullery and yard."

I didn't want Larry to see Vinny's room – I thought it was a mess and smelled bad. Gran said it was because of his condition and he couldn't help it. Once I said I wished I had a condition and could get away with being so messy, but Gran said I should feel sorry for Vinny and that made me feel guilty. Today I didn't feel sorry or guilty – just ashamed. I knocked gently on the door and called, "Vinny, you in?". No answer. I held my nose, opened the door an inch and slammed it shut again.

"All clear!" I shouted.

"All clear!" Larry came in from the yard, and we both leaped down the basement stairs.

The back basement room was the kitchen. None of my mates had been in there. I threw my head in. It was dark and disgusting – layers of grease over everything, holes in the brown lino, tattered lace curtains draped in greasy cobwebs. It smelled of grease, piss and cockroaches. I was filled with deep shame. I slammed the door quickly.

"All clear!"

We burst into the front room – our sitting and dining room evenings and weekends, family party room on Saturday and my bedroom at night. It was dark. The whole room was lined with brown-painted wooden panels to shoulder height and peeling nicotine-thick wallpaper above. On the right wall, an ornate brown mahogany sideboard where fresh black coal dust settled after every delivery into the coal cupboard in the corner, and where grey ash from the fire settled during the rest of the week. Above it a row of family photographs including one of Dead

Uncle Louis – only 21 when he died in Italy – and beside him a photo of his grave and a framed message from the King.

"Gunner Louis Angel. 6969469, 81 Bty., 25Lt. A.A. Regt., Royal Artillery, gave his life for King and Country on Thursday, 10th December 1942."

Next to the sideboard was a brown mahogany fold-down dining table and chairs that hosted Saturday night's card games and Sunday dinner. To the left my put-u-up bed, folded back into a brown fabric settee with mousy holes gnawed in the arms. On the far wall, the fireplace with more family pictures above, and under the window a tattered brown armchair, slung with an untidy pile of my clothes.

The window overlooked the airee. The bottom half was obscured by rubbish; the top gave a view of the damp airee wall four feet away. A little light squeezed down from the street above.

"Oi, this is good," Larry said "You can look up girls frocks!"

"Come on, help me open the window."

It hadn't been opened for years. It was jammed with layers of paint. We shook and banged and managed to lower the top pane a little until it jammed on the rubbish outside. Larry was ready to climb out.

"Just a minute. Lets make sure everybody's out." I banged at the coal cupboard door.

"What are you doing?"

"Giving Ratty a chance to scarper." I joked about it, but the rats scared me. I had to sleep with them every night.

Larry was too big to get through the gap in the window, so I told him to go upstairs and climb down from above. I could easily squeeze through. In fact I was so thin Uncle Vinnie said I was the original "seven stone weakling" in the Charles Atlas adverts.

Mr. Atlas guaranteed that if you tried his *Dynamic Tension* system for just seven days, he would turn you into a New Man. I didn't dare send off the coupon for his book, *Everlasting Health and Strength – Free on Approval*, in case Gran opened the parcel first and I'd have to explain what it was. So instead I invented my own Dynamic Tension method. Every day I'd pump my hands together as if squeezing a ball, hoping it would improve the strength and size of my chest. I'd grab my right wrist with my left hand and alternately push and pull with all my strength to grow my triceps and biceps. I did it for seven days. Nothing. I gave up and resigned myself to being a weakling.

I climbed through and passed rubbish up to Larry who hung inside the railings and lobbed it over to the pavement. Then we piled it on his go-cart and dumped it on the debris.

Among the piles of rotting wood, soggy cushions and disgusting wet masses of unidentifiable grot, we found a whole armchair and we commandeered the cushions for our camp. Under the chair I found a flat square box – white with a silvery floral pattern and something white inside. It was lacy, folded carefully. It was a wedding veil. Despite being near the bottom of the rubbish it was perfectly clean – like it had never been worn.

On the back of the box was a scribble *Sylv Angel 44*. It said Angel so it must be something to do with the family, although I couldn't work out what *Sylv* meant. Perhaps it was short for silver.

I also found a framed photo wrapped in brown wrapping paper. It was a pretty girl, about four years old. It was hand-coloured. She wore a red velvet dress with a white scalloped collar. She had blond hair in ringlets, blue eyes and a big wide smile. I didn't know who she was. Perhaps she was Poor Dead Katy. I ran off and hid it with the veil in the air-raid shelter in the back yard. We'd look at it properly another day.

We found some damp comics, which we hung to dry over the railings. We told any kids who passed by they could have one if they helped, and soon we had the whole gang – Davy, Ronny, Viv and Errol.

Davy modeled himself on Dennis the Menace. He was big and loud and dangerous. He enjoyed shouting, so he gave the orders.

Ronny never got his hands dirty. If we were the Bash Street Kids, then he was a chubby Lord Snooty. He appointed himself lookout, in case any adults came along, and, so we wouldn't think he was totally lazy, he also took charge of light entertainment. He fulfilled this roll by leaning over the wall and doing The Goons and Journey Into Space. The natural echo in the airee helped with the sound effects.

Viv was energetic and quick, like a squirrel digging for nuts. She stood on the pile of rubbish and grabbed the smaller items from between her legs and swung them over her head, high in the air in a single movement. Most of them fell back to the airee, but after a while, she realized why rubbish was falling on her head and changed her trajectory, so the rubbish landed in the street. From that moment she worked at a furious pace.

Errol was eager to prove his value. He ran all over the road catching Viv's flying rubbish and piled it on the go-cart. Larry, Davy and I handled the larger things and collected the treasure.

By four o'clock we had the airee clear. Most of it – that is. We'd found nine coal sacks among the rubbish. Larry wanted to throw them, but I had other plans. We folded them in half and made a neat and conspicuous pile right in the middle of the otherwise empty airee.

"Why we doing this, Tommy?" Larry asked.

"Come round tomorrow at ten and you'll find out."

We shared out the leftover comics, bike parts and other swappable stuff just as a wave of black cloud swallowed the sun. The temperature dropped, the wind came up and it began to snow.

When Gran came home from Great Aunt Betty's, it was dark. She didn't look into the airee and even if she had, it was too dark to see what we'd done.

That night as I turned out the light and sat on the edge of my put-u-up bed, I had something on my mind – the little blond girl in the photo. Was it Katy, Gran's baby, who died when she was three? Gran never mentioned her, and there were no photos in the house. But I once heard my aunts talking about her. They didn't say much – just that she was unwell and didn't live long. They stopped talking when they saw me.

The sounds were different that night. It was snowing heavily and the wind howled through the railings. The top window, now free to move, rattled loudly and little clouds of powdery snow puffed in through the cracks. There was more scuffling in the coal cupboard than usual. I didn't want to look at the cupboard door in case it was moving. I looked towards the armchair by the window, piled high with my clothes. A shaft of yellow streetlight sloped through the window.

"Oh God!"

There was a girl sitting in the armchair! I sucked a lungful of cold air. A hand clutched at my stomach. I broke into a sweat. My heart thumped wildly.

A white cloak fell loosely around her shoulders and a white hood partly covered her dark hair. Her little face was sodium yellow, her eyes sunken and dark. She had a sad smile. She looked about three years old. It was Katy! It was Poor Dead Katy – Gran's lost baby! I dived from the bed and fumbled for the light switch.

It was just a pile of clothes. My legs were wobbly and I felt sick as I padded to the armchair. I folded the clothes neatly then switched off the light and looked back. Just clothes. I scanned the room. No Ghosts. No dead children. I flicked the light on again and climbed into bed.

I lay thinking about Katy, a poor lost baby and it dawned on me that she would have dark hair, like Gran and Granddad used to – not fair hair like me. The blonde girl in the photo wasn't Katy. So who was she?

But the answer would have to wait. Tomorrow was coal day and I fell asleep with a big grin on my face.

Rebecca's Lies

Although Gran constantly complained about how badly off we were and how the price of coal was a disgrace, we always had half a cellar-full. I didn't think about it until we found the empty sacks in the airee and it made me curious. I knew she was up to something. I didn't know what, but I had an idea she was on the fiddle, and today I'd find out.

I called for Larry. He was glad to see me. His Mum was so delighted with his cleaning she offered him a shilling to do it every Saturday morning while she was at the dress factory. He gave me thruppence for the idea.

By the time Coalie arrived, Larry and I were watching from behind a low wall on the debris opposite Gran's.

"So, what's up?" Larry asked.

"Well you know my Gran's always saying other people are thieves?"

"Yes, rogues and rascals, cheats and robbers."

"Yes, well I think *she's* been fiddling the coalman."

"Blimey!"

"And we're gonna catch her out!"

"How?"

"Not sure how she does it, but I think it's to do with those sacks in the airee."

As Coalie slowly worked his way from the top of the street I told Larry how almost every week Gran would get into a row with the coalman about the number of sacks we'd had and I usually got caught up in it. It was the same every time. Coalie would arrive by the underground station riding proudly on his dray with its bright red wheels. At the start of his round the coal sacks were stacked double against the headboard and then single height over the flat bed. His big black dray horse, Soldier, could easily pull the full load and he knew how to stop at each house, so when Coalie had delivered a few sacks, Soldier would pull the cart to the next house without being told. The little kids would skip around old Soldier and make a fuss of him, but he'd keep his huge head in his feedbag and crunch on regardless, steamy breath rising around his ears. The kids would run ahead down the street shouting.

"Coalie's coming! Coalie's coming!"

Gran's house was half way down.

The landing in front of the street door had a round cast iron coalhole cover, about a foot across. Every third or fourth Wednesday when Gran bought the coal, it was my job to lever it open with a screwdriver I got from Vinny's bedroom.

Coalie's face and hands were black with years of ingrained coal. His eyebrows were black. His mustache was black. He wore a black railwayman's hat with a leather flap sewn on to the back so it looked like a foreign-legion hat. The flap fell over his neck and on to his thick army jerkin that had metal studs running down the back to protect him from the knobbly coal.

He was a big strong man and could easily lift a hundredweight sack of coal, balance it high on his shoulders with one hand, and carry it to the coalhole, then he'd bend forward with a twist and drop it over his shoulder, right on to the hole, throwing up a small cloud of black dust. The coal would roar into the cellar like an underground train. He'd then catch the corners of the bag, give it a quick shake, and in one movement, throw it in the air, grab the centre, let it fold exactly in half and toss it fold-first to land flat in front of the door. He repeated this until he'd emptied four bags and stacked them in a neat pile.

Gran would sometimes say, "Go on then, we'll have an extra this time." Coalie would throw in a fifth and add the empty bag to the pile.

"That's five then, Becky, All right?"

When he'd finished Gran would smile and offer him a cup of sweet tea.

"Thanks, Becky. It's a dusty old job."

He would gulp it down in one, and as he descended the steps, Soldier would shuffle on to the next house.

When he'd delivered to the whole street, he would return for the empty sacks. Coalie would sit up on the cart holding Soldier's reins, while his mate, a scrawny sixteen-year-old called Sammy would count the sacks and make a note in his little book that had a page for each customer. Then he'd throw the empties on the back of the wagon.

We all liked Coalie, but the women didn't trust him. He'd been caught a few times delivering a bag or two short and sometimes the women said the bags looked light and made him reweigh them on his big scales in front of their eyes. He'd measure a quarter weight of coal on to the scales and then tip it into the spare sack he kept for the purpose, until he'd done it four times and the lady was satisfied she'd got full weight

Granddad said you couldn't blame him for a bit of fiddling – everyone was short of cash and did what they could to make ends meet, but the women watched him very closely.

On Fridays Coalie would return on foot without his hat and with a slightly cleaner face and hands, carrying Sammy's little book, a pencil behind his ear and a leather money pouch slung round his waist. The kids would skip ahead of him. "Coalie's coming! Coalie's coming!"

By the time he got to number 90, Gran would be on the doorstep in her paisley pinny and hair net with her purse in hand. Coalie wouldn't look at the book, but would trust his unfailing memory. "Number 90. Five 'undredweight." He would sing.

"No four." Gran would say.

"No it's five sacks, Becky. You asked for an extra. You stood 'ere and watched me tip it in."

"I only had four." Becky would say, folding her arms over her bosom.

"Ah now, don't come it, Becky, Tommy was here, he'll tell you. Hey, Tommy, you saw me do five bags, didn't you?"

I'd open my mouth to agree, but Gran would interject, "You tell 'im, Tommy, there was four."

"Well... I really thought there were fff..." but my cheery commitment to the truth would fizzle away under Gran's stare.

"Well..." I'd pretend to recall, "maybe it was fff..." but Coalie would look me in the eye, honest, pleading, hands-open and I wouldn't be able to bring myself to lie – not even for Gran. "Well, maybe... Er... I'm not sure. I dunno."

Then there would be a big row with me stuck in the middle, flushed with embarrassment, getting the blame from both of them for being a *luftmencsh*, thick as two short bloody planks with a brain full of nonsense and a memory like a blooming sieve. Their voices would rise higher and higher. Neighbour women would come to their doors in pinnies and hairnets to fold arms on bosoms, tut-tut and shake their heads. Then the kids would gather round laughing, mimicking, and jeering. This would make Coalie really mad, and he'd shout at them.

"Gerroff yer little buggers! You're like bloody flies round dog shit!"

Mrs. Kutchinski would protest, "Now then, don't you start swearing at the kids. It's not their fault you can't count!"

All the pinnies would smile and nod in agreement.

"You mind you own bloody business, Missus. You 'aven't paid me for two weeks!"

"Oh go on then, tell the 'ole bloody street, why don't you!"

When the row had escalated to a crescendo of abuse involving all the pinnies and hairnets within range, Gran would shout above them, slowly, one word at a time, as if she was talking to a foreigner.

"Why... don't... you... look... in Sammy's... book?"

Coalie would shrug and open the book, while the spectators fell silent. He would check Gran's page, and sure enough, find that Sammy had written four bags. "I could've sworn I dropped you five." Coalie would scratch his head, "Aw, all right. Four then!"

Gran would pay up, fold her arms, and with a big told-you-so smile, shout to all the pinnies, "Bloody *ganef*! All thieves and villains. You gotta bloody watch 'em or they'll fiddle you rotten!"

"Too bloody right Becky", the ladies would reply.

Gran would triumphantly wave to the kids in the stalls and the women in the gallery and make her regal exit, closing the street door slowly behind her.

But today was going to be different.

"So how does she do it?" Larry asked.

"I'm not sure," I said, "but we'll soon find out."

Coalie was now at Gran's House. I'd already removed the cellar lid. So we watched as Coalie delivered five bags, folded the empties in a neat pile, replaced the lid, drunk his tea and went off to deliver the rest of the street. Gran went in. Then, when he was at the bottom end of the street, Gran came out again, took the top sack and threw it down the airee.

"Look at that!" Larry said.

"Gotcha!" I said.

As the sack hit the bottom of the airee, it made a sound Gran didn't expect – not the usual dull flump on to the pile of rubbish, but a sharp echoing smack as it belly-flopped on the wet flagstones below. Gran looked into the airee and her face turned white. There was the sack in the airee – visible for all to see and near it a neat pile of nine more. Gran looked puzzled for a second and then the light reached in. "Tommy!" She shouted to the open street, "Tommy Angel, you get in here! Right now!"

Larry and I ducked down behind the wall, giggling and poking each other. When Coalie came back on the cart five minutes later, Sammy leaped up the steps and counted out four sacks in front of Gran.

"Oh... Er... it was five actually, Sammy," Gran said, "Tommy must have dropped one down the airee. Stupid boy, always larking about."

"I'll get it for you, Missus."

Before she could stop him, Sammy had climbed down the airee, to retrieve the sack and he saw the pile. He looked up at Gran. "There's a few more here, Missus."

Gran looked worried. "Oh that's Tommy for you. He's been collecting from round the streets."

Sammy said nothing. He brought up all the sacks and counted them out as he stacked them on the kerb. "That's ten, Mrs. Angel." He said raising his eyebrows.

"Really?" she said nonchalantly, scanning the street – probably looking for me.

He scrutinized her for a while, turned to look at Coalie and Soldier who'd moved on to next door and then turned back to Gran. His brows were creased in a deep frown and her brows were raised in surprise and innocence. He shrugged and grabbed the sacks, flung them on the back of the dray and went on to the Needlemans'.

Although she knew that I knew what she'd been up to, Gran never said anything. I just got an extra long keep-your-mouth-shut glare whenever Coalie came round and for the rest of the winter we made do on four sacks of coal a month.

Running Away

My Gran was an imposing woman, taller than Granddad, big boned and well padded. She had big forearms like Popeye the Sailor. When she stood with both hands on her hips and glared, she was formidable.

Her relationship with me was complicated. While she was usually complaining and judgmental, she'd often say, "Tommy, you're all I've got in the world. What would I do without you?"

At least five times a day she'd say, "Tommy, you know my legs play me up. Run me an errand, will you."

I never seemed to have a moment to myself. If I was listening to the radio, drawing or writing, she'd say, "You bored, Tommy?"

"No. Gran, I'm busy."

"Busy doing nothing. Run me an errand will you." She'd send me round Great Aunt Betty's for half a cabbage.

If she caught me reading, she'd say, "What a *luftmensh* – always got your head in a book. It's not healthy. Why don't you get some fresh air? Run me an errand will you. Pop round to Aunt Betty's."

She'd have me running out time and time again for single items. I'd go to Great Aunt Betty's for one onion, an apple, or just two potatoes. Gran always said, "Tell her to put it on the slate and I'll see her right at the weekend." Great Aunt Betty would hand me the food and say "Yea, she'll see me right into me grave!"

I'd sometimes have to borrow a cup of sugar from Mrs. Bresslaw – which I hated because Mrs. Bresslaw always complained that Gran never returned anything. Half an hour later I might have to run to the grocers for a packet of tea. Then back to Mr. Levy's for the paper.

Once she sent me for a loaf of bread. The queue at the bakers' stretched twenty yards down the street. I joined at the back and shuffled slowly forwards. It took ages and by the time I was in the shop, I was busting for a pee. I dared not give up my place in the queue, so I hopped from foot to foot, crossed my legs and quietly whistled, but the closer I got to the counter, the more the pressure built until I couldn't hold it any longer. I wet myself, right there in the middle of the shop surrounded by ladies. A hot trickle ran down my leg, filled my left shoe and spilled into a growing puddle. There was nowhere to hide.

The only thing to do was ignore it and pretend it wasn't me. I squelched to the counter, holding my head high, bought a large seedy loaf and squelched out with a nonchalant smile. As I stepped into the street I heard an explosion of laughter inside.

What I hated most was fetching the stew. Usually by Tuesday or Wednesday Gran would complain to Granddad that the housekeeping had run out. He'd always chuckle and say, "Well you'd better run after it, Girl, 'cos there's no more till pay day!"

"Sunday bones and brown stew tonight then." She'd send me round the neighbours with a shopping bag. I'd knock at Mrs Bresslaw's and say, "Gran says, she's making the stew but hasn't got any onion. Can we borrow an onion to finish the stew?"

Mrs Bresslaw would look to the sky, shrug and fetch an onion.

Then I'd go to Mrs Levy's and say, "Gran says, she's making the stew but hasn't got any carrots. Can we borrow a couple of carrots to finish the stew?"

Mrs Levy would fetch a few carrots. Then I'd get potatoes from Mrs White and a couple of tomatoes from Mrs Kutchinski. By the time I got home I had a basket full of vegetables Then Gran would say. "We've only got bones, so pop down to Morris's and ask for six penn'orth of blue bits to tie together to make a joint."

Mr. Morris kept the discarded meat trimmings in a basket behind the counter and when money was tight people would by a bag of bits. But I wouldn't want him to think we were penniless, so I'd ask if he had any scraps for the dog. The meat had usually been in the basket a few days and Mr Morris would say,

"Now you know Tommy, it's not fit for human consumption?"

"I know, Mr Morris. It's for Sally."

When I'd get home I'd tell Gran, "Mr, Morris says it's not fit for human consumption?"

"Be all right for you then, Luftmench." Gran would say. "Don't you worry Tommy, any harm'd be cooked out."

"Yes, any good too!" Granddad would say.

Twice a week Gran sent me to the newsagent on Burdett Road, with small brown envelopes containing coins and marked "Mr. Levy". She told me not to tell Granddad about it. I'd hand the envelope over to Mr. Levy, and lately I'd taken the opportunity to make sure Mrs. Levy hadn't been decapitated. "Hello, Mr. Levy."

"Watcher, Tommy."

"How's Mrs. Levy?"

"Nice of you to ask, Tommy, She's fine."

"How's your Gran?"

"She's fine."

I must have done the trip almost every week for the past year, but now my curiosity overcame my diminishing fear of Gran's big glare. On the way I opened the envelope. Inside was one-and-six and a scrap of lined blue Basildon Bond, and in Gran's spidery capitals, *"1s 6d E.W. GOOD HEALTH 3 O CLOCK CATTERICK"*. She was betting with Granddad's wages!

Granddad worked very hard for every penny and I hated Gran for wasting his money. I ripped the envelope and paper into the tiniest pieces and dropped them in the gutter. I knew I'd be for it, but I didn't care. I pocketed the money and vowed to return it to Granddad.

Either Gran forgot about the bet or Good Health lost – anyway she said nothing. I forgot about the money and it stayed in my pocket for weeks. Every time I touched the two coins, I vowed to return them to Granddad and tried to imagine what I'd say. I couldn't work out how to tell him Gran was betting his wages. I knew Granddad also put money on the horses or greyhounds, but then, I thought, he earned it so he could do what he liked.

I was confused and I became more confused when I overheard Aunt Hannah telling Aunt Marlene in Gran's kitchen one Saturday night, that Gran was "betting Tommy's social money". I didn't know what social money was, but apparently it was mine and it was going on the horses.

The following Saturday night, when the family came round, I asked Aunt Hannah, "What's the social money?"

Aunt Hannah was Gran's eldest daughter. She was dignified, intelligent and well spoken. She had a thin strict face. She stood straight and tall and was morally upright too. She could be trusted to tell, if not the whole truth, at least as much as she thought a boy could understand.

"It's what the welfare pay Mum to look after you."

"Do they pay for everybody – Louie, Joey, Lucy, Alice…?" I rattled through a long list of cousins.

"Oh no. Just you. You're special."

"Because I went to the Muller?"

"Well, yes" she said.

From the age of five to nine, I lived in the Muller Home in Broadstairs, Kent. I didn't remember much about it – just a few snapshot memories. I slept in a big room with lots of kids, mostly older than me. After lunch we had to lie outside on rows of stretchers. Matron walked around between us. You could open one eye and peep at her bloomers. She smelled musty like Gran's bedroom.

I remembered falling over and cutting my knee when I fell on a boot scraper – loads of blood. I fingered the scar. "Why was I in the Muller, Aunt Hannah?"

"You were unwell" she said "It was a convalescent home, where children go to get better."

Yes, I remembered singing in a big room. The teacher played the piano and we had to sing. Once the teacher asked the kids if any of us could play the piano. I said I could and marched up front. She sat me on the stool and I tapped the keys just like she did. I was dismayed and embarrassed when no tunes came out, but she was kind and said I had a nice touch and one day I could be a real musician. Then we all sang the Muller Song, to the tune of *Men of Harlech*. I remembered a fragment:

"Five and twenty years have seen

Many boys and girls upon this scene

Restored to health and ..."

Yes, that's what I was there for – to restore my health.

Aunt Hannah looked like she'd had enough of the conversation, but my curiosity was unstoppable and I was out to light up every shadow. "Why was I sick, Aunt Hannah?"

"You ask too many questions." She said, "You were... undernourished."

She anticipated my next question. "It means you weren't growing properly."

"Why not?"

"It happens to... children who don't get a good start in life."

Maybe that's why I'm so skinny.

"So now the welfare gives Mum some money and the social worker comes to make sure you're looked after."

"Is that Doris?" I asked?

Doris was a nice lady who came to see me now and then. She was soft-spoken, kind and intelligent. She always asked if I was OK and if I needed anything. Gran told me I wasn't allowed to ask for sweets or comics – only for things I didn't really want, like socks, vests or shoes. Once she said I could ask for a winter coat. I asked, but I never got the coat.

"Yes. Doris is the lady who gets the social money."

"And Gran spends it on the horses."

I realized as soon as the words left my lips that I should have kept quiet. Aunt Hannah glared. "Why Tommy Angel! That's just nonsense! Don't ever let me hear you say such things again!"

"But, Aunt Hannah…"

"Not… another… word!" she said and bustled off.

I kept running Gran's errands, until that winter in 1956, after I'd spoken to Aunt Hannah. The next time she asked me to take another envelope to Mr. Levy, she held it out and I suddenly shouted, "Why should I?" She snatched her hand back.

"You cheeky little bleeder!" she said, and I ran out and stayed out with my mates until late that night.

During the days that followed I did my best to stay out of sight, so she wouldn't be able to send me on errands. By now she was wise to my hiding with the lodgers and she'd shout me down when she heard me patter up the stairs.

One time I hid in the narrow gap behind the put-u-up, where I could draw for a while but she found me and sent me on an errand.

I took a cushion from an armchair and made a den in the coal cupboard. There were rods of dusty light filtering through the ring of holes in the coalhole cover – just enough to read by. When she found me I got a good yelling for making the cushions filthy. I said they were black to start with, but she still sent me on an errand.

My best hiding place was the air raid shelter in the yard. It was dark in there and full of boxes. I piled them up to make a wall to squat behind and hid some matches and candles so I could read. She only came into the yard to hang the washing and collect it, and she did that to a predictable pattern. For a while, between hanging and collection I had a few hours of peace, but she eventually discovered my last hiding place.

I was reading the Eagle Annual – "*How to Make Your Own Crystal Set – One Exciting Way to Spend Your Winter Evenings – by Ernest Meadowcroft*". We'd had no radio for the gang since Larry broke his mum's transistor. Journey Into Space had finished, but we were missing the Goons. Perhaps this could do the trick.

All you needed was some wire, a variable condenser (*.0005 mF with a knob*), a germanium crystal, 75ft of aerial wire and a pair of headphones (*high impedance*). I'd read the article eight times. I even gathered a few of the components including a variable condenser from an old radio I found on the debris. I didn't know if it was *.0005 mF*, but it did have a knob. I had no idea where to get a germanium crystal. Mr. Meadowcroft wrote that the parts could be bought from "*any general radio shop*", but I had never seen a general radio shop. Then I read you had to drill holes in a Bakelite chassis and solder some of the pieces together. I didn't have a drill, a soldering iron or a Bakelite chassis.

Despite these limitations, I'd imagined Larry and Viv's faces when I turned up with a home made radio. I resolved to move the project one step forward each time I re-read the article.

I'd found a reel of thin paper-insulated wire in the pile of junk in Vinny's room and I was winding it carefully round a roll of cardboard to make a coil, like Mr. Meadowcroft said you should. I had to wind 60 turns. I was on forty-five when I sneezed violently. The coil shot from my hands and flew across the shelter trailing a spiral of wire. Gran was in the yard. She heard me and peered into the darkness.

"Tommy? You there?"

I blew out the candle, sat still and held my breath. She screwed up her eyes and scanned the gloom. "Vinny!" she shouted, "We got rats again! Get down here!"

In a few seconds, Vinny was standing at the doorway brandishing a bicycle pump. Gran mocked, *"Toig ahf kapores.* What you gonna do? Catch the bloody rat or pump it's bloody tyres up?"

Vinny's form filled the doorway and he slowly advanced.

"S'OK. It's not a rat. It's only me!" I jumped up in front of Vinny – barring his entry to stop him getting any closer to my treasures.

"I was looking for… my comics." I said, grabbing a small cardboard box with the comics we'd found in the airee – the ones nobody wanted.

Vinny lowered his pump, backed off and let me out.

Gran looked at me. "You are a quandary," she said, shaking her head.

I walked to the house, hoping she'd lose interest in the shelter.

"Tommy, do an errand for me will you."

Now there was nowhere left to hide. My whole life would be spent running back and forth to the shops or begging from the neighbours.

That night I took a candle to bed and I lay there digging through my box of comics. I found a complete Beano and I read the Bash Street Kids, Rodger the Dodger and Dennis the Menace. I'd claimed half the pages of a newish Beezer with Pop, Dick and Harry and the Kings of Castaway Island. I'd also kept a few inside pages of a old Knockout and read Tod and Annie. They were my favourites after Bash Street. They were orphan twins, running away from the cruel orphanage, sleeping rough under bridges, in barns or in haystacks and hiding from nasty farmers. Every week they did a good deed like finding lost children and rescuing wounded lambs and then ran off somewhere else.

I could do that.

It was late February and it had been bitterly cold for a long time. Next morning there were twelve inches of snow and we couldn't play out because of the icy winds. The scullery taps had frozen solid, so Vinny had to heat them with a blowtorch to get water for washing clothes. The kitchen taps were all right, but the water was achingly cold.

That evening after Vinny and Grandad had gone upstairs I asked Gran if I could put some coal on the fire.

"You know you're not allowed to after bedtime."

"But it's really cold."

"It's cold for everyone. And anyway, we're a bit short of coal."

She gave me a look that said "and you know why".

It was impossible to keep warm in bed. I wrapped the sheet and blanket around me to make a tight roll, but my face and feet were frozen. I woke early and lay there, too cold to move, exhaling steam. It was hunger that forced me out of bed. I dragged my clothes on as fast as my shivering would allow and walked to the kitchen. I placed a chair under the dresser and climbed up to reach Gran's bread pudding pan. I took a knife, cut a slice and stuffed it into my mouth.

There was nothing unusual about being cold and hungry. It was always cold and my mates and I were always hungry. We gulped our food and guzzled our drinks, as if they were the last we'd ever get. We didn't chew or savour food – we needed fuel and we needed it fast. We needed energy for adventures.

This day felt good for an adventure. I decided to go. I took more bread pudding and half a sliced loaf in a brown paper bag. I stuffed a box of matches and a candle in my coat pocket – in case I had to hide in the forests and make a campfire. I sneaked out to the air raid shelter and took the photograph of the little girl from its frame, rolled it carefully in newspaper, secured it with an elastic band and put it in the paper bag.

I stood outside Gran's room and listened for her flubbery snoring. I sneaked in quietly and took her purse from the piano. I grabbed a handful of change and stuffed it in my shorts. I padded out, along the passage and closed the street door gently behind me.

I marched with ridiculously high steps through the deep new snow up Eric Street to Mile End Road. It was freezing. My shoes were soon full of snow. My knees were already red with cold. I jumped on the first bus I saw heading west towards the City. I ran upstairs and sat in the front seat to be furthest from the stairs.

Sometimes the conductors were too lazy to drag all the way upstairs to collect the fares, and if you got off at a busy stop you could hide in the crowd and get away without paying. I was usually honest and paid up, but today I needed my money to go as far as possible.

I took off my shoes and shook out the snow.

"Where to, Son?"

The conductor stood above me.

"Where can I go?"

He said the bus went to White City.

I imagined a steep mountain covered in fresh clean snow with a fairytale city perched on the highest peak, with castles and towers crafted in sparkling white marble.

"Yes, White City, please" I said with a smile and poured Gran's coins into his hand. He took the fare and gave me the change, pushed some buttons on his ticket machine, spun the handle and handed me a green ticket. I rode to the end of the route.

All the time I was worried the conductor might realize I was a runaway and call the police and I'd be arrested. People got on and sat beside me, then got off. I was frightened one might be a policeman, so I looked out the window so they wouldn't see my face. I was terrified but excited. I was a runaway orphan, just like Tod and Annie.

The White City didn't quite match my fantasies. It was just another part of London, but it was a lot posher than Mile End. When the conductor announced the last stop, I leaped off the bus and ran as fast as I could, in case he reported me. I found myself on a suburban road between very large semi-detached houses, protected by high green hedges, topped with snow, like icing on a Christmas cake. The grass verges, were knee-high in snow – clean and white and soft. To walk I had to lift my knees almost to my chest.

I must have walked for an hour. My emotions swung between fear of being caught and the excitement of the adventure. I realized I was so intent on running away, I hadn't thought about what I was running towards. I didn't know where I was going, or what I'd do when I got there.

I was getting colder. I cursed all grownups for making kids wear shorts and telling us fresh air was good for us. I'd like to see Gran in deep snow in a pair of shorts.

I came to a main road. Davy had told me a bit about hitch hiking. With great embarrassment I stood at the roadside, held my arm straight up above my head, stuck out my thumb, and looked pleadingly at the drivers flashing past through the brown slush. They ignored me and I felt increasingly stupid and despondent. Perhaps I wasn't doing it right. I started waving my arm like it was a flag. Then to my amazement, a lorry and five vans stopped all at once. It was a huge Bedford Carrimore double-decker transporter loaded with Austin vans. I couldn't believe my luck. I loved transporters. My best toy was a Dinky transporter. It cost me 14/6d and I'd saved a whole year for it. I'd never ridden in a lorry, never mind a transporter, and this one looked brand new.

The driver was a burly man with a round red face and a purple nose pitted like a strawberry. He leaned over and shouted above the engine.

"Where do you want to go?"

"Wales." It was the first thing that came into my head.

"Hop in, Son." I climbed up the outside of the monster vehicle. It was hard to get a grip on the metal step with my shoes caked in ice and snow. It was hard to open the door without knocking myself off the step. Once I was in he drove on and asked me a stream of questions. Where was I from? How old was I? Where was I going? Who was I staying with?

I only answered the final one. "My sister." I said.

"What's her name? Does she know you're coming? Where does she live?"

I didn't answer. I thought he might turn me in. After a few miles, he stopped the lorry, poured me some hot tea from his flask, and told me to stay where I was while he called his depot. He climbed down and walked to a red telephone box beside the road. I thought about running off. I opened the door.

"Wait there, Son!" he yelled back, and I shut it.

He made the call and came back and sat beside me.

"I'm meeting someone. Won't be just a minute. Then we'll see about Wales."

We sat there for five minutes and he kept me occupied with stories about his travels around the country. He had delivered cars and vans everywhere – Watford, Sidcup, Swansea, Dartford, Bristol. I was getting more and more worried.

In the side mirror I saw a flashing blue light. A policewoman walked up to the lorry. She smiled, waved at me and opened the door.

"Come on Sonny. Come with me."

I was done! The driver had turned me in! I was arrested for running away. I was bound for prison or at least borstal.

On the way to the police station, the policewoman asked my name and address. She was gentle. I liked her. I felt safe with her, so I decided to own up.

"My you've come a long way!" she said. Despite my fears I felt proud.

At the police station she sat me in a wood-paneled waiting room, brought me orange juice and a couple of Nice biscuits and then left me – for an hour. I unwrapped the picture of the girl in the red dress, so I could see her smile, and then stuffed it away under my coat when I heard a noise in the next room.

I was frightened, bored and very cold and I hated Nice biscuits – like eating cardboard. I sat with my coat huddled round me, hands in pockets, fiddling with the matches. She came back into the room and saw me fiddling between my legs.

"Don't do that," she said, "you'll go blind."

I was embarrassed. I looked down. What did she mean? How do you go blind playing with matches? When I looked back at her, she was staring at the bump in my coat.

"What's that?"

"It's just my stuff."

"Show me."

I reluctantly took out my brown bag and the picture.

"Show me."

I handed her the picture. She flicked off the rubber band and unrolled it. "Who's this?"

"It's… It's just a girl."

"She's pretty." She smiled, head slightly to one side, eyebrows raised in question, waiting for more.

"Yes." I said, "She's my…"

A policeman poked his head round the door. "His Grandmother's here."

The policewoman returned the photo and I quickly wrapped it up and hid it away. She took my hand and led me to the next room. Gran was sitting in her grey overcoat, crying. As I walked in she cried out, "Tommy, I love you so much. You are all I've got in the world. What would I do without you?"

I looked down and talked to my feet. "Run your own errands, I s'pose."

She cried louder.

I felt guilty making her cry, but rather than apologize, as I knew I should, I blurted out, "You don't love me. You're just saying that for the police lady. You didn't give me a good start in life. You didn't give me any food when I was a baby. You starved me, made me sick and then sent me away to a home to restore my health. You didn't even give me my new coat! And you spend Granddad's money on the horses!"

Gran looked flabbergasted, upset and then angry. "Why you ungrateful little…" she spluttered and her lips pouted and cycled in such violent contortions that her top teeth fell down and she had to stop to push them back. She turned to the policewoman.

"He makes it up in his head. It's all in his imagination."

She looked to heaven. "Oh dear God, tell me please. Why did you give me a boy like Tommy? What did I do that was so wrong? Why do I deserve this heartache?"

"He's just upset." the policewoman said, smiling at me and touching Gran's forearm.

They must have decided not to arrest me, and instead they called a driver to take us home. It was a long way and I sat silent. When we arrived, Granddad opened the street door. I felt ashamed and stupid and couldn't look at him. I ran past him and out to the yard and sat in the darkest corner of the shelter. I ignored Gran's calls and stayed there for hours, past teatime and then well past bedtime. I lit a succession of candles to keep my hands warm.

I took a long look at the picture of the girl.

"Who are you?"

I replaced the photo in its frame and held it in my folded arms. When my last candle died, I hugged my knees to my chest and stared into the dark. Before me I could see years of slavery – run me an errand, get this, do that, run round Aunt Betty's for something else. As my arms and legs got colder and stiffer, my mind froze on a vision of a boy imprisoned for life in Gran's dark, cold basement with the rats, let out only to run her errands.

I was determined to stay in the shelter in protest against my cold, hungry loveless life, but the cold began to hurt. It felt like my fingers would crack if I moved them. My toes felt like they'd been hit with hammers. Reluctantly I mobilized my frozen joints, stretched my limbs and slowly stood up.

I hobbled into the house carrying the photo under my arm and crept down to my basement room. Before I switched on the light, I glanced towards the window. Granddad was sitting on Poor Dead Katy's armchair, his white hair haloed in streetlamp yellow. I jumped.

"It's all right, Tommy. I'm not a ghost… yet."

I shuffled stiffly towards him like a guilty prisoner in leg irons, my head hung in shame. "I wasn't running away from you, Dad."

I didn't cry aloud but tears dribbled down my cold cheeks.

"I know, Son. I know what you were running from."

He smiled and winked at me, and I knew that he knew.

"Of course you don't have to go quite so far for a bit of peace next time." he said, "I understand there's a nice quiet spot for a boy, just across the road." He smiled.

I looked puzzled.

"Nobody in this house knows about your little camp. Except me of course and I believe a boy should have a secret place of his own where no one can find him."

He stood up, and squeezed my shoulder as he left the room. I watched his back as he faded up into the dark stairway.

I set the photo of the girl on Poor Dead Katy's chair, so I could see it from the bed and stared at it until I fell asleep.

Tell the Girls Their Daddy Loves Them

I took Granddad's advice. To avoid being Gran's errand boy I stayed out of the house, and out of her sight as long as possible. As the weather improved I spent more of my evenings, weekends and holidays in the street with my mates.

In 1944, after the D-Day landings, the Germans launched thousands of V1 doodle-bug rockets from France, aimed at London. Vinny told me one of them had *90 Eric Street* written on it, but luckily it stopped just short of Gran's house and blew up six houses opposite.

The whole block was destroyed right through to Mossford Street. Vinny said whole houses just disappeared and lots of people were killed by the blast, but our family was miles away, evacuated in East Hanney.

The bomb site was now a wasteland of rubble, bricks, splintered planks and twisted metal, the last remains of bedroom walls with peeling flowery wallpaper, smashed toilet bowls, discarded furniture and rubbish.

It was a backdrop for my growing up and a perfect playground –a place where we could pick sides and play endless war games.

Larry Black and Viv Cohen and I were the English. Ronny Needleman, Errol White and Davy Yude, were the Germans. We made barricades from old furniture, doors, dustbin lids and planks and lobbed bombs and grenades at each other with accompanying whistling and explosions.

I don't know how we survived without injury. The sticks and rocks we threw were real and we aimed them straight at each other's heads, but we were innocent of the laws of cause and effect and we had no real understanding of the possible bloody consequences. Mostly we were wide of target, or we ducked to safety just in time.

Davy was the best shot. He was a year older than most of us. He was nearly as tall as Larry but heavier and squarely built. He had curly hair, bright green eyes, and a big wide grin with a twist of cruelty in it.

There was some anger and wildness in him. He would often go a step too far and cross the line from fun into danger. As our war games progressed, he would throw larger and larger stones, building up to half bricks. That was the signal for the English to take cover behind the barricades and let the Germans win.

There were a few direct hits but somehow the blood and pain always came as a surprise to the victim and the bomber. We would have been mortified if anyone really got hurt, and miraculously nobody did.

As time went by we graduated from building barricades to making camps. We started with simple wooden tents made by leaning two doors together. These evolved into long tunnels made from four, six or eight doors. Larry was the architect for our first 'room'. Errol and I held one door upright on it's side, while Davy balanced another parallel. Larry roofed these with two more doors, which he nailed on to the upright walls. It was pretty wobbly, until we piled rubble around the outside – enough to stabilize the walls and camouflage the construction.

Over a few weeks, we extended the camp and cleared rubble from the middle of the floor, until it was just deep enough inside to take the cushions from Gran's armchair and a mattress. We couldn't stand up, but eight kids could hide in the camp for hours on end, loll about in comfort and make plans for adventures, invent stories and tell jokes.

We extended the camp with door-tent tunnels and added an emergency entrance. We balanced one end of a door on the roof at the opening and propped up the other end with two sticks. We piled rubble on top of the door and tied ropes to the sticks, if we were ever being chased, we could dive into the tunnel, tug at the ropes and the door would collapse, the rubble would slide down and cover the entrance.

We planned to dig out an underground hiding place below our main room. Larry, Davy, Errol and I spent the whole of one Saturday digging away at the floor. I returned early Sunday morning to find them already digging. We set up a chain – Errol passed the bricks to me, then I lobbed them out to Larry who piled them on the roof as camouflage.

After half an hour Errol screamed. In the gloom all I could see was his bum in a cloud of billowing dust. The top half of his body was missing.

"Pull me out!" His voice was strangely distant. I tugged at his feet and dragged him towards me. He twisted round and his face, covered in white dust, was a mixture of fear and excitement.

"It's a tunnel!"

"Yes I know." I said, "It's our secret tunnel."

"No. It's a *real* secret tunnel!"

The others had squeezed into the camp and were peering into the dark and dust. We crawled carefully to where Errol's body had disappeared and gaped down into emptiness.

"Cor!"

"Wow!"

We'd broken into the basement of the bombed house.

Davy ran home and nicked his dad's torch – a big long powerful silver one that took six batteries. I found a smaller one we'd hidden in the orange box we used as a cupboard. We sprawled around the hole and peered over while Davy circled his light in the gloom. At first we could see only dust in the beam, but it slowly settled and we saw an open room with a small pile of rubble in the centre.

"Let's get a ladder!"

Davy and Errol ran off to explore their yards, but came back empty handed.

"I know" Davy said, "Viv's Dad's a window cleaner! He's got ladders. I'll get Viv."

"Don't tell her dad anything." Larry said.

"'S'all right he won't be in."

Ten minutes later Davy returned with Viv and a ladder. It was a rotten old wooden thing about twelve feet long. Viv said her Dad didn't use it anymore.

"If it's any use you can keep it…"

"Thanks Viv."

"… but only if I can come down with you." she said.

Like Errol, she was younger than Larry and me, and sometimes she got left behind on dangerous missions.

"Course you can." Davy said, and she beamed.

It took some time to get the ladder in place between the exposed joists. It reached to the cellar floor with a foot to spare.

We argued about who should go first.

"I found it." Errol said.

"I rescued you." I said.

"'S'my ladder." Viv said.

"I got the biggest torch." Davy said.

"I got the biggest willy." Larry said.

"What if there's gas?" Viv asked, and she dived for the orange box, took out her gas mask and said as she pulled it on. "I'll go first becauuuu hmmm humm hmm."

Viv went first, then Davy, me, Larry and Errol.

The room below was dark, cold, damp and dusty.

"Wow!" Larry said, "the Bat Cave!"

"No one must say a word. It's gotta be our secret." Davy said.

We made a circle and placed our hands in the centre, one on another "All for one and one for all." Larry took Davy's torch and held it under his chin so his face looked ghostly. "Pain-of-DEATH!" he hissed. We laughed and bundled each other, excited, delighted and a bit scared.

Davy cackled like a witch. Larry danced around screaming "Pain of DEATH! Pain of DEATH!"

Errol and Viv got spooked and fought to get to the ladder first. Viv won and scampered up with Errol behind. Davy and Larry followed, leaving me alone in the dark. I stumbled towards the ladder.

"Pull it up!" said Davy, "leave 'im down there!" and I felt it lift through my hands. I was terrified of being there alone. I pulled sharply at the ladder with my whole weight.

"Blimey, Tommy. Nearly pulled me arms off!" Davy said. "Can't you take a joke?"

I climbed up the ladder fast, but paused once my head was above ground.

"S' great innit!" I beamed, hiding my terror under a big grin. Their knowing smiles suggested Davy and Larry were not convinced by my performance.

"Hold on a bit. See you in a minute." I forced myself to climb down again. I'd never felt such terror in my life. Every rung of the ladder was one step deeper into fear. I could feel skeleton hands clawing at my ankles, hear the gurgles and moans of dying souls in the dark below. It was little relief to set foot on the floor.

I didn't want to let go of the ladder, so I held on with one hand and probed the darkness with the torch.

"What you doing Tommy?" Larry yelled.

"Oh, you know… just exploring." I said.

"Better you than me!"

When I was sure they wouldn't lift the ladder I let go and shuffled a few steps away. As I circled the torch, I could see the room wasn't empty. I could see a wall with paisley paper, hung with pictures and a sideboard just visible under the dust.

I wasn't surprised to find a living room in the cellar. Most Eric Street families used their basements for storage, but the poorer families, including mine, lived below and sub-let the upper rooms to lodgers to help with the rent.

I brushed some rubble from the sideboard, making a clatter.

"You alright Tommy?"

"Yea. It's only a ghost!"

Beneath the rubble I found a picture frame, glass broken, with a photograph of a group of soldiers. I looked at the other photos on the wall and brushed away the dust to reveal a man in his twenties, a pretty bride and her groom, a vignetted old lady with her hair in a bun.

I was so absorbed I forgot I was afraid. I opened a drawer in the sideboard. It was stuffed with papers – bills, notices and blue airmail letters. One was addressed to Rachael Isaacs, 65, Eric Street. I opened it. Much of the letter was smudged and unreadable and words and phrases had been blocked out in black ink but I could make out the start and finish.

> *Rachael, my love,*
>
> *Sorry I have not written for a while, but it's getting difficult here. More ---- ----- ---- and night. We can't move out of this stinking trench. Some of my mates have caught it. Remember Jackie Levy – we lost him. He was ----- ----------- ----- couldn't save him. I'm OK though. We have a laugh and a fag and we get through. I think about you and little Daisy and Rose all the time. You are what I live for. Without you I'd ------ ----*
>
> *Kiss the girls and say Daddy loves them. I'll be home soon. Make sure you got the tea on the table.*
>
> *You are my heart's love – all I live for.*
>
> *Love and kisses,*
>
> *Tommy.*
>
> *XXX*

I wanted to show the others, but I didn't. He had my name and I felt the letter was somehow private to me. I replaced it in the drawer. I opened the cupboard. It was full of baby stuff – a toweling bib, toweling nappies and clothes. The other cupboard had plates and cups, a silvery coffee percolator and cutlery.

I shone the torch around to the sofa with cushions and a coat slung over the back – all covered in a thick layer of dust. On the seat was a baby's dummy.

And then I remembered. Granddad told me about this family. The Cohens lived here with their daughter Rachael. She was seventeen when she married Tommy Isaacs. They were married a year and had twins – two little girls. Tommy was called up for the army. He had to leave them behind and go to France. There was a big air raid one night. Rachael and the twins went to the shelter in the yard, but they took a direct hit from the V1 that was meant for our house. They all died.

Tommy knew nothing about it until he came home. He found the debris where his house used to be, and the neighbours told him his wife and little girls had died in the raid. Granddad said he didn't say a single word. He just turned and walked away and he never came back. That was over eleven years ago – just before I was born. They say he's still walking.

I noticed a cardboard box on the sofa, next to the baby's dummy. I blew the dust off and opened the box. It was full of photos. Most of them were tiny black and white prints, about one by one-and-a-half inches – someone's mother, aunts, uncles, brothers and sisters. There was one of two babies sitting end to end in a pram with two hoods, folded open. One had a rattle in her hand and a big grin. The other was asleep. I guessed it was Daisy and Rose – Tommy's lost babies. I thought about Katy. I slid the box under the sofa and looked around the room for the ghosts of lost babies. I saw nothing and realized I was no longer scared.

I explored a bit more and found a hole in the wall, which led to the cellar of the bombed house next door – that's what I'd tell the others about – nothing else. I climbed the ladder and peeked out from the cellar. The others were lying around chatting.

"Boo!" I made them all jump. The sight of me covered in white dust added to the shock.

"You sod!" Davy shouted.

"Scared you!"

We slid a door over the hole, and covered it with the mattress, leaving just the ladder top visible and we hid that under an orange box. Now we had a secret bolt hole to escape from parents or grandparents whenever we wished. In subsequent forays, we explored the opening to the shell of a house next door. It led to a basement room with an intact door that could be opened from the inside and jammed shut from the outside.

Larry said it might come in useful some day and he was right.

The King and Queen Were Drinking Gin

Errol was young, and sometimes irritated the other boys. He was unsure of himself and afraid of being left out and that made him eager to please – too eager. We teased him a lot, but we all liked him.

One morning, Errol crawled into our camp. His face was covered in white stuff. We took it for Calamine lotion.

"What's up Errol? Caught the dreaded lurgie?" I asked.

"Been stung?" Davy asked.

"No" Errol said, "I wanna be white."

"What? You are White – Errol White." Larry said.

"My name's White but I'm… black", Errol said.

"What do you mean, you're black. I'm Black – Larry Black. You're White – Errol White. Right?" Larry said.

"Yea my name's White but my *skin's* black." Errol said.

"Where?" Ronny asked, "Got a bruise?"

"Did you fall over?" Viv asked. "I've got a nurse's kit with special scissors and cotton wool and bandages and ointment and injections and those rubber things you put on your thumb. I got everything. I'll go and get it now."

Errol shook his head. Viv looked disappointed.

We had no idea what Errol was on about. We looked at each other for clues, but saw only puzzled faces.

Ronny said, "Who wants to play gobs?"

"Yea, come on", Larry said, and we gathered stones to play.

Gobs was a game about picking up stones. I never understood it. You threw one stone in the air, picked up another from the ground, and you had to catch the stone you threw before it hit the ground. Then you threw up two, caught them on the back of your hand and you had to pick up more stones between your outstretched fingers. I couldn't get the hang of it. It was too serious, so I'd tickle the others when their stones were in the air and make them miss. The game always ended in a bundle, which was much more fun.

While we were playing, Larry started a rhyming contest. The idea was to recite old rhymes or make up new ones – as rude as possible, each taking a turn to add a new line.

"How about this… Errol White had a fright."

Ronny continued, "In the middle of the night."

I added, "He saw a ghost eating toast"

Errol concluded, "Halfway up a lamppost!"

We laughed.

"OK, here's a new one." I said, "Davy Yude was a dude…"

They all giggled and pointed at Davy.

"Went to Soho in the nude." I said.

"Whooooah!" the gang chorused – wolf whistles.

"All the girls would scream and shout." Larry said. "Davy's willy's 'anging out!"

Larry jumped up, unbuttoned his fly and strutted around us shaking his willy.

"I thought you said 'his willy' not a his caterpillar!" Ronny said.

"You can talk" Larry said.

"What's this then?" Ronny jumped up, flipped out his willy and gyrated his hips.

"It's a disgusting little maggot!" Viv said.

"Yea well… show us yours then." Ronny said.

Viv popped up and dropped her trousers and pants. There was nothing there.

"You ain't even got one!" Larry said.

We were helpless with laughter. We collapsed in a heap of giggling bodies.

"All right Tommy, your turn…" Errol said, launching into an old favourite, "Tommy Angel did a fart…"

Ronny took it up. "Right into a jam tart…"

Larry said. "The fart went rolling down the street…"

Davy said, "Knocked a copper off his feet."

Errol said. "The King and Queen were drinking gin."

Ronny said. "Opened their mouths…. and the fart rolled in!"

"Yeah!" they cheered.

"Hold on. Hold on," I shouted "How about this … The pong it made them scream and shout. So they went to the lav and the fart blew out!"

"Hang on. Hang on!" Larry yelled above the laughter, "In walked Tommy in his Gabardine Mac, saying… that fart's mine I want it back!"

"No. No. Not done yet…" Davy screamed over the helplessly giggling gang. He stood up and mimicked a lady, holding the hem of his dress, and he said in a posh soprano,

"The Queen said, George, it must be his. All right Tommy here it is!"

Davy spun round lifted his imaginary skirt, pointed his bum in the air and let out a real whopper fart.

We rolled about on the cushions. Tears streamed down our faces. I could hardly breathe. We were a bundle of young humanity – five kids with a single soul, joined by humour and friendship.

And then we noticed Errol. He sat apart, looking down at his knees.

"Dad's had trouble at work." he said quietly. "They said he was stealing their jobs. Called him a nigger. Pushed him about."

"What's a nigger?" Ronny asked.

"Mrs. Bresslaw's dog's called Nigger." Davy said, "It's black."

"Yea." Errol said, "Dad said we're niggers and we're treated like dogs because we're black."

Until that moment we hadn't noticed Errol was black, in the same way we didn't see Viv as a girl – they were just mates. Now we saw it. Errol was different. We looked from one to the other as realization spread across our faces.

His house was different – each brick was painted bright blue with white mortar. The window boxes were bright with pink flowers. The house smelt different – Mrs. White's spicy food. She talked different and her hair was different, like Errol's – tight little curls. Although we'd seen Errol every day for years, we'd never noticed that his skin was the same as his mum and dad and other black people we'd seen around – doing the bins, on the buses and the underground.

"You're not black!" Larry said. "I am!"

Errol ignored Larry. "I wanna be white." he said.

"So, what's on your face then?" Ronny asked.

"Whitewash." Errol said, "I want to be white like you."

We were bursting to laugh but for Errol it wasn't funny.

"You are like us." I said, "You don't need to paint your face. You're our mate. Come on."

I took Errol across the road to Gran's house. We pushed open the street door, ran down the passage.

Gran called out "What are you up to now?"

We ignored her and ran to the scullery. I gave Errol a flannel to wash his face. I told him how Granddad stuck up for black people. He went to see Oswald Mosley march through the East End with his fascist blackshirts. Granddad said he had a sneer on his face like the whole place stank. Granddad threw rotten eggs at him and one hit Mosley on the forehead. The egg dripped all the way down his face and he pretended it didn't happen and kept marching with the same look on his face, but now he had a real stink under his nose.

"That's better," I said, "Now you're really one of us."

Errol looked up at me with a huge smile.

"Here, have a hankie and blow that snotty nose." I picked one from the top of the pile on the ironing board.

"Blimey. You've got a few hankies."

We had more handkerchiefs than anyone I knew. Granddad found them in the park and brought a few home every night. At the weekend Gran boiled them, hung them to dry, ironed them and added them to the huge pile in the scullery. I thought everyone had piles of hankies until one day at Ronny's house. I had a cold and I asked Mrs. Needleman for a hankie. She said, "Ronny's got his. Mr. Needleman has his, and I have mine but we don't keep a spare. Sorry!" She offered me a Kleenex.

Ronny was much better off than we were, with all his Meccano and model aeroplanes, and his dad had every tool on the planet, but they only had three real hankies!

Granddad also collected combs. We had hundreds in a box – every colour you could think of – red, green, white and blue plastic, brown tortoiseshell and silver metal. I swapped them with the other kids for sweets and comics. When James Dean films came out, they jumped in value. James Dean always combed his hair back at a dramatic moment in the film. The kids liked to copy his exact move – elbow high over his head combing backwards through his quiff. This meant that combs were *in* and I could swap a good comb for two old Eagle comics instead of one.

I looked at Errol's tight curls and wondered if a comb would work on his hair. I gave him a nice shiny steel one. Like the nit nurse used.

"Thanks! Beat you at gobs." he said.

We ran back to join the gang.

Deceiving Mrs. Green

One Thursday morning in March I caught the bus to school as usual. But this was not a usual day for two reasons.

First, it was Purim and that meant missing maths after play for a special festival lunch with turkey. Second, I had, in my pocket, a carefully forged note for Mrs. Green that would be the key, either to my freedom or to a prison of humiliation and dishonour.

I was full of mixed feelings when I leapt off the bus and walked along Stepney Green. I was happy to see Benny just ahead.

Benny Jacobs was my best friend at school. He was in my class, but you wouldn't think so looking at us. He was much bigger than me and well built, with broad shoulders – he must have had a good start in life. He was square-faced and handsome like Clark Kent, with jet-black Brylcreemed hair. He was cleverer than me. He read a lot, listened to classical music and played the recorder. He got good marks for arithmetic and was good at Hebrew and he didn't drop his aitches or tees. He could swim really well and even play proper football. In fact he was better than me at everything, but I could make him laugh.

His parents must have been well off. They had a nice flat on the Ocean Estate with modern furniture and bookshelves full of books. I liked his Mum and Dad and his little sister was good for a laugh. I often went to his house after school and stayed there as long as I could to avoid going home.

"Oi Cream Crackers!" I ran to catch him up.

"Hi, Tommy. Ready for the test?"

"What, Hebrew?"

"Yes. You have to do a translation Hebrew to English and then English to Hebrew. I've been practicing."

"I know," I said, "Louis Nyman told me yesterday. With luck I'm gonna get off."

"How?" Benny asked.

"You'll see. Come on."

We skipped, ran and danced our way to school, ragging each other, fighting with our satchels.

"Oi! Jew Boys!"

Four kids from Ben Johnson Secondary barred our way.

I didn't understand how they knew we were Jews – we looked much like them, except we had caps with the Stepney Jewish School crest. I whipped off my SJS cap and held it behind me, but I was too late. As one kid grabbed Benny's satchel, another snatched my cap. After a bit of teasing and a game of piggy in the middle where we lunged helplessly as they threw our things between them, they ran off, throwing our stuff over the park fence. The chain link fence was ten feet high. We had to run back to the park gate and scrabble among the bushes until we found our things. Our leisurely meander to school had now become an anxious dash to get in before the bell.

Being late meant three whacks with a ruler across your knuckles from Miss Goldberg. If you were late more than once, you were sent to the headmaster, Mr. Rosen, who used to turn kids upside down and wallop them on the bum.

The ruler and the smacks didn't worry me. They hurt like hell, but only for a few minutes. I was more worried about eternal damnation for the sin waiting like an evil genie to pop out of my pocket at Hebrew, second lesson.

Miss Green taught Hebrew and ran Cheder classes every Thursday after school. Benny talked me into going because he said you got a break halfway through and everyone went to the shop over the road, where you could buy a huge bag of broken crisps for tuppence ha'penny – food from heaven.

When you finished a normal bag of crisps, you always had a residue of broken bits at the bottom of the bag. These were a precious bonus. They were greasier and saltier – altogether a more intense if short-lived experience. Now imagine a bag stuffed full of *only* the broken bits. That was the great attraction of Mr. Newman's shop. Benny shared a bag with me once and I was convinced I needed extra Hebrew.

Mrs. Green was fascinating. For one thing she had real blonde hair and blue eyes, like me, which was very unusual for a Jew. She wore a red dress, when other teachers wore black or grey and she smiled more than anyone I ever met. She was a bit like the little girl in the photo, but grown up.

I really didn't believe in Hebrew. If God was all-powerful and knew everything, surely he could speak English, so what's the point of talking to him in an ancient language from another country? So although Mrs. Green was very nice, I was neither motivated nor capable.

When I started classes, I hoped Gran's Yiddish might come in handy but I was disappointed to find that none of the English-to-Hebrew translation exercises included the phrases I knew, like "boring old fart", "loud mouthed gossip" or even "head in the clouds". I did manage to learn a few short words I could recognize in any Hebrew text like "mah" means "what" – or was it "why"? But that wasn't enough for translations. I learned a few prayers, which I recited without understanding.

When I got home after my first Cheder class, Gran asked what I'd learned. I was really embarrassed to recite a prayer in another language in front of her, and because I didn't have a kappel, I put one hand on my head, closed my eyes and walked in a circle reciting my first prayer.

"Sh'ma Yisrael Adonai Elohaynu Adonai Echad."

I sounded the guttural "ch" in "Echad", which further embarrassed me because it felt and sounded like I was going to cough up some phlegm.

"And what does it mean?" She asked.

"Hear, oh Israel, the Lord our God, the Lord is One." I said.

She looked slightly impressed. "Do you know any more?"

I continued my gyrations.

"Er... Borukh shem k'vod Malcolm Toe, Leo Lamb va-ed."

"Mmm." She sounded doubtful, "What does that mean?"

"Erm... Blessed be these names in His glorious kingdom for ever and ever."

I was hoping she wouldn't ask for any more because I'd only learned the first two lines.

"Well," she said, "You're good at the English. I don't know about the Hebrew."

She turned to go. With great effort I buried my embarrassment and suppressed my pride and called after her.

"Gran? Who's Leo Lamb?"

She turned to me shook her head, then looked to heaven, shrugged her shoulders and sighed, "Oh God, what did I do so bad that you send me such a boy as this?"

I managed to fake it for six weeks, since Mrs. Green mostly got us to recite Hebrew phrases from the board or passages from our books. I just made sure I sat at the back of the class and mimed in time with the others. In fact Mrs. Green thought I was her best student, because whenever she tried to engage us in the meaning of a passage, she'd ask related questions, like, "In Israel long ago, people lived in houses made of stone, wood and mud. What are our houses made of?"

I always jumped up first with my hand up straining, aching to answer, "Please, Miss. Me Miss!"

"OK, Tommy?"

"Bricks Miss. Our houses are made of bricks."

"Right, Tommy. I can always rely on you." She said. Actually she cooed – like a pigeon. "I can aaaalways rely on yoooooo."

She gave me the kind of soft smile you give to a puppy when you pick it up. I'd seen mothers in Burdett Road market do that smile when they lifted other people's babies from their prams. I was addicted to her smile. It filled me with a warmth that flushed right through my body, heart and soul for a brief moment, and as the warmth faded, it left me with aching black emptiness, which had to be filled as soon as possible.

If her question was about the Hebrew, I just looked across at Benny with a big smile that intimated, "Oh yes I know this, but I'll give one of the others a chance this time." Benny always got it right.

I got away with being the brightest-dumbest kid in the class for a full six weeks. Until Louis Nyman told me we had a test coming up. I'd have known about this, had I been listening to Mrs. Green's announcement during last Thursday's class, but I was too anxious to get out and tuck into the crisps.

What could I do? I'd score nothing in any Hebrew test! I couldn't let Mrs. Green down after I'd basked in all those lovely smiles. She might get upset, and possibly angry. She might even report me to Mr. Rosen and he'd do the Ten Commandments on me.

Once I spilt ink on Zennia Simon's frock and her parents came up to school and got me into trouble. Mr Rosen said I did it on purpose and I was a born sinner and he dragged me out in front of all the kids at morning assembly and made me stand in front of him while he did the Ten Commandments.

"ONE!" He bellowed, his voice echoing round the hall. "I am the Lord thy God who brought you out of the Land of Egypt!"

He shouted really loud and pointed his finger at me.

"TWO! Thou shalt have no other God before me!"

When he said that, I thought Mr Rosen wanted me to bow down and worship *him*.

"THREE! Thou shalt not take the name of the Lord in vain!"

I was beginning to feel guilty. I had asked God for help sometimes when I was in serious trouble with teachers, but it never made any difference, so perhaps I *had* been talking to Him in vain.

"FOUR! Remember the Sabbath Day and keep it holy!"

He was on to me. I disobeyed that one lots of times – riding on busses on Saturday when you shouldn't, spending money going to the pictures and I hardly ever went to the Synagogue.

"FIVE! Honour thy father and thy mother!"

Now he'd got me. How could I honour my father or my mother when I didn't have either?

"SIX! Thou shalt not kill!"

He shook his finger violently at me.

Did he know about Mrs. Levy? I felt so guilty standing there, I thought perhaps she'd poked her head out of her window again and it had been cut off. I opened my mouth to say "I didn't mean it, Sir, honest, it was an accident!" but he went on.

"SEVEN! Thou shalt not commit adultery!"

I didn't know what that meant, so I hoped I hadn't done it yet.

"EIGHT! Thou shalt not steal!" He pointed the fingers of both hands at me.

Now I was for it – all that stuff we'd taken from people's airees and hidden in our shelter. Was that stealing or just finders-keepers?

"NINE! Thou shalt not bear false witness against thy neighbour nor covet thy neighbour's wife!"

Davy's Granddad, Abe Yude, lived next door at number 92. His wife Dorrie was a very big lady and as old as my Gran and I know I didn't covet her.

"TEN! Thou shalt not covet thy neighbours house nor his servants male or female or his ox or his donkey!"

There were no servants, oxen or donkeys in Eric Street, so I was all right there.

"ELEVEN!"

This was Mr Rosen's very own commandment.

"Thou shalt not dishonour the Holy Language of God!"

He used that one for kids who didn't do well in their Hebrew lessons.

I'd broken most of the commandments, but I couldn't work out which one said no spilling ink on Zennia's frock. But anyway, I felt humiliated in front of everyone and the most overwhelming sense of guilt.

"Let that be a lesson to you boy!" Mr Rosen bellowed. He brushed me away and turned to the whole assembly. "And to any of you who break God's holy commandments!"

I wasn't keen on the wrath of Rosen. I had to get out of that Hebrew test. So I wrote a note on Basildon Bond from my Gran:

> *"Dear Mrs. Green, I'm afraid Thomas won't be able to do Cheder classes any more. I am crippled with arfritus and he has to be at home in the evenings to help me. I know*

he has enjoyed the classes and learned a lot. Yours Truly, Rebecca Angel."

It wasn't a lie. Well not completely – Gran often said she was crippled with arthritis and I was her arms and legs, when she sent me for errands.

At the end of the morning Hebrew lesson, I hung back and gave Mrs. Green the note.

"It's from my Gran." I looked down to avoid her eyes.

"Thaaank yoooo, Tommy." She cooed.

Time slowed to a crawl as she carefully opened the envelope. Fear welled up in my chest. First my ears and then the rest of my face started glowing. My mouth went dry but the rest of me broke into a sweat. I needed the lav.

What have I done? What would she think? What will she do?

I could hear Mr. Rosen's lecture in assembly.

"ONE! This boy lied to his teacher!"

"TWO! He cheated in class."

"THREE! He dishonoured God's Holy Language. Just for a bag of crisps and FOUR! He exploited his poor crippled Grandmother and forged her handwriting to cover up his sins!"

In my stomach emptiness grew like hunger.

She unfolded the letter and read silently. Her eyebrows, first raised in a question, quickly lowered into a frown. She looked down at me with that grownup resignation that's usually followed by a deep sigh of disappointment.

I heard her say, *"Whaaat on eaaaaarth have yooooo done?"*

But that was only inside my head. She looked me straight in the eye.

"I'm sooooo sorry about your Grandmother, Tommy."

And then she filled my gaping, aching emptiness with that warm smile, and said, "You're one of my best boooys, tooooo. Never mind. I dooooo hope you enjoy Puuuurim."

Then she did the most terrible thing.

She held my shoulders, reached down and kissed my forehead. I was mortified. My crime was compounded a hundred-fold. What had I done! I stared at her, my mouth dangling stupid. I forced a weak smile, blushed again and looked back at my feet.

"Thank you, Miss... You too."

I walked to the door a free man, but locked in a prison of shame.

"Oh, Tommy, just one thing", she called after me, "That's not how you spell arthritis."

I turned to her. I wanted to confess everything, fall down on my knees and beg her forgiveness, but Benny and Louis rushed up and dragged me into the playground to kick a can.

I was useless and kept missing. I was thinking about that kiss. I had seen Benny's mum kiss him and his sister like that. It was a parental kiss – from a mother to a son like I never had before. Gran never kissed me like that. In fact she never kissed me at all – in fact she never even touched me and it would be disgusting if she did. Larry's mum kissed him every morning as she left for work. Viv's mum kissed her when she came in for tea. That's what mums did, but not for me.

"Come on Tommy. You're in goal." Benny yelled, kicking the can towards me. He knew something was wrong. "What's up?" he asked.

I couldn't tell him I was thinking about the amazing all-accepting unconditional love that's in a mother's kiss and I couldn't tell him how I lied to Mrs. Green to escape the Hebrew test and how I wished she was my mother and that's probably number TEN! – coveting thy neighbour's wife, because although she doesn't live next door, she is someone's wife and she does live somewhere around here and I coveted her for a mum.

"Nothing."

That lunchtime, instead of sitting at the top table, the teachers sat with us, to celebrate Purim. To my relief, Mrs. Green sat on the far side of the room and we got Mr. Baldwin, who I liked a lot because he let me make cardboard models of old temples instead of doing real work.

At the end of firsts, which included a slice of turkey each, the teachers left to do something important in the staffroom, and we all got Hamantaschen. These were flattish triangular lumps of dough filled with sweetened poppy seeds supposed to be shaped like Haman's hat. He was the baddie in the bible story of Purim, and we were all supposed to hate him for trying to kill Queen Esther and the Jews. Well we did hate his buns, at least the school variety. They were big, tasteless, heavy and boring – but perfect for throwing.

David Benson, one of the older kids started it. He flicked his bun across the room at Harvey Kutner. That was it. Permission granted! Suddenly the air was filled with flying Hamantaschen – hundreds of them. It was war – all against all. Chairs went scraping and kids scuttled under tables collecting ammo, then popped up and threw them indiscriminately. Some of the younger kids hadn't finished their firsts, and soon the buns were supplemented with over-boiled potatoes, limp cabbage leaves, carrots and turkey. It got messy – time for me Benny and Louis to retreat behind the notice board screens, where we could watch the fun, safe from leftovers. Well, not quite. A slice of turkey came spinning through the air from our left. Benny pulled me down in time, but it thwacked into Louie's ear, dribbling gravy down his shirt.

It was wonderful and terrible, and becoming more serious by the minute, as some of the more reckless kids started skimming plates across the room. Something had to be done before someone was decapitated. Benny made a pathetic attempt to put on a big deep teacher voice and shouted above the din.

"Children, that's ENOUGH! I said, E-NOUGH!"

No one was fooled, but the distraction injected a short pause, into which stepped, by a miracle of perfect timing the only teacher whose presence alone would, like Moses parting the Red Sea, still the barrage of missiles. Mr. Baldwin appeared in the doorway and asked quietly, "What's going on?"

Shocked silence. The last few flying Hamantaschen floated to the floor and a plate smashed against the wall. A hundred faces flicked to the crash site and back to Mr. Baldwin. On every face an expression of surprised innocence, as if they had just been beamed down from the planet Mars and materialized in this strange room and had no idea what had happened.

It took some time to clean up the mess – all our dinnertime play, in fact, but luckily there was no inquisition. Probably a waste of time – no one would have seen anything – no one would have thrown anything and everyone would claim they tried to stop it.

It wasn't even mentioned in assembly. It's like it never happened. And we all knew it wouldn't happen again. Not until next Purim.

And Benny, Louis and I wouldn't be there – we'd be at the Grammar if we were lucky or the Secondary Modern if we were not.

Mrs. Levy Loses her Head

Riding the bus home after the Purim party. I was feeling good about escaping Cheder classes and avoiding the wrath of Rosen's Ten Commandments, but I was also feeling bad about lying to Mrs. Green and that lead me to thinking about Mrs. Levy.

I'd been worried about her getting her head chopped off for a long time. As soon as I got home, I grabbed my pocket money and ran round to Mr Levy's shop.

I squeezed through the queue and went straight to the sweet jars. I took ten minutes choosing sweets for the weekend and then put them on the counter with my money.

"Hello, My Levy."

Mr Levy was the opposite of Mrs. Levy in every possible way. She was tight featured and thin. He was round featured and fat. She was tight-fisted and tight-lipped. He was generous and talkative. She affected a posh accent and he reveled in his barrow-boy cockney.

"Wotcher, Tommy."

"How's Mrs. Levy?"

"I'll tell you what, Tommy, you boys did such a good job of cleaning that bloody airee, she's got me making her a bloody window box to go down there and she's planted bloody pansies."

"That's nice."

"How's your Gran?"

"She's fine thank you."

I walked out quickly, imagining Mrs. Levy leaning out the window tending to her pansies, the cracked pane hovering over her head. I decided to save up my pocket money to pay for the window.

A couple of weeks went by and I had bad dreams of Mrs. Levy being guillotined and her head falling into a basket of pansies or Mrs. Levy with her head on the chopping block and the executioner's axe falling on her scrawny neck.

When I'd saved 2s 6d I ran round to the shop intending to confess and give the money to Mr. Levy. But once in the shop I was tempted by a packet of Rolos and spent sixpence. One more week, I thought. I'll save up again and then I'll pay for the window.

The following Friday I came back to the shop and waited outside until there were no other customers. I went straight to the counter clutching my 2s 6d.

"Hello, Mr. Levy."

"Wotcher, Tommy."

"How's Mrs. Levy?"

"She's gone."

"What?"

He looked down. "I suppose it's all your fault, Tommy."

It's happened, I thought, I've killed her!

"Er… What happened, Mr Levy?"

"Well, Monday morning she goes down the basement to water them bloody pansies. Five minutes later. There's a scream and an almighty crash. I run down and there's bloody glass every-bloody-where and she has her bloody head sticking out the window."

Oh no! Oh God forgive me! Mrs' Levy's head's been chopped off and it was all my fault. I cracked the window and then I scoffed the Rolos instead of paying to fix it and now she's dead! "SIX! Thou shalt not kill!"

"You all right. Tommy?" Mr Levy asked.

I couldn't speak. What could I say? I just stared at him with my mouth open.

"Well anyway," he went on, "I says to her 'What's up?' and she says 'Crick in me neck. Can't move". So I pulls her in and sits her down. 'Dropped me water jar!' she says. 'Never mind the bloody jar.' I says, 'Better get you to the bloody doctors'. But she won't go will she. 'I'll be all right in a couple of days', she says, and hangs around the house all week giving me a bloody headache complaining about her bloody neck.

"So yesterday, I'd had enough. I says to her 'It's all that bending down under the bloody window what does it'. I says 'You'll have to give up on them bloody pansies. So we has a row, don't we, and she goes right off her head, opens her mouth and shouts loud enough for the whole bloody street to hear that I'm the biggest bloody pain-in-the-neck. 'Ha ha very funny!' I says and then I bloody nails it shut – the window I mean.

"Then she has the bloody cheek to say I cracked the window with me hammering. Well, I didn't bloody notice did I. And who cares about a little crack in a bloody basement window. I'm not forking out ten bob for a new pane. So I says 'Right, that's it!' and I drags her round the doctor.

"So, anyway. She's just gone for her bloody appointment up the bloody hospital – physio-bloody-therapy. You just missed her."

"Oh thank God!" I said.

"What?"

"Er… that she's… OK."

"Oh, yes, she's OK, Tommy."

I promised God I'd go to synagogue tomorrow and every Saturday from now on and I wouldn't even take the bus. I'd walk all the way.

"You sure you're all right. Tommy? You do look a bit pale."

"Oh no. I'm fine, Mr Levy."

"Well, Tommy, since this was all your fault for cleaning the bloody airee in the first place, perhaps you'd like to make up for it?"

"Oh yes, Mr Levy. Anything you want."

I must have looked a bit frightened. He reached over the counter and mussed my hair. "Only kidding, Son. Tell you what I'll give thruppence a week if you keep an eye on them bloody pansies. You can climb down the airee and give em a drink when they need it. How about that?"

"OK Mr Levy" I said, "But you don't have to pay me."

"You're a good boy, Tommy." He said. "Here, have a Rolo on me."

The Lone Ranger and the Bedspring War

Every Saturday morning, as I lay late in bed, Granddad would come quietly into the room and leave a pile of coins – eighteen pence – on the mantelpiece. When I wasn't saving up to fix broken windows, one and sixpence kept me in sweets and comics for a week and paid for Saturday morning pictures.

But that pile of coins meant more than money. It was our secret. Every time he left my room, he ruffled my hair and said, "Don't tell your Gran."

I am sure Gran really knew, but the secret was a bond between us. It joined me to Granddad and my uncles and the history of their Saturday night stories. I was one of them – Solly the Motor Magician, Sammy the Grenade Catcher and I was Granddad – Daniel Angel the Champion.

On Saturday mornings our gang always went to the pictures – the Odeon on Mile End Road. But this Saturday I'd promised God I'd go to the synagogue and I wouldn't even take the bus. This was one promise I was absolutely determined to keep. So I set off walking down Mile End Road with that intention.

"Oi, Tommy!"

Outside the cinema, a snaking mass of anarchic kids queued to see the latest episode of the Lone Ranger, Superman, some cartoons and a Cowboys and Indians film. Larry had a good place near the front of the queue. He beckoned me over to join him.

I pushed in front of Larry, ignoring the moans from the kids behind us. We wrestled and boxed each other, pulled hair, nicked sweets, bombed and machined-gunned each other for what seemed like eternity, until at last we paid our sixpences to enter the darkness.

Usually, while the trailers were running, we tucked into our sweets, stuck chewing gum under the seats and had farting competitions.

Unusually, this time, we heard little whizzing noises and the odd howl of pain from kids around us. It was as if a swarm of bees had been released in the dark and were streaming in our direction. We ducked behind the seats to take stock of the situation from safety. Davy, always the bravest among us, told Ronny to pop his head up and look around.

"Blimey", Ronny said, "its Ropery Street. They've got catties!"

One by one we ventured a peek.

Half a dozen Ropery Street kids were sitting together about four rows in front of us. They had bedspring catapults and were firing at us!

You could usually find a discarded iron bedstead on the bomb site. Some had those spiral springs that went "Boing!" on cartoons. We stapled them to planks to make jumping shoes, which never worked. But some bed frames were fitted with a mesh of y-shaped wire springs. We pulled the springs apart and strung them with elastic bands to create perfect mini-catapults to shoot spit-soaked wads of paper at each other.

We thought we had invented these weapons, and we had a blood-brother pact to keep them a close secret. We were convinced no one in Mile End knew about them, but Ropery Street must have been spying on us – they had our secret weapon.

Errol popped up and got hit on the chest. He slapped his hand over the missile, took a look and shouted, "Duck!"

It wasn't a paper spit ball, which might sting a bit if it hit your face, but a staple nail, with two sharp points that could draw blood or put your eye out. We kept low and listened to the little thuds as staples hit clothing or seat backs and heard yelps as they hit boy flesh.

Eventually the victims triangulated on the enemy position and mounted a spontaneous counter attack from all angles. The Ropery Street mob disappeared under a swarm of angry fists and a chant went up, "Fight! Fight! Fight!"

While pandemonium was exploding Uncle Joe was on the stage with a few volunteers from the audience, making animals from sausage-shaped balloons. It was a competition, with a bag of assorted chocolate bars for the winners. When the kids had finished they held up their animals and Uncle Joe asked the audience to vote for the best. His timing wasn't good.

A hundred kids, bored with twisted balloons, converged on the bundle. Most of these blood-lusting boys had no idea what the fight was about but that didn't stop them from joining in, perhaps in a more light-hearted and opportunistic way than the original combatants, who had justice and pain on their side. The fight spilled into the aisle and then into the no-mans-land in front of the stage. It seemed as if the whole audience was bundled into one crushing mass, four or five deep on top of the Ropery Street boys, who, while safe from flying fists, were now struggling for breath.

The Manager marched on to the stage and ordered everyone back to their seats – no effect. He asked nicely – no effect. He pleaded – no effect. He threatened to ban everyone – no effect. For life! – no effect.

He called for the three usherettes, who stood in front of the stage with their trays of choc-ices and lollies. They waded into the outskirts trying to cut a path through the centre of the fight, but they couldn't control writhing boys and ice cream trays at the same time. Trays tipped and choc-ices went flying. One boy shouted "Scramble!" and dozens of kids dived for the floor searching for the ices. A kid struggled up through the mass holding an orange lolly triumphantly above his head. Another snatched it from his hands and a new fight broke out, and then another and another.

It was madness and it was escalating wildly. Only one thing could stop this melee.

I'd been jostled to the front – right under the stage. I looked up at the Manager who stood helpless on stage with his hands on his hips, mouth open, and eyes wide.

"Mister!" I shouted. "Mister!"

He looked down at me.

I mimed a man riding a horse, pulling rhythmically at the reins. I ran my hand around my head to suggest a cowboy hat.

He looked disdainfully at first, then puzzled.

I mimed a mask over my eyes and shot my six-guns at him.

And then he realized.

He waved at someone high at the back of the cinema and whirled his hand in a circle.

The William Tell Overture blasted at full volume and the Lone Ranger flickered to life on the screen. His faithful horse reared and he cried "Hi Ho, Silver…"

In a split second the kids stopped fighting and cheered in unison "Awaaaay!" and scrambled towards their seats. We settled down to boo the baddies, cheer the goodies and jeer at the crushed and embarrassed Ropery Street gang.

Just before the end of the show, we raced out to avoid the Ropery boys who might be looking for revenge. We ran into the blinding light and charged across the big open square outside the cinema, holding hands in a wide arc, oblivious to everyone else and cheering "Hi Ho Silver… Awaaay!"

A tall slim woman, with long dark hair, wearing a black fur coat stood in our path, with a girl, about a year older than me. We noticed them too late. I was in the middle. I stopped dead in front of them, but the others, victims of centrifugal force, flew out of control, wrapped around them and fell in a bundle about their feet.

I thought we were in for big trouble, but the girl who was blonde with blue eyes just looked straight at me and laughed.

Suddenly I had tunnel vision. Everything was blurred except her face. Every movement was stilled except her smiling and every sound was silenced except her laughter.

Her mother glowered down at us and stepping over our bodies she dragged the girl away. The girl looked back over her shoulder. She waved. I lifted my hand to wave back, but her mother spun her round as they hurried off and she didn't see.

I wanted to follow her, but the gang had other ideas. It was mid-day and we were hungry and we went wildly snaking across the Mile End Road towards Eric Street where we dispersed into our houses for food.

Saturday Night

Every single Saturday night from as far back as I could remember – the whole family came round to Gran's.

They all gathered in my bedroom. With the put-u-up folded away and the drop leaf table opened and extended for cards, it became a living room. As a compensation for getting the room ready every week, my cousin Louis (the younger) and I were allowed to roast chestnuts on the fire for all the kids.

There were lots of kids – Gran had six surviving children, all married except Vinny, so I had eleven uncles and aunts and twelve cousins. Everybody came on Saturday, plus Great Aunt Betty. With Gran and Granddad that meant twenty-six people crammed into the basement.

Little Louis and I squatted on either side of the hearth and speared chestnuts on toasting forks. When they were blackened, we threw them across the room to our various cousins, making sure they were still hot enough to burn their hands when they caught them.

From the hearth we could see everyone and make fun of them.

Auntie Hannah – tall, thin, dark and dignified stood with her back to the fire, skirt lifted, warming her bum. The uncles jeered, "Let the rest of us see the fire, Hannah." But she just lifted her nose higher and surveyed the family. She was our moral guardian and was allowed and expected to make judgments on everyone else.

Louis was giggling about her blue knickers and the red blotchy patches on the back of her legs. I made him shut up. I liked Aunt Hannah – she stood up for me many times, and tonight she would come to my rescue again.

She was the oldest and wisest, among the aunts, and the most religious of the family – not really *frum* like the Jews from Stamford Hill and Golders Green – she shopped and traveled on the *Shabbat* – but she mostly ate kosher food and went to synagogue Friday evenings.

The family were Jewish by culture rather than religion. Gran was the only one who spoke any Yiddish and she only knew insults.

Most of them only went to synagogue for funerals. Some had married English husbands or wives. Everyone celebrated Christmas and Easter as well as Chanukah. Some of the kids had even been christened. Auntie Hannah and her Harry were the only ones who spoke Hebrew properly and could follow all the services. She did *Pesach* and *Rosh Hashanah* at home and fasted on *Yom Kippur*. Her son, Big Louie was the only cousin to have a *Bar Mitzvah*.

Aunt Hannah's husband, Uncle Harry Diamond was short, round and smiley and well off. He collected silver ornaments for their sideboard. Big Louie was one of the cousins but he was so old he counted with the aunts and uncles. He was very intelligent, preferred Frank Sinatra to Buddy Holly and wanted to "get on in life". He became a jeweler, married a pretty English girl called Shelley, and they had three Great Danes and two little girls.

Aunt Miriam sat close to the fire, near me. She was always cold. She looked much older than her sisters. She had a thin face, full of sorrow or disappointment. Like most of the family she smoked, but she had the worst cough and you could hear gurgling in her breathing. Her skin was wrinkly grey paper and the whites of her eyes were yellow with spidery red veins.

Her husband, Uncle Arthur was a docker – a jolly man who kept budgies and when I did or said something he thought clever, he called me, "Pretty Boy, Tommy. Pretty Boy!" like I was one of his birds. They had two girls, Esther and Rita, who tended to play together or hang around Aunt Miriam.

Uncle Solly and Uncle Sammy were twins, but like Rebecca's twins Jacob and Esau, they didn't look alike.

Uncle Solly had playful eyes and a wicked sense of humour. The Uncles revered him for his legendary ability to strip any lorry engine down to nuts and bolts and put it back together in better condition than when he started. He smoked cigars, which gave him an air of authority. He didn't shave at weekends and by Saturday night had a chin like Desperate Dan, which he scraped on the kids' delicate faces. Connie was his victim tonight. She screamed loudly and cried, but she really loved being the one chosen for his attention.

I always thought that Uncle Solly's wife, Aunt Marlene, looked French. Her real name was Marlena – that must be French. Her clothes were flowery and shapely – as I imagined French women might wear and she moved, chuckled and talked with a sauciness that certainly was not like any Jewish or English woman I knew. She ran a bed-and-breakfast at their old house before they moved to Brokesley Street, and some of the aunts said she flirted with her lodgers. I don't think she did – it was just that they weren't used to Aunt Marlene's ways.

Their daughter, my cousin Connie was only nine. Her little sister, Sarah, was just six – both too young to be interesting.

My other twin uncle, Uncle Sammy worked in the Davis Bros. Road Haulage yard behind Gran's house, with Uncle Solly and Vinny. He was very good at finding things that fell off the backs of lorries. He would bring them over on Saturday and give them away or sell them.

Miraculously, nothing was ever damaged by the fall. This explained why, no matter whose house I visited in the family, they all had the same red Formica fold-down kitchen table and a weird foreign coffee machine that no one could work.

I loved Sammy and Solly for their stories and jokes, but they scared me.

Vinny told me that Sammy and Solly were very brave soldiers and had fought side by side throughout the war. When it was over they went AWOL and commandeered a lorry. They filled it with army equipment, weapons and rations and drove it back to England, where they sold most of the stuff and stockpiled the rest. He said that's how they started their business.

Connie once told me Uncle Solly had a shed full of army guns at the end of their back yard. I didn't believe her, but whenever I was round their house I noticed no one was ever allowed to go near the shed. Once, playing football with Connie, I deliberately kicked the ball down the end of the yard and ran after it, towards the shed, hoping to take a peep inside. Uncle Solly suddenly appeared at the kitchen door and shouted in his deepest darkest voice, "Tommy. Keep away from there!" No one disobeyed Uncle Solly. After that, whenever I played in their yard I was careful not to even look at the shed.

Uncle Sammy was always joking with the men, but was frighteningly gruff with the children. If one of the kids fell and cut a knee, his wife, Aunt Nina would run to comfort them, but he would laugh. I know he loved his kids, but he didn't seem to show it. He was always telling them off, although, to my puzzlement, at the same time he laughed at them whatever they did wrong.

The previous summer, during the school holidays, I went to stay for a week at Uncle Sammy's. I loved staying at his house. It was on a nice clean street in Romford, with trees and grass verges. They didn't have a concrete back yard with an air raid shelter, but a grassy garden, which spread all around the house, with a little goldfish pond and flower beds and a brightly coloured climbing frame and a swing for the kids.

The house was modern and clean and full of light. All the kids had real beds and there were no bed bugs, mice, rats or cockroaches.

There was a bathroom with white tiles on the walls, a proper white bath and a white sink to wash in, with hot water coming straight out of the taps. There were coloured towels and little plastic dishes with soap. It smelled of perfume.

Aunt Nina's kitchen had diamond-patterned lino – not the thick brown peeling stuff Gran had. She also had the latest kitchen units, all in a line, fixed to the wall.

Next to the kitchen she had another small room with a washing machine and the latest stainless steel sink. She didn't have to pummel the clothes and use a washboard and soap like Gran. She just put them inside the machine, closed the door, poured some powder through a hole and then watched them roll over and over, through the round window.

We used to eat at the red Formica kitchen table. It was a squeeze with seven of us and the baby.

We had roast dinner on Sunday, but it wasn't like at Gran's. They cooked a smaller roast, even though they had more people to share it. Aunt Nina put less on the plate, and the meat potatoes and veg were all separate. They didn't have mash – just roast potatoes.

They finished off the leftover meat at Sunday tea. From Monday they had various combinations of spam, eggs peas and chips for tea – every day. I liked spam. I never had spam at home. Lucy complained every night and by Thursday she really had the hump.

"Spam again!" she said.

"Just you think yourself lucky there's food in your belly." Aunt Nina said.

"Yea, I know, lots of kids are starving." Lucy said.

"Alright, you can have pilchards instead."

Lucy retched.

When we finished tea, all the kids asked permission to get down from table. Uncle Sammy teased each one in turn for a while and then let them go. "Oh all right then, get off out of my sight."

I never had to ask to get down at Gran's and I was so scared to ask Uncle Sammy that I stayed long after all the others had gone. I had to join in their conversation, which was mostly about their friends – local people I didn't know. It was strange to think that the adults had friends because I'd only ever seen family in Gran's house. Eventually Uncle Sammy left, Aunt Nina cleared the table and sent me out.

"You're a good boy Tommy," she said, "the others never want to stay and talk with us."

I played with Louie in the garden for a bit and then I asked him why they always had spam for tea.

"Only Monday to Thursday," he said, and he led me to the utility room. At the opposite end to the washing machine was a pile of cardboard boxes, stacked almost to the ceiling.

"Look." he said, "Dad said he liberated it from the army."

Every box was stenciled "Spam x 100".

"Blimey, Louis" I said, "That's a lot of spam."

He beamed.

I counted the boxes. "Let's see… twenty four boxes times a hundred tins is…"

Louis looked up at me with his eyes wide and his lips pursed in anticipation.

"…Two thousand four hundred tins."

Louis grinned.

I had watched Aunt Nina open two cans that night.

"So that's… about eight cans a week. Two thousand four hundred divided by eight is …" I couldn't do the division by eight in my head, so I divided by ten instead. "Two hundred and forty. You're gonna eat spam for two hundred and forty weeks."

"Blimey!"

"That's… five years!"

Louis's grin widened and then faded as admiration for my mental arithmetic was replaced by appreciation of what five years of spam would be like. He liked spam, but not that much.

"What's this?" I asked, pointing to another pile of twelve boxes, with no stencil markings.

"Pilchards." He said, "We have 'em on Fridays. Lucky we go to Nan's on Saturdays."

While Uncle Sammy was respectful to Aunt Nina in his own home, on Saturday nights at Gran's house, he constantly teased her in front of the other men. This disturbed me, because Aunt Nina was soft and warm and was always on the kid's side – a safe haven for us all. She was light and giggly in a way that the Jewish aunts never were. She had lots of children:

Lucy was ten – a serious little girl, born middle-aged with a sense of morality – more like Auntie Hannah than her mum. But she did have Aunt Nina's giggle, and was easily persuaded to join in any mischief her brother Louis and I got up to. Louis was seven and like a puppy – eager, with an up-for-anything sparkle in his eyes. He was full of life and great fun. Alice was eight, bonny and enthusiastic. Joey was only two and very quiet – watching everyone. Debbie was just a baby.

Aunt Stella was the youngest of the Aunts gathered at Gran's. She was dark haired and had a pretty round face. She spent most of the evening asking Granddad if he wanted more tea, or a biscuit or something. She had the same wheedling smile that my mate Ronny put on when he was trying (always successfully) to get round his dad to buy him more Meccano.

Her husband was Lionel. Gran called him a *groyse macher* – a big shot showoff and said she didn't trust him because he smoked the new filter tips.

Great Aunt Betty Levy was Gran's sister. She sat in the chair by the fire opposite Aunt Miriam all night. She was very old, very wide and a bit scary. Her face was hairy, warty, dark and deeply furrowed like a walnut. Her voice was gravelly like the witch in Hansel and Gretel. But she was also kind to all the kids – gave us sweets which were always welcome and lung-crushing hugs and wet kisses, which were not.

So, with Uncle Vinny and me, that's the whole family. Gran saw all her descendants every Saturday night. Except for the dead ones.

I knew about Uncle Louis who died in the war and Katy who died too young to become an Aunt or have her photo taken. Aunt Hannah told me her ghost came back the night Gran heard Uncle Louis had died in the war.

Great Aunt Betty asked me to fetch a cup of tea. When I got back from the kitchen, I asked her how many children Gran had altogether.

"Nine"

I recited them and counted them off on my fingers. "Sammy, Solly, Vinny, Dead Uncle Louis, Aunt Miriam, Hannah, Stella and Poor Dead Katy – that's eight." I said

"You forget Sylv." She said.

"Sylv." I remembered the box with the wedding veil, "Sylv Angel."

"That's right, Tommy" she whispered, "don't you forget Sylvie. They'd all like to forget Sylvie. They pretend she doesn't exist." That was the first time I heard that name said aloud.

Three generations crowded into the basement front room. The oldest women including Gran had the armchairs and pouffé near the blazing fire. Throughout the evening they exercised their matriarchal privileges, ordering any nearby child to turn up the radio, fetch tea, or a shovel of coal.

The kids kept moving most of the night to avoid being caught for more tea or coal. We played cowboys and Indians behind the settees, under the table, in the coal cupboard, up and down the stairs and out in the street.

The radio played the Archers, where Dan Archer and Walter Gabriel spoke a foreign language about "heifers, ewes, silage, and milk quotas". The men around the dinner table smoked and drank beer and played cards – Klabyash. They spoke another foreign language – words like "trump, yoss, manel, and misere of aire".

Granddad sat at the head of the table smoking Woodbines. Everybody loved him. He was kind, gentle, unassuming and full of humour. He was always making jokes and he told them like they were secrets.

One of my jobs was tearing up the newspaper for the toilet. I had to tear it into six inch squares and spike it on a butcher's hook, which hung over a pipe on the lavatory wall. The job was boring and took too long, but Granddad could make anything into fun. He used to encourage me to use the saucy pictures from the News of the World, just to annoy Gran. Whenever I filled the butchers hook, I'd shout "Finished" and Granddad would say,

"So Tommy, now you're the tallest boy in the world."

I'd ask, "Why's that, Dad?"

"'Cos you can wipe your arse on the Evening Star!"

We'd laugh as if we'd never shared the joke before.

Granddad had been a boxer. He had a bent squashy nose and cauliflower ears to prove it. When Rocky Marciano retired undefeated-six-times-world-heavyweight-champion in April, Uncle Sammy said Granddad was better than Rocky, because Granddad never lost a fight and Rocky lost three out of forty nine.

Granddad was small like Rocky, slighter of build and he had a quiet strength that won everyone's respect. The Uncles ribbed each other constantly, but they never teased Granddad. The Aunts argued about everything, but when Granddad spoke they listened without contradiction or protest, and Gran could go only so far with her continuous nagging and complaining – then Granddad would look her straight in the eye and she'd fall silent.

He would tell me "Tommy, you must take the best from everyone and let them keep the worst to themselves."

I hoped I took all his best – his quiet strength, his kindness, his humour. I never saw any of his *worst*.

As the card games progressed the men would raise their voices and argue every trick. The room would fill with their bellowing protests, teasing and laughter. Granddad never raised his voice. Nor did he appear to be very interested in the game, until he'd smile quietly and play a flurry of tricks, win the hand and leave his sons speechless for a moment until they chorused "He's bloody done it again!"

I usually kept an eye on Granddad's pale ale. When the glass was empty, I'd ask, "Want another, Dad?" and fetch a refill. I had always called him Dad, even though I was confused and sometimes embarrassed about it. I knew he was my Grandfather, but Gran and Vinny called him Dad and so did I. No one seemed to mind. It gave me a special place among my cousins, who called him Granddad. They all thought I was their uncle, and Gran and Granddad were my Mum and Dad. I knew that wasn't true, but until the summer of 1956 I didn't know what *was* true and I went along with it. When I asked him, "Want another, Dad?" he'd respond with the same kindly, teasing tone he used with his sons, "Fill 'er up, Tommy!" and I'd feel privileged and proud.

The Aunts took turns to lift their skirts and warm their bums by the fire, but spent much of their time in the kitchen. They all had neat, clean kitchens at home and were revolted by the thick layer of grease in Gran's kitchen. It was everywhere, on the floor, walls, shelves and especially thick on the gas cooker. I'd tried to clean it many times, but it was beyond me. I'd run a cloth under the cold-water tap and scrub away at the grease. I had no effect. Later I found out about Brillo pads and, when I was old enough, I boiled kettles of water and learned how to mop the floor.

It wasn't Gran's fault. She was old, over sixty. She had been a very robust young woman – had a fish stall on the market and she was proud of it. She said our family, were fish people back through the generations – fish porters, fish traders and we knew everything about fish. She said she'd had her hands full of ice-cold cod and halibut for most of her life and now she was suffering for it. Now she was slow and weak. She had arthritis in her hands and diabetes, her eyes were bad and she was forgetful. She regularly made a big pan of bread pudding, stood on a chair to put it right on top of the dresser to cool and then forget it was there. Months would pass and the crust would get thicker and harder and covered in dust, grease and cobwebs, but the middle stayed edible, moist and succulent. I used to sneak in at night and cut a chunk for a midnight feast.

"I know she's old, but this is really disgusting." Auntie Hannah would say, "Why doesn't Vinny do anything?"

"Are you joking?" Aunt Stella would sneer, "Have you seen his room? That boy needs a good woman to sort him out."

They complained, drank gin and made huge piles of sandwiches – cheese, egg, ham (which Auntie Hannah always refused) and spam (which Uncle Sammy never refused) all served up on big oval platters, and endless pots of tea for the fireside matrons.

As the evening rolled on the men laughed louder and argued longer, until they lost concentration on the cards altogether and distracted into stories.

Granddad told how he worked for Costains the builders and used to put dead mice in his mate's sandwiches. Sammy and Solly loved to tell stories about fights they had been in – during the war and since. They'd laugh loud when Solly told how he'd smashed his fist in an Italian's face and his nose exploded. They told two versions of how Sammy's hand was blown up when he either (depending on who you believed) saved his mates by catching a grenade and throwing it back at the Nazis or nearly killed his mates while messing about with one of his own grenades.

The men never spoke seriously about the war, and if Louie or I asked what it was like they'd say it was years ago and best forgotten. Instead they told the same stories every Saturday and argued over the same details.

I wanted to know more. I wanted to know how these men had been changed by the war. Sometimes I saw something in Uncle Sammy's face, when he got annoyed at his kids. At first he'd laugh at their antics, then he'd pretend to be annoyed and growl at them, but sometimes he got really angry and shouted wildly. Then I'd see him suddenly stop and a look would flash across his face as fast as a blink – realization, horror and then composure – all in the tiniest fraction of a second. I imagined he was remembering what it was like to kill people. Uncle Solly and even Granddad must have killed people and they must have buried that horror somewhere inside them. That's why they kept to a safe ritual of funny stories – to distract them and protect us from darker memories when they were their best and their worst.

Once I asked Uncle Sammy what the war was like, he said, "It's not the last one you need to worry about, Tommy. The next one will be over in two minutes."

"That's all right," Uncle Solly said, "we'll get four minutes warning. So that'll give us six minutes all together – just time for a quick one. *L'chaim*!" he raised his glass and finished his beer.

Under Sammy and Solly's humour I suspected there was a darkness and something hard. I once overhead Aunt Marlene say that if it wasn't for the Krays, Sammy and Solly could be running London. I didn't know who the Krays were and what running London meant, but it frightened me.

While the men drank beer and became more merry, the women drank gin and became more melancholy. Aunt Marlene sat halfway up the stairs crying with Auntie Hannah comforting her, while Aunt Nina had a row with Aunt Stella in the kitchen. Granddad asked me to fetch more ham sandwiches. As I skipped in to the kitchen, I saw Aunt Stella sneering at Aunt Nina, whose eyes were red and tearful. Aunt Nina saw me enter and ran out. Aunt Stella twisted round to look and me and snapped,

"What do you want?"

"Aunt Stella. Dad asked if he could have some more ham sandwiches."

"Haven't you kids stuffed yourselves enough?"

"No, not for me… for Dad."

"Little liar", she said and her pretty round face distorted into a sneer.

"Honest, Aunt Stella, Dad sent me!"

"Honest, Aunt Stella, Dad sent me." she mocked.

"Oh yes", she said, "don't we all know it. Little Tommy. Apple of his Daddy's eye."

I didn't understand what was happening. I came in for sandwiches and now Aunt Stella was angry with me. She suddenly took my ears roughly in both hands and looked straight at me, eyes blazing,

"Well he's not your Dad. He's my Dad, right? You? You're a bastard!"

"Why what've I done?"

"Nothing." She pushed me away, with a look of disgust, "You can't help it. You were born a bastard and you'll always be a BASTARD! A bastard son of a WHORE!"

My face flushed, my eyes filled and my chin start to wobble. I couldn't understand what I'd done to her. I shouted, "Sorry!" and ran up the stairs, out into the yard and climbed on top of the air-raid shelter, where no one could see me. I stayed there, head in hands, sobbing until the fire in my head began to subside. I dried my eyes and went to find the only adult I knew I could trust.

Auntie Hannah was with Aunt Marlene on the front doorstep. She said, "I know, Marl, all men are useless. You can't trust any of them."

I took her hand and pulled her into the dark passage.

"Auntie Hannah, I think I've upset Aunt Stella."

"Why?"

"Well she swore at me."

"What did you do?"

"I don't know. I didn't do anything. Honest. I just asked for Dad's sandwiches."

"What did she say?"

"She said he's not my Dad. She said I was…" I hesitated to say a swear word to an adult "…a bastard."

Aunt Hannah looked shocked and angry. I thought it was because I'd said the bad word, and I was in for a good telling off. But, no, she glared, not at me, but over my head into the darkness of the house and marched away towards the kitchen.

I don't know what happened between them. Louis and I ran off to the air raid shelter. I showed him my treasures – some rifle shells, the gas mask, which he tried on and then the picture of the little blond girl in the red velvet dress. I watched his face when he looked at the photo. He was the first in the family to see it after me. He turned with his wide grin and said, "Pretty girl."

I also kept a box with paper and coloured pencils we used to draw things together – cars, planes, mountains. We grabbed the box and ran upstairs to the lodger's. Joe and Maurice were out, but they said I could use their living room whenever I wanted. There was a special reason tonight. I turned on their radiogram. I tuned into Radio Luxembourg, medium wave 208. Tonight, 25th May 1956 was the last episode of Dan Dare. We'd missed the beginning. We lay down on the floor in front of the speakers and drew Dan Dare and his spaceship.

"Oi, Louis. What's a bastard?" I asked casually. He was younger than me, but at home he hung around with some rough kids and he knew things I didn't.

"It's a kid who ain't got no Dad." he replied just as casually, "Do a lady for me. Tommy."

"What?"

"An old fashioned lady."

"OK." I knew what he liked. I drew a knight's lady in a long flowing dress with long gloves, a pointed hat with ribbons flying.

"OK. Let me do it." He said.

Louis drew a lady, more elegant than mine, with a fine profile, big soft eyes, and long lashes. She had flowing wavy hair and long sensitive hands. Her dress was delicately patterned with tendrils of vines. She stood alone on a rock looking over a calm sea, as the sun dipped into the water. It was beautiful.

"That's really good, Louis."

"She's lost someone." he said, "I wanna be an artist."

"You can be Louis. You've got it in you. You can be anything you want."

Fear of Dark and Vermin

The last Dan Dare finished. We ran down to the front room as Granddad was singing one of his songs. Louis and I grinned at each other. We loved it because it was rude, it made Granddad happy and it drove Gran wild.

"My wife's a cow. My wife's a cow. My wife's a cow... keeper's daughter."

Big smiles all round, except for Gran who glared at Granddad.

"I saw her arse. I saw her arse. I saw her arse.... king for water."

The men joined in with the song and the women tutted and giggled. I looked for Aunt Stella, who was sitting on the arm of a settee next to Uncle Lionel, scolding Jessica for something, gripping her thin wrist tight. I felt a hand on my shoulder. It was Aunt Hannah. I looked up. She smiled.

"Don't worry, Tommy, she was just a bit merry. She didn't mean anything."

I smiled. If she was merry, I thought, why was she so angry? If she didn't mean anything, why did she swear at me?

"It's nothing." She looked straight in my eyes and smiled, the way that Mrs. Green did. "It's nothing Tommy."

But it wasn't nothing. It was everything.

Granddad launched into the song I loved best. I slid into the corner, by the coal cupboard, where it was dark, because it always made me cry.

"I leave the sunshine to the flowers,

I leave the raindrops to the trees

And to the old folks,

I leave the memory

Of the baby upon their knees...

I leave the moon above

To those in love,

When I leave the world behind,

When I leave the world be... hind."

Please, Granddad, Please. Never leave me behind.

One by one as the evening closed to night, my cousins, with their brothers and sisters, mums and dads, went home and left me behind. Vinny, Gran and Granddad went to bed. I folded the table away, cleared the chairs to the edges of the room and opened the put-u-up.

I lay in the dark and re-lived every moment of the evening like it was a play and I was a spectator. I'd always known that I didn't belong in the family, but I didn't know why. Apart from Aunt Stella, they were all nice to me, but something was missing. Perhaps they had taken me, in like a stray puppy, as a favour.

That was it. I was a favour. I had no *right* to be there. Louis, Joey, Lucy and Alice – they all had a right to be there. No matter what they were or what they did. No matter how angry Uncle Sammy got with them, they knew he was their Dad and would never leave them behind. Aunt Nina was their Mum and would always smile, even when they got into trouble. It was a given, a certainty.

It wasn't a matter of choice. They didn't choose each other; they belonged with each other – and they'd belong always and forever, no matter what. I had a feeling that I didn't belong, that maybe I was… chosen. Yes, perhaps, someone chose to take me in and they could choose to turn me out.

Louis was an eager boy who loved to play and wanted to learn how to draw, but whether he became an artist, or a gangster, he would always belong with his Mum and Dad and his brothers and sisters.

This Saturday night, I realized for the first time, that I had no real Mum and Dad – only Uncles and Aunts. I had no brothers and sisters – only cousins, and every Saturday night, they went home together and left me behind in the dark.

Louis said a bastard was a kid with no father. Up to now I'd pretended I had lots of fathers. When I was at home it was Granddad. When I stayed with my cousins, I pretended it was my uncles. I told kids at school my father was a Spitfire pilot.

If Aunt Stella knew I didn't have a real father, then everyone must know! So they all knew I'd been pretending. But they didn't let on they knew, and they never told me.

Why? Were they hiding something, ashamed of something? Did something bad happen? Did I do something bad? Was it my real Mother or my real Dad? Was he bad?

My head spun with possibilities. Suddenly all that was solid in my life was melting away; my bed wasn't real – it was a settee, my bedroom was really a living room; my home, my place with Gran and Granddad. None of it was what it seemed.

The solidities gave way to vague and ghostly half-thoughts, suspicions, unanswered questions, whispered names, fleeting looks on Aunts' faces, glimpsed from the corner of my eyes.

As the real world melted, the half-world took its place and all the fears I'd ever had, came back in a huge wave. Perhaps the next war will come tomorrow and I'll be blown up by the H-bomb in two minutes, or be left behind in a radioactive desert, to rot. Perhaps the faces I could see in the pile of clothes by the window really were the faces of ghosts. Perhaps Poor Dead Katy did wander the house at night, with other ghosts to keep her company. What if there really were, as I always imagined, skeletons under the bed, waiting to grab my hand if I let it drop?

I know there really were rats in the coal cupboard. I could hear them scratching at night but Gran always said it was just the coal settling by itself. I know there were cockroaches in the kitchen, because I padded in there barefoot when I got hungry in the night and fancied some bread pudding and I felt them scuttle across my feet. But they didn't matter right now. I was in bed.

But what about the bed bugs?

I shouted, "Gran! Gran!" louder, "Gran! Gran! Come here!"

I heard her scuffling for her slippers in the room above.

I shook my feet convulsively and pulled my knees to my chest.

She came slowly down the stairs. She walked like a toddler – two feet landing on each step, a pause for a couple of breaths and then the next step. "I can't do with this at my age." She shuffled into the dark room and switched on the light.

"What's the matter now?" she scowled.

"Bed bugs, Gran. They're in the bed."

"Get on with yer. We ain't got bed bugs." She turned to leave. "*Meshugener!*"

"But we have, Gran. Look!"

I threw back the covers – right off the end of the bed, so she could see the bottom of the mattress. Dozens of red bugs, the size of peppercorns, some dead flat, some distended with my blood. They slipped out of the light and disappeared into the folds of the covers.

"I can't see nothing." She said with a sigh.

"But there, Gran, look. You can see the spots." I pointed to the round spots of blood, where some of the bugs had burst when I kicked them.

"There's nothing there. Just your imagination. Go back to sleep."

She turned and reached for the light switch as she left the room.

"No leave the light, Gran."

"Gran?"

"What now?"

"Why don't I have any brothers and sisters?"

Caught by surprise she answered without thinking. "You d'…" She stopped and turned away. "Get on with yer. You're full of daft questions."

"But Louie's got three sisters and Connie's got Sarah and Jessica…"

She paused at the door, looked back over her shoulder her face pinched and severe. "Go to sleep and let me get some rest."

"And who is Syl…?"

"Enough already! Enough!" She said, with an urgency and distress in her voice that made me stop.

She shuffled back up the stairs, along the passage. I heard her door creak open and close. I heard her say something short and muffled to Granddad. Then nothing.

I went to the kitchen, peed in the piss bucket by the door and came back to bed. I lay there with the light on and the covers thrown back to keep the bugs away.

Two possibilities, I thought. Either she really couldn't see the bugs – her eyes were getting worse with the diabetes, or she saw them and pretended not to, like the whole family pretended that her daughter Sylvia didn't exist.

I was alone with the rats, cockroaches and the bugs and I knew for certain that anything any adult had ever said to comfort or reassure me, no matter how well intentioned, must have been pretense.

It was a long time until daylight.

Ring of Silence

When I woke the next morning, I checked the piss bucket, which was full to the brim. I struggled upstairs to the toilet, one step at a time, trying not to spill anything on the way. But I splashed a little on the stair carpet. I poured the remainder down the pan and flushed it away.

Gran always said that a healthy family needs a good hot dinner once a week. On Sundays we had a joint of beef or shoulder of lamb. Gran started cooking about nine o'clock. She prepared a big black greasy roasting tin and poured in an inch of rice. Then she settled the joint on top of the rice, scattered lumps of lard, half tomatoes, half onions and half potatoes around it. She sprinkled it with plenty of salt and pepper, covered the rice with water, added more lard, slid the tin in the oven and left it to cook all morning. Now and then she'd check the oven. The rice and potatoes soaked up all the meat juices and fat. If she thought the rice looked dry, she'd add more water and lard.

While the meat was roasting, she boiled potatoes for mashing, and cabbage charged with Bicarbonate of Soda – which was supposed to bring out the colour. She boiled the cabbage until it was almost white and so soft and glutinous you didn't have to chew it. She boiled the potatoes until they started to disintegrate in the water. They were very easy to mash, with a couple of lumps of lard. That was my job – because Gran's wrists hurt with the arthritis.

We ate at the foldaway dinner table in the front room. Gran ladled a mound of mash and rice on each plate, covered it with a layer of cabbage, then roast potatoes, onions and tomatoes. Granddad sliced the meat and shared it out. Vinny ate as fast as he could – which was very fast, and then went off to a football match at Millwall.

Granddad stirred his mash, cabbage, rice, onions and tomatoes, like he mixed concrete at Costains, breaking everything down to small lumps, pouring gravy into a pool in the middle and then folding the mix in from the outside until it was a homogeneous mass. He saved the roast potatoes and ranged them around the edge of the mix. He always enjoyed his food and he always said at every meal, "When we were in the trenches up to our arses in shit and mud. This was what we dreamed about."

He would make a special place for his most succulent and crispy roast potato. "Save the best 'til last." He would clear his plate, leaving the last potato. "I'm full. Who'll help me with this one?" and he winked at me – my cue to scoff his best potato. Like the last crisp in the packet, it was heaven.

I had to clear the plates after dinner. Some leftovers went into Sally, Gran's dachshund. She was so fat her belly trailed on the ground and was worn hairless when she walked. Granddad sliced the leftover meat and Gran served it cold for several days. Everything else including the bones, leftover greens, potatoes and rice, went into the big brown stew pot with the vegetables I'd gather from the neighbours. Gran added water, OXO cubes, and several bottles of HP sauce, some peppercorns and barley. She left it to simmer constantly on the range, and she served it up in the evenings with suet dumplings and bread.

Most Sundays we had family round for dinner. Sometimes Great Aunt Betty, but usually Uncle Solly, Aunt Marlene, Connie and Sarah, who lived around the corner in Brokesley Street.

The conversation was mostly jokes and family stories and a comprehensive running down of everyone in the family who wasn't at the table. I was usually relieved to slide off and play with Connie and Sarah. But this Sunday I was listening – for clues.

It wasn't what they said that mattered, but what they didn't say – the names they didn't mention. For half an hour they had the usual ritual conversations, and then...

"Who is Sylvie?" I blurted out.

There was silence. They looked at each other, then at their plates.

"I'll give you a hand, Mum". Aunt Marlene stood up quickly, scraping her chair across the floor and started collecting the plates even though it was my job.

"Woodbine, Dad?" Uncle Solly asked. He lit a cigar for himself and offered the cigarettes to Granddad.

"Thanks, Sol," said Granddad, tapping the cigarette on the packet and then sucking a light from Solly's match, "How's the new motor?" They talked about engines and gearboxes.

Like the rats, cockroaches and bedbugs, and Katy's ghost, it seemed that Sylvie really didn't exist and if I said her name, I didn't either.

I played out all afternoon with Ronny, Errol and Davy around the bomb site. We installed a couple of newly salvaged armchair cushions in our camp and crawled in. Snug and hidden, we joked and chatted about everything and nothing.

"What did you do last night?" I asked. I listened for what they said about their mums and dads and brothers and sisters. Mostly they complained about being told what to do by their parents and being annoyed by brothers and sisters, but I knew they could only complain like that because they belonged.

That evening I went to the air raid shelter and found the picture of the little blond girl in the red velvet dress. I carefully took the frame to pieces to clean it. While re-assembling, I noticed for the first time a pencilled note on the back of the photograph. It read,

"*Carol Angel, June 48*"

I hadn't heard that name. We had no Carol in the family. Who is she then? Did she die like Katy or is she alive somewhere? How old is she then? June 48. 49, 50, 1, 2, 3, 4, 5, 6 – that's eight years ago and she looked about four or five, so now she's twelve or thirteen – older than me, older than any of my cousins except Big Louis. Who is she – a secret cousin?

Whoever she was, it was a secret – one of those names nobody ever said aloud. I decided to do something dangerous. I needed a hammer and a nail.

I'd seen a hammer balanced on top of Vinny's Austin 6 gearbox. I sneaked into his room. I'd always thought of it like the bomb site or the airee – a rich, if smelly, source of treasures. Now I saw it for the first time as my uncle's bedroom. Around the gearbox, the floor was scattered with oily car parts, repair manuals, crummy old books, a couple of deflated leather footballs, a pile of Millwall football club programmes, cycling magazines and bike parts. He had two old bikes against a wall, one with a broken chain trailing to the floor. The window to the yard was thick with grime and hung with grubby lace curtains that were hard to distinguish from the cobwebs. I delved in the dust on the windowsill for a nail.

Although I'd looked at it a dozen times, I had never seen his bed before. It was a low wooden base strewn with brown blankets. Beside the bed was a brand new copy of Picture Post with a picture of Marilyn Monroe on the cover. She wore a man's shirt. Her arms were folded and she had a nice soft smile. With her blonde hair, blue eyes and red lips she looked very pretty. It was the only clean and pretty thing in the room.

On the floor near the bed was a loose parcel, half wrapped up in the Evening Standard with a picture of the A-bomb explosion on Bikini Atoll. Strange medical things spilled out from inside – flesh-coloured rubber tubes, some with bladders attached, like on the inside of proper footballs. The room smelled of dampness like a bombed-out cellar, but laced with pungent and dark smells I'd never known before or since.

Months later I plucked up courage to ask Auntie Hannah why Vinny's room was like that. She told me he'd missed his education. He had a hole-in-the-heart condition as a child and had to have lots of operations and spent most of his childhood in hospital and now he has a bowel complaint and has to wear a colostomy bag instead of going to the toilet. I asked how a colostomy bag worked and she told me, but a few sentences into her explanation I began to feel ill and ran off in the middle of a sentence. I determined not to miss my education.

The pictures on the walls in the front room had been there for as long as I could remember – Uncle Louis, who died in the war, so couldn't stay upstairs on Gran's piano, Uncle Louis's gravestone, The letter from the King, Uncle Sammy, Solly and Granddad in a group of soldiers, and others of older people I knew nothing about and wasn't interested enough to ask. For as long as I could remember no picture had been moved, none taken away and none added to the family gallery.

I nailed the picture of the blonde girl in the middle of the wall above the sideboard.

Over the days that followed, Vinny, Gran and Granddad came in and out of the front room. They saw the picture and said nothing.

The next Saturday night the whole family saw the picture. I watched for their reactions. Most of them looked straight at it and appeared to see right through to the wallpaper. Aunt Stella sneered for a second, and looked away. Auntie Hannah looked quickly from the picture to me. A shadow of concern flashed across her face then she too turned away. The Saturday night ritual played as normal, the same stories, jokes and arguments. No one said a word about the picture.

When all the aunts and uncles and cousins had gone, and I was climbing into bed, Granddad popped his head round the door and said, "I'm at the park in the morning. Want to come?"

"Not 'arf, Dad!"

Granddad worked at Victoria Park as a parkie. He'd had years of labouring and bricklaying on building sites, sweating through summer and freezing through winter, blistering his hands with picks and shovels, skinning his knuckles on bricks and concrete. He used to say he was building "homes fit for heroes" and he had the hands to prove it. I loved his hands – gnarled like tree roots, so strong but so gentle on my shoulder. I was relieved when he got the park keeper's job. He deserved to be in the green park, in the open air with the sparrows and pigeons and people walking their babies and their dogs. I'd asked him a dozen times to take me with him.

On Sunday morning I was up with the sun and we walked together to Victoria Park. We walked round the lake along with the mums pushing their babies in huge Silver Cross prams. The mums stopped to chat and coo at each other's babies or boast about how many new teeth they had, how clever they were or how well they slept through the night.

Granddad chatted with a few, telling each in turn that their baby was the prettiest he had ever seen. He smiled as each mother feigned modesty "He might look like an angel now, but he can be a little devil sometimes, can't you Booboo."

Granddad loved to see them so proud. He turned and winked at me.

"Nothing matters more, Tommy."

"What's that, Granddad?"

"Kids need love." He said.

He took me to the keeper's hut – a small wooden shed. The park visitors would never suspect it existed, because it was hidden behind a maze of bushes. Inside Granddad and his mate, Johnny, had a little stove where they burned coke to keep them warm in winter. The walls were covered with postcards and pictures and notices from the park authorities. There was a bench piled with small garden tools, old newspapers, shanks of hairy string and tangled spirals of galvanized wire. They had a couple of worn armchairs, an orange box table. It reminded me of our camp on the debris. On another box they had a small electric ring and a long twisted brown cable that plugged into a two-way adaptor in the ceiling light socket. There was a kettle, a dark brown teapot, and jam-jars of tea, sugar and biscuits.

Granddad made us a cup of tea, gave me a biscuit and we sat – the three of us – talking. They didn't treat me like a kid. They included me as if I knew who and what they were talking about. It was one of the best moments of my whole life. I belonged to my Granddad.

They talked about people in the park and the things they got up to.

"I had to tell them, I did. You can't do that here. Go find somewhere else more comfortable." Granddad said, "And anyway, I told 'em, you'll get bitten on your arses when the midges wake up in a few minutes."

I had no idea what they were talking about, but I loved just being there. I stayed with him all day, helping to move flowerpots from here to there, empty rubbish bins and collect litter. We found a couple of hankies abandoned on the grass, which he stuffed into a plastic bag to take home.

At the end of the day, Granddad brewed another cup of tea in the hut. His mate had gone. He sat on a box, leaning forward, elbows on knees, cradling the mug in both hands. I sat opposite and copied him. He stirred his tea and watched the bubbles spin. I stirred my tea and watched the bubbles spin.

"Your Gran's not well."

"What?"

"She's not a well woman, Tommy. The arthritis. It makes her... well, you know. She can't deal with things, gets irritable."

He slowly stirred his tea. I slowly stirred my tea.

"She's had a lot of heartache in her life. Can't take it anymore."

"Yes, she told me."

"Well, so long as you know.'

"Know what Granddad?"

I looked at his face. He looked up from the spinning bubbles. He smiled, reached over and put his hand on my shoulder.

"She's your Carol."

I didn't need to ask. I knew who he was talking about. I couldn't stop a huge grin spreading across my face.

"Come on. I've got something for you." He walked out. I followed. At the back of the hut he'd hidden a bike frame.

"Kids've pinched the most of, but it's a good frame Tommy. You could build a good bike on that."

It was a good frame – all scratched up and with some surface rust, but it would clean up fine. Kids had stripped it bare of handlebars, seat, wheels, gears, chain, brakes and pedals, but it was a good frame.

"Cor, thanks Dad!"

I hoisted it over my shoulder and we walked home. I still had that big involuntary grin I couldn't control. I had my Carol and a bike. I was so proud that my Granddad had found the bike and saved it for me. I was an expert on bikes, but never had one of my own. Already I could see my first bike with sparkling chrome-plated cow-horn handlebars, racing saddle, lightweight alloy wheels, and derailleur gears. I'd make the best bike in the street and Granddad would be so proud!

I spotted Ronny Needleman squatting at the edge of the boating lake.

"Hiya Ronny!"

Granddad waved his arm to say "Go and play." and I raced off.

Ronny was trying to start the motor on his model boat. He often spent whole days trying to start motors on model boats. Sometimes the motor would start and the boat would steam across the lake a few yards. Then it would splutter to a stop and he'd have to paddle out to get it back. I'd been to the lake with him a few times, but I'd get bored of Ronny trying to start the motor and I'd leave him to it.

"Look at this!"

I lowered my bike and held it proudly in front of him.

"What's that?" he pushed it away with his fingertips, not wanting to get grease on his hands,

"It's my new bike." I grinned.

Ronny screwed up his face and blew through pursed lips, like someone had just farted.

"Well, it's not a bike yet, but it will be when I've finished it." I said.

"Some hopes!" he said. "I'm getting a new bike tomorrow. It's my birthday. Wanna come and see it? Have a go?"

"Yes, not 'arf" I said, "See you tomorrow."

The Tower Hill Mob

The next day Ronny Needleman, who I thought, already had everything a boy could wish for, got a new shop-bought racing bike from his dad – A Raleigh Lenton Sports with Reynolds 531 lightweight frame. It was painted Special Chromatic Green and had light alloy mudguards, Sturmey-Archer 4-speed hub gears, dynamo lighting, drop handlebars whipped in white tape, and a special racing saddle. Ronny didn't say how much it cost, but we guessed it must've been fifteen to twenty quid.

Although we all thought that hub gears and mudguards were for girls and old people, it was a beautiful bike and the first brand new one any of us had seen or touched outside of a shop. Ronny posed proudly in the middle of the pavement outside number 84, while Mr. Needleman, watched grinning from his doorstep.

We called Ronny's dad Mister Fixer because he had a basement lined with workbenches and hundreds of tools all neatly laid out on shelves, in trays and on little hooks on the walls. He had thousands of see-through plastic boxes with every kind and size of nut, bolt and washer, nail, screw, hinge and bracket possible. He made absolutely everything in their house, even Ronny's bed.

Mr. Needleman was a portly man, who was always kind and welcoming. He must have been very rich. Larry said he made and cleaned suits for famous people. He had photographs of his famous clients on the mantelpiece in his living room. I once asked him who they were. He told me about each one while Ronny stood by looking at the ceiling. There was an actor, an opera singer, a comedian, and two politicians. But he was most proud of a small picture of himself between two serious men, one with glasses. He said one was Ronny and one was Reggie. He said that's where Ronny got his name. Ronny looked away embarrassed.

These men looked... different, like Al Capone in the movies. I asked, "Are they gangsters, Mr. Needleman?" Ronny glared at me.

Mr. Needleman chuckled, "I only ask two things of my clients – have they got the cash, and which side do they hang!" He laughed until his belly bounced.

"Hang what?" I asked and he explained the asymmetry of men's testicles. Ronny covered his face with both hands and turned away. I was embarrassed to hear a grown up talk openly about rude things but even more disturbed that he worked for crooks.

"Oh and they both hang left if you want to know."

Ronny headed for the door.

"Look, Tommy. I'm not here to judge a man – just to measure him."

He laughed again. This time I laughed with him. I didn't quite understand what he meant, but I thought there was something wise about him.

"I'll tell you what, Tommy," He was beginning to enjoy his captive audience, "What I say is this. No matter how much money these men make and no matter how much treasure they pile up in this life, they will only take one thing with them when they go…" He paused for effect.

Ronny looked back over his shoulder and shook his head– he must have heard this a hundred times. "Come on Tommy, let's play out." I waved him to wait.

"What's that, Mr. Needleman?" I asked.

"Well Tommy…" He savoured the moment. "The only thing they'll take to their coffins will be…" He took a deep breath and said proudly, "one of my suits!"

Ronny ran upstairs.

I liked Mr. Needleman.

Ronny and I had one thing in common – neither of us had brothers or sisters, but Ronny was lucky – he had a real dad and they did things together. They made huge model aeroplanes – not the plastic-and-goo Airfix models the rest of us made, but real ones made from balsa wood and tissue and painted with dope. They had real little engines and they really flew. They also made the model powerboats that Ronny floated in Victoria Park boating lake.

Ronny was a bit chubby like his dad, soft-faced, with a long lugubrious nose. He took himself seriously and had to be an expert in everything and he had to have everything. He had every possible piece of Meccano plate, strip, nut and bolt, axle and cogwheel, all neatly laid out in labeled trays in a cabinet his Dad made and while the rest of us had to make bikes from bits we found, swapped or nicked, Ronny had shop-bought bikes and the Raleigh Lenton was the last in a long series that started when he was five and had the first new tricycle in the street.

Larry, Errol and I circled, whistled and cooed at Ronny's new bike and stroked it all over. With its shiny chrome and green paint it glinted in the sun like a jewel. We tested and savoured everything. Larry pinched the thin racing tyres, lifted and spun the front wheel, which ran fast and free with a beautiful hiss. I flicked the pedals and they spun into a blur. Errol curled his arms under the drop handlebars and squeezed and released the brake levers while we traced the cable path and admired the smoothness and precision of the caliper action.

Ronny brushed us off and threw his leg over in an attempt to mount the long thin racing saddle, but it was too high and we had to steady the bike to help him to the seat. Larry and I held the seat stem and Errol stood at the front and steadied the handlebars. Ronny sat there grinning widely, proud as King George, on his wobbly steed, pedaling backwards.

Larry teased, "Blimey, Ronny, if you go over a bump on that saddle, it'll cut your arse in half."

Laughter broke our concentration. I let go of the bike. Ronny balanced unsupported for a moment, frantically scrabbling to reach the ground with his outstretched toes. Errol tried to hold on to the front, but lost control. Ronny fell towards the railings and the bike clattered away beneath him.

It wasn't a serious fall. Ronny had a small graze on his right knee and the bike was just a bit scratched, but Mr. Needleman ran down the steps, took Ronny in one hand and the bike in the other and yanked them upright.

"Needs a little adjustment."

He carried the bike into the house and down to his workshop.

Of course Mr. Needleman had every type and size of bike spanner. He had metal claw-things for taking tyres off and putting them back, little clamps for replacing broken chain links, special keys for adjusting the tension of spokes and cans and cans of Duraglit. He had everything he would need to make Ron's bike perfect in every way.

"Well, Ronny," Larry said, "You won't see that again in a hurry."

Ronny shrugged.

We felt sorry for Ronny. He was lucky to have a dad who worked at home and had time for him. He was lucky he and his dad shared hobbies together. But he was also over-protected and spoilt. His parents always wanted to know where he was; who he was with; what he was doing. The rest of us were happy to be left to roam the streets wild and free. If he wanted something he only had to ask and he got it. The rest of us had the fun of finding, making, scrounging and swapping.

I was good at swapping. I'd been collecting stamps and swapping carefully for a few years and I'd built up quite a big collection.

To start with I saved up to buy the Stanley Gibbons collection they advertised in the Eagle. You got a selection of 400 stamps from all over the world, complete with a packet of hinges, a super-high-power magnifying glass, a pair of tweezers and a Stanley Gibbons catalogue for identification – all free on approval.

Most of the stamps were really boring, like the French ones, with women's heads in dull browny-greeny-grey, greyey-browny-green or greeny-greyey-brown. I swapped these with more serious collectors at school for my favourites - from places like Antigua, Trinidad and Tobago or the Cayman Islands. We all thought these weren't real countries and so the stamps were sort-of-fake, but I loved their impossibly colourful and intricate images of birds and butterflies and my album became a miniature art gallery, which I pored over with my super-high-power magnifying glass for hours and hours.

But right now I'd swap anything for parts for my new bike.

Larry told me that Nathan Isaacs, a boy from Ropery Street, had some spare alloy wheels and he collected stamps. We both went to see him.

Nathan had a round face, sparkling eyes and a grin – well not really one grin, but an endless series of grins that constantly played across his face as he leapt from one joke to another. Before I even said Hi he asked, "What's the cheekiest football team in London?"

"Er..."

"Tottenham Chutzpa."

I didn't get it. In fact I didn't get any of the jokes he rattled off one after the other – mostly with Yiddish words I didn't know because they weren't in Gran's collection of insults. But that grin infected me and I had to laugh along.

I told him I was looking for bike parts. He led us through to his yard where he had a pile of old bikes and spares, "Here you are Tommy, " he sang "bikes for tykes, seats for cheats, wheels for deals – anything you want."

While I picked over the bike bits, he leafed through my stamp album, constantly quipping. "It's Stanley Gibbons – you can't monkey with him. Anyone who's Hungary can have a slice of Turkey and cook it in the Greece. Ceylon, mate – see you later, OK me old China. Brazil – they're all nuts out there. India... if you met a girl from India would you rubber? France – let's dance. Belgium – sounds like bubblegum. Ah, where do you go to buy a new potty? – Poland!"

Nathan's clowning kept Larry and me giggling and ten minutes later we were walking home having swapped my whole stamp album complete with 5 packs of hinges, the magnifying glass and Stanley Gibbons catalogue for a couple of slightly buckled wheels.

Larry thought I'd been done, but I didn't care I could borrow a spoke key from Ronny's dad to fix the buckles and some Duraglit would shine them up nicely and I'd have a decent pair of wheels to go with my frame – a good start.

Larry and I were determined to find everything we needed for two complete bikes. We toured all the bomb sites in Bow, Mile End, Commercial Road, Stepney Green, Whitechapel, and Aldgate. It took two weeks of our summer holiday and we got into a few scrapes with the local kids, including a very scary confrontation at the Tower Hill bomb site.

We circled the whole bomb site opposite the Tower of London, looking for a gap in the fence. It was a fairly new wooden fence about eight feet high. They were getting the site ready for demolition. We found only one slim gap where the fence butted against a wall and two planks were missing. It was tight, but I squeezed through, and although Larry was bigger and it took a while, he also made it.

Inside was a perimeter wasteland of rubble – low mounds of broken bricks, crazy up-thrown slabs of concrete and eye-poking rusty metal rods twisted randomly. We picked our way carefully across the ankle-cracking terrain to a concrete floor slab with a scattering of low broken brick walls.

We darted deftly in and out of what were once the rooms of a building until we came to a clump of Rose Bay Willow Herb, forming a long barrier, taller than us, humming with bees and hover flies and sprinkled with tiny blue and white butterflies. I led as we padded through, silently parting the tall stems, keeping our heads low like an Indian war party. All we could see was blue sky above and green on every side and for a while I was carried away with the intoxicating sense of isolation and secrecy spiced with the dusty scents of summer.

We parted the last curtains of Willow Herb and saw the factory just yards ahead. It was a tall building, perhaps ten stories high. Most of the interior had been destroyed by the bombs. The roof had gone completely, but the outer shell of grey brick was standing, supported by the adjoining buildings to the left and a network of heavy wooden buttresses and metal scaffolding to the right.

Although three walls towered above us untouched, the nearest wall was mostly obliterated. Larry and I gripped each other as we tipped our heads right back to look up and up, through a skeleton of exposed floor joists spanning the dizzying void, open to the racing sky above.

Looking down, half of the ground floor was missing and we could see a gaping hole two storeys deep into the cellars, which looked like Aladdin's caves full of the kind of treasure we were looking for – old prams, car tyres, arm chairs and such – all of which suggested it had been used as a local dump – just the place we'd find old bikes.

But that could wait. Right now, our minds were on something else.

"What d'ya think?" Larry looked up with a wide grin at the web of wood and scaffold towering above.

"Come on!"

We raced towards the scaffold and started to scramble up. This was the closest we ever got to heaven – challenge, adventure, danger and freedom. The scaffold took us up two storeys, and then we transferred to the trickier wooden buttressing. There was a row of six triangular buttresses supporting the wall. They were about a foot square in section, splintery and hard to hold, but they were connected by a network of smaller beams offering precarious, but manageable, foot and hand holds. We climbed to the fifth floor, and stood in a stone windowsill. Inside the hulk, exposed joists spanned the gap to the far side, about thirty feet away.

"Dare you, Tommy!"

I was fearless and experienced. I was the best climber in the Muller, the best in the street, the best in the school. I didn't hesitate a moment. On hands and knees, I straddled two joists and started to cross the sixty-foot chasm below. After a few seconds, Larry started out directly behind me and we inched across together.

"Whatever you do, Tommy, DON'T FART!"

It's not a good idea to giggle when you're trying to concentrate on every muscle, but I couldn't help it. I shook with laughter for half a minute, until my arms and legs felt like jelly and a nail head digging in my knee reminded me where I was.

It was only when we were halfway across that I realized this was scary. The joists were eighteen inches apart. It wasn't possible to sit and rest, I had to grip hard because of the shifting layer of grit and dust, and keep my eye on every movement to avoid puncturing my already sore knees with a rusty flooring nail and when I looked down it was a long way to fall. What's more crawling backwards would be impossible – we could only go forward.

"Okay Larry?" I asked.

"Eeee-sy! Hi Ho, Silver…" he sang.

"Awaaaay!" we chorused.

We were the Lone Ranger, Dan Dare, Superman, Audie Murphy and John Wayne again. The other side seemed nearer and our confidence returned – but not for long.

"Oi! You!" A loud ugly yell from below.

"What'cha doing up there?"

Four rough kids appeared from a doorway far below.

"This is our bloody camp!" one shouted – a big, burly boy with a round face.

"Oi, Donkin," a smaller dark haired boy yelled, "I hope they can fly!"

"Let's 'elp 'em!" said a thin blond boy.

They started throwing small lumps of concrete and broken bricks. Most of them fell short – we were a long way up, but the biggest kid, Donkin, who looked two years older than us, got his range and began to hit the joists around us. The terror on our faces must have inspired them. The smaller kids collected rocks and fed them, to the bigger ones, who kept up a constant barrage of missiles and abuse.

A lump of powdery concrete hit the joist to my right and exploded in a cloud of dust and grit in my face – in my eyes and mouth. For a while I could do nothing but hold my eyes tight shut and spit grit.

"He's spitting. How rude!" the dark-haired boy jeered.

"Yea, disgusting innit! 'it 'im, Frankie." Donkin yelled.

I pushed my lower lip forward and blew upwards to try to blast the dust from my eyelids and shook my head to loose it from my hair.

"Oww!" a whelp from behind me. Larry was hit.

"You SODS! Let's get out of 'ere, Tommy!" Larry shouted.

I groped blindly forward and got moving very slowly. Larry didn't know I was blinded and he soon caught up.

"Come on, Tommy. It's alright, they're getting tired."

I had to concentrate hard on my blind crawling, but Larry seemed to get braver:

"Just you wait," Larry yelled down at the gang, "My dad's a copper and he'll get you all locked up."

"Oh yeah, Lanky, where is he then?" Frankie taunted.

"He's right outside waiting for us. He'll be here in a minute to see what's up."

"Oh yeah? How's he gonna get in? Is he a skinny little mouse like you?"

At least while they were jeering they stopped throwing. Larry yelled at the top of his voice, "Oi, Dad, you can come in now!" His plea echoed around the building.

"Listen lads," Donkin jeered, "Baby's calling for his dada!

"Made it!"

We were at the far wall. There were a few loose floorboards to sit on and protect us from the artillery below and at last my hands were free to rub the dust from my eyes.

"Now what?" Larry asked.

"Well they can't get up, unless they climb where we have and that will take ages and they're too yellow."

"And they can't see us now." He added.

"But they know where we are. They might just wait."

"Or get reinforcements!"

"Yeah, or air guns or catties."

We sat back against the wall, knees clasped to chests.

"Oi, Laz, what was all that about your dad being a copper. You don't even have a dad." Larry went quiet. He never spoke about his dad – perhaps he died in the war or perhaps he left."

"Nor do you." he said.

Larry knew Granddad wasn't my father.

"Yea. Well. My real Dad's a… a pilot."

"Oh yea! What – like Dan Dare?"

"No he's real. He's in… the air force."

"Really, where's he based?"

"America." I said.

He knew I was making it up, but he didn't let on. "OK then, get Squadron Leader Angel to bomb this lot!"

Despite the danger, there are few times in my life when I was happier than at that moment – in the middle of an adventure, backs against the wall, invisible, high above everyone and joking with my best mate. We were reckless. We were wild, dangerous and invincible. We could leap tall buildings and catch bullets in our teeth. We were intrepid climbers, supporting each other physically and mentally through mortal danger, our humour dispelling our darkest fears. We were two fatherless boys, alone in the world but closer than brothers.

"And I think I've got a sister." I said.

"You haven't."

"I know. I haven't really. But there's this girl and Granddad said she's my Carol."

"What girl?"

"In the photo. The one we found in the airee."

"That's your sister?"

"Well, I dunno. No one talks about her. No one says her name, but Granddad said she's my Carol. Why is she mine if she's only a cousin?"

"Where is she then?"

"I dunno. Maybe she's dead. We got lots of dead people."

"Yea, but what if she's alive? You gonna find her?"

"Maybe. One day. You wanna come with me and…"

"Is Daddy's little baby sucking his thumb now?" – Donkin's voice.

"A policeman's lot is not a nappy one." – The thin blonde boy..

There was an explosion of laughter far below and a few rocks flew in our direction.

"Now what?" Larry asked.

"We better get out. Create a diversion."

"How?"

"Drop some bombs!" I said.

"Good idea, Squadron Leader, and then we'll see if we can get through that window at the end." Larry said.

"Is baby having a little rest before he comes back for more?" Donkin jeered.

Now the height was working to our advantage, I felt a little braver:

"You're gonna get it if you don't go away!" I shouted.

"Oh, listen boys it's Lord Snooty. He wants us to go away." Donkin jeered.

"Come on Snooty. Time to go home." Frankie said.

"Time to go home. Time to go home. Andy is waving goodbye. Goodbye. Goodbye." They sang.

"Come on Snotty, we're waiting." Donkin jeered.

"We're waaaiting!" wailed another.

"Why are we waaaiting? Why-y are we waaaiting? Why are we waaaiting oh why oh why? Why are we…?"

"Here you are then!" Larry grabbed a loose floorboard, about five feet long, swung it out between the joists and let it go.

We peered over the edge and watched it flutter over and over, then glide a bit, then fall into a nose drive and crash to the floor ten feet from the enemy. They scuttled for shelter. "Bloody 'ell!" one screamed.

"No don't go, boys. There's more. How about this?" Larry tore a loose brick from the wall behind and lobbed it into the void. It exploded with a thump in the dust below.

"And this…" I heaved another plank.

Screams from below: "Bloody SODS! You're bloody DANGEROUS! You could KILL someone!"

I tipped one more floorboard over the edge and cried, "The Angel of Death is upon you!"

And then silence.

Larry led this time, scurrying on all fours over the remaining floorboards by the wall until we reached the window at the far end. We looked out and to our relief there was a tiled pitched roof sloping away beneath the window. We shuffled carefully to the left, where the roof met the towering wall of the adjacent building.

With left hands groping for maximum friction against the wall and right hands on the tiles, we wedged our bums into the corner and inched carefully down, knees to chests, gripping with our plimsoles.

At the lower edge of the roof, the left hand building finished and there was a drop of perhaps thirty feet onto the rubbish-strewn floor of another roof-less bombed-out building.

There was no easy way down, but there was the remains of an exterior wall that must have held the roof. It ran as a continuation of the wall to our left. It was eighteen inches wide and stretched away from us for a few yards, level with the roof. Then it stepped down steadily, as brick courses had been blown off, ending level with a six-foot perimeter wall around the yard of the building behind.

I eased carefully on to the wall and sat astride it. Larry shuffled up behind me. We stayed close like motorbike riders, so we could steady each other if we lost balance.

We edged along the flat part with our legs dangling in space on either side, until we came to the damaged section. It was trickier than it looked from the roof. The wall sloped of at a steep angle and was covered with powdered bricks and mortar. As we slowly inched down, we found some of the top layer was loose, so I kicked at the wall ahead of me, showering loose bricks and dust.

About a third of the way down, we came to flatter section followed by a near-vertical five-foot drop. It wasn't visible from the top. Perhaps if we'd known we could have come another way. But it was too late. Like many times in my life before and since, I'd taken just a few steps too far from safety and found myself in danger with no turning back. I twisted to look at Larry. He look worried, but shrugged his shoulders to say we'd no alternative.

I scuffed off the loose rubble on the edge of the drop to give us a safe grip. I twisted on to my stomach and lowered myself backwards to the edge. I gripped tightly with my fingers on the top of the wall and slid my feet over, gripping the vertical edges between my insteps. Larry held tight to my wrists. I slid under control at first, but as I accelerated I just had to trust that my feet would land on the wall below before I lost my grip on the edge above.

It didn't work out like that. My feet slipped on loose rubble and flew into space on either side of the wall. I fell legs apart and yelled "Laaaarry!".

Everything went slow. I was falling in slow motion. I saw every brick rising past my face, every speck of dust. Larry's eyes and mouth slowly opened wide. I imagined myself crashing crotch first on to the wall below and anticipated the pain. I imagined how I would land and fall to one side and topple off into the void. I saw tomorrow's headline "Stupid boy falls from wall and dies." I stopped in mid air.

Larry was very strong. He kept hold of my wrists and held me at the end of his long arms. I dangled with my crotch 12 inches from the wall. I lifted my feet, scrambled for solid brick and took my own weight, hugging the vertical wall like a baby monkey locked on to its mother. It was a moment of utmost fear, followed by instant joy. I looked up at Larry with a big grin.

"You bloody *meshugener!*" He laughed.

Larry followed me. I clamped his feet tight against the edges of the wall as he slid down.

"Made it!"

"Oww!" Larry yelled.

A small lump of concrete flew by, just scratching at his calf. It was the Tower Hill mob. They were in the building with the pitched roof behind and above us, leaning out of a window – a menacing mass of flailing arms and snarling faces. They had a couple of serious catapults and were firing marble-sized chunks of concrete.

We turned and threw ourselves down the rest of the sloping wall, sliding on our bums, scrambling on all fours, sending up a cloud of dust and raining down a curtain of rubble.

The damaged wall gave way to a solid wall about six feet high with a ridge of broken bottle glass set in mortar along the top. We raced lightly across the wall like tomcats, picking our steps between the blades of glass, until it joined a smaller wall at right angles. We dropped down to the lower wall and ducked into a yard – protected from the catapults.

"Wow! Look at this!" Larry had stopped beside a couple of bike wheels.

"Hi Ho Silver!" I shouted.

We grabbed a wheel each and ran through an alley into the street.

"Awaaay!" We ran and ran without looking back, expecting the Tower Hill mob to appear behind us any moment. We ran all the way to Aldgate station, and nipped into the entrance for a breather and our first look backwards. No one. We set off for home.

The Invasion of Eric Street

It was late afternoon, almost evening, when we arrived back from Tower Hill. As we crossed the bomb site Errol, Davy and Vivien greeted us.

"Whatcha got?"

We showed off our new wheels.

"Cor! Where did you get 'em?" Davy asked.

"Tower Hill." we chorused proudly.

"Blimey – that's miles away!" Errol said.

"Yea, and it's full of thugs and murderers." Davy said.

We picked our way towards the camp and Larry launched into an heroic tale.

"We found this huge bombed factory place and we climbed right to the top. You should've seen us. These kids came and started aiming rocks and we had to crawl across... Oh no!"

Larry stopped in his tracks.

"What?"

He stared towards the Mossford Street side of the debris. We followed his gaze.

"Blimey! They must've followed us."

Four of the Tower Hill kids on bikes skidded to a stop in close formation, sending up a cloud of dust with their rear wheels.

"Well... look who it isn't." Donkin drawled like John Wayne as he dismounted. Then he spotted me. "Hello, Tommy. Long walk innit! Didn't 'cha see us? Right behind ya all the way. Must be blind Jew boy!"

"Come on!" Davy led a scramble for the camp. We flew over the rough ground, dancing between twisted girders, leaping over low walls. We knew the debris intimately, which gave us an advantage over the Tower Hill boys who threw their bikes against a wall and picked their way carefully between the hazards. We made it to the camp and dived into the tunnel. Vivien was last in. She pulled the inner door closed and tugged at the emergency ropes, pulling the props holding the rubble trap. The sticks collapsed and the entrance roof crashed down along with half a ton of dusty rubble.

"That'll keep 'em busy for a while. Come on." Davy shouted. We slid the trap door open, grabbed two torches and climbed into the cellar. Larry was last down and he closed the trap door above us.

"Will they find us?" Errol asked.

"Yea" Larry said, "but it'll take a while."

We'd spent many happy hours planning our emergency escape, and we all knew it by heart, but we hadn't imagined the combined terrorizing effect of four raging bullies screaming abuse and threats above, and the clammy darkness of the cellar.

"They'll kill us." Errol said.

"What if they come down after us?" Vivien asked.

"That's the plan, stupid." Davy said. "Come on."

We picked our way through the Isaacs' living room as we heard the trapdoor slide open above us.

"Down 'ere" one of them shouted, "Found 'em."

"Yea come and get us, bloody cissies." Davy jeered, shining his torch back towards the ladder.

"I see 'em." one of the enemy shouted. "Down 'ere".

They started to climb down.

"This way." Larry led us over piles of bricks and planks, through the hole in the wall, into the next-door ruin. Davy stayed at the back, shouting abuse and daring the Tower Hill kids to follow. They were slow and clumsy in the dark, but desperate to get their hands on us. We scrambled over the rubble and through the doorway. Davy was last.

"Right. Now block it up."

We wedged a pile of broken joists against the door.

"Come on. Gotta be quick."

We couldn't get out of the building on the ground floor. Every doorway and window was nailed up with planks. We climbed up the wooden shoring that supported the crumbling party wall, climbed to the edge and dropped through a hole, down to the debris.

The Tower Hill boys screamed, "Oi you fuckin' Jew Bastards!" They hammered hard against the door, but they'd never shift it.

We were intoxicated by an emotional cocktail of fear and exhilaration. We cheered, laughed, danced and whooped in wild celebration.

"Not done yet." Larry said, "Come on."

As we came back to the camp, we saw the enemy had cleared most of the rubble. The upper door was propped up with one stick. We dived through into the tunnel. When we reached the trap door, we could hear the Tower Hill kids shouting in the darkness below. They were still hammering at the door to the neighbouring house.

"Let us out, you Jew bastards. Open this fuckin' door!"

Larry and I quietly pulled up the ladder and slid it along the tunnel.

"Now we've got 'em." Davy gloated. "Yooo hooo, boys." he shouted down the hole.

"This way, kiddies." Davy shone his torch into the dark. "Come to Daddy!" he sang.

The ruffians were drawn towards the torchlight like moths. We could hear their cursing and occasional cries of pain as they bumbled into walls, tripped over rubble, twisted ankles between planks. At last four faces stared up to the light, covered in dust and dirt, streaked with tears. One had a bloody cheek.

"You fuckin' Jew bastards. We'll fuckin' kill you when we get out!"

Their voices trembled with anger and fear. "Come on let us up!"

"Can't. Sorry. Lost the ladder. Must've fallen down there somewhere." Larry said. "Why don't you look for it? Can't be far away."

Larry slid the trap door shut.

"Can't see in the bloody dark!" one of them screamed.

"You're dead Jew boy. We're gonna put you in the fuckin' gas chamber like the rest of 'em."

"Good idea!" Davy scrabbled amongst our orange boxes. "This should do the trick!"

He emerged with a tin box of tricks we'd bought from Ellisdons magic shop. There was a nail-through-finger trick that fooled my Gran once, an electric shock machine I had tried out on Ronny, some very disappointing indoor fireworks and a couple of stink bombs, which we'd bought but hadn't dare use. We thought about dropping one at school in assembly, but we were sure we'd get caught. We'd tested one on the debris. It was putrid, like rotten eggs, but the wind quickly dispersed the smell. We had two bombs left. Davy slid the trap door open a few inches, quietly dropped the stink bombs and slid the door back. He turned and grinned his wide grin and we all waited in silence.

"Awww fuck me! Who did that?"

"Wasn't me. It's not a fuckin' fart. It's gas. There're gassing us!"

"Oh my Gawd. They're fuckin' gassing us!"

"It's your fuckin' fault, Donkin – what you said about gassing Jews!"

"Shuttup Frankie, fuckin' stupid Itie!"

Someone, probably Frankie, crashed to the ground.

"Oi! Oi you up there. We didn't mean it. Just kiddin'" Donkin pleaded.

"Let us out! Come on. Please! Oh Gawd it fuckin' stinks down 'ere!"

"We're gonna die!"

"Don't be a bloody cissy, Bullen. Jimmy – hold your fuckin' nose."

"I want my mum!"

We laughed until our sides ached. Vivien giggled until she wet herself. When we'd calmed down, a shadow of guilt crept over us.

"What we gonna do now?" Errol asked.

"Leave 'em there all night." Davy said.

"No we can't, they'll starve." Vivien said.

"Serves 'em right." Larry said, "Bloody Nazis. Their lot gassed us – millions. In the camps."

"Not them though. Not those kids." Errol pleaded.

"Would've done if they'd had the chance." Larry said.

"OK", Davy said, "we'll let 'em out, but not yet!"

He shouted into the cellar, "Sorry about that boys, but we're going for tea now."

Their screams and curses were muffled by the trap door and mattress.

"I'm off." Davy said.

"Me too." Larry said, "Whose gonna keep guard?"

Errol, Vivien and I stayed to guard the prisoners.

"Whatever you do," Larry said, "don't let them out – we'll be back after tea. I'll bring you something."

The boys disappeared through the tunnel and we three sat looking at each other. Suddenly it didn't seem like fun. There were four murderous ruffians under our feet and we felt vulnerable. Errol, the youngest broke the silence.

"What if they get out through next door and come for us."

"They won't" I said, "It would take a tank to shift that door."

"What happens when we let them go in the end?" Vivien asked, "They might come back another day and get us."

"That's true." I said, "So we'll have to make sure they don't."

"How?"

I slid the trap door open a few inches.

"You boys still there?" I yelled.

"Har Har! Very funny! Where else, Jew Boy?"

"We're gonna let you out…" I said.

"No!" Vivien yelled. The prisoners cheered.

"…but we need some information first." I said.

"Oh... what?" one of the boys asked suspiciously.

"Just your names." I said.

"Fuck off!"

"OK Mr. Fuckov" I said, very matter-of-fact, "You can stay there." and I slid the trap door shut.

"NO! No all right. I'm Donkin."

"I know that, and Frankie's down there, Jimmy and Bullen. I want your full names please."

"Arthur Donkin."

"'Alf a Donkey?" Errol said, "Which 'alf the 'ead or the arse?"

"Fuck off you! It's Arthur Edward Donkin."

"Thank you." I said, "Where do you live – full address please."

"What's it to you, Jew boy?"

"You wanna get out?"

"OK, OK, 166, Peabody Buildings, Tower Hill, London, E1, England, Great Britain, the world, solar fuckin' system, uni-fuckin'-verse!"

"And the others?" I demanded.

Donkin continued, "He's Terry Bullen, 168 – that's next door. Jimmy Rutter – upstairs in 232. And the Itie's Franky Costa – 91, downstairs. We all live in Pissbody – bloody dump! Satisfied?"

"Not yet. Parents full names."

"You're pushing it, Jew boy." Donkin hissed.

"Come on," I coaxed "just want to get to know you better. Your mum's name."

"Dunno. I forget." Donkin said, "What's yours?"

I dunno either! I thought, "None of your business. I'm asking the questions."

"OK. Me mother's Dora. Me dad's dead-in-the-war." Donkin said.

"What about you, Terry?" I asked.

"Mum's called Irene. Dad's Joe. Gotta war injury. Stays home drinking all bloody day and belts *us* for being lazy."

I continued to interrogate the prisoners, who, despite their protests, gradually revealed their school and their teachers' names.

"So, Donkin. You must be the toughest kid in your school." I said.

"Yea!" Donkin leered "and you're gonna find out why, Tommy Boy."

"No he's not." Frankie squealed, "Abbot beat 'im up."

"Shuttup, Frankie."

"Well he did, didn't he, when you wouldn't give 'im your penknife. He thrashed you all round the bloody playground. You were crying for your bloody mum."

"Shut up, Frankie." Donkin sent Frankie flying again.

"Thank you, gentlemen." I said.

"Is that it?" Donkin asked.

"Not quite." I said. "Just one more thing."

"Ohhhh!" they moaned.

"Might as well have some fun while we're stuck here. Tell me the most embarrassing thing that ever happened to you. Your most secret of all secrets."

"I can tell you about Frankie." Donkin jeered. "He shit his pants in prayers." Terry and Jimmy Rutter joined his mocking laughter.

"Shuddup!" Frankie screamed, "You said! You said you'd never tell. I was ill, couldn't 'elp it. You promised!"

"'ad to mate, matter of life-or-death." Donkin said.

"Well what about you." Frankie retorted, "When you wet the bed and your Mum chucked you out on the balcony bare bloody naked, and locked the door and wouldn't let you in!"

"Yea, fuckin' cow!" Donkin said, "And fuckin' Bullen told all the kids in the fuckin' block. You fuckin' bastard, Bullen. I said I'd get you for that."

Donkin lashed out at Terry Bullen who yelped like a dog and scrambled away into the darkness.

"Made 'er pay for it." Donkin said. "Found out where she kept the social money, didn't I."

"Yea," Jimmy said, "He nicks five bob a week."

By the time they'd finished, we had a sordid tale to hold each of them to ransom.

It was dark when Davy and Larry returned with a couple of sausages and some corned beef, sneaked from their teas. Davy had a broad wicked grin. "OK time to let them go."

"Alright. We'll let you go."

"Hooray!"

"But you gotta promise no trouble."

"We promise... honest." said Donkin.

We glanced at each other nervously and shrank away from the hole. Davy opened the trap door. Lowered the ladder and the Tower Hill Mob started to climb up. They were a very sad looking mob, battered and bloodied like war wounded. They slumped down around the trap door, looking at us with dark, doleful eyes.

"Bloody clever you Jew boys. I'll give you that." Donkin said.

"We're not all Jews." Errol said.

"We're not all boys!" Vivien chirped, which further puzzled them, since she looked exactly like a boy.

"And we're not all clever" said Davy who loped around making monkey noises.

"Yea, well," said Donkin. "We'll be off then."

"And you won't ever come back." I said.

Donkin pushed his face in front of mine. His breath smelled like sour milk. "Might do."

"If you ever come within a mile of here," I said slowly, "our mates will tell us and we'll tell Abbot everything you told us – pissing the bed and all."

Donkin moved back and grimaced.

"And we'll write letters to your mums and your teachers." I said.

"Alright." Donkin said, "Come on." and he crawled out of the camp, his mates following. They shambled across the debris towards their bikes. Davy and Larry stood watching, with their backs to Vivien, Errol and me. Davy held a bike spanner behind his back and wiggled it so we'd notice.

When the Tower Hill Mob got to their bikes they stepped back in horror.

"We'll fuckin' kill you cunts!" Donkin screamed, picking up his bike with no wheels. Terry Bullen's bike had no chain. Frankie had lost his derailleur gears and Jimmy Rutter had no handlebars. They exploded with rage and frustration.

"Fuckin' cunts!"

"Bastards!"

"Thieving Jews!"

Davy and Larry twisted round to us with big grins. Donkin and his mates shouldered the remains of their bikes ready for the long walk home.

Vivien was worried. "What if they come back, with more murderers?"

"Dear Mrs. Donkin," I shouted after them. "I wonder if you know what happens to your social money."

"Alright. Alright." Donkin shouted over his shoulder.

"They won't be back." I said.

That night Larry and I had a selection of new parts for our bikes. I took the handlebars and gears. No pedals yet but the bike was taking shape.

In the weeks that followed we found more discarded bike parts. With help from Vinny, who gave us inner tubes, puncture kits and stuff from his bedroom, Larry and I built two complete bikes.

We spent weeks making them work, and reached the stage where just any old handlebars wouldn't do. We wanted cow-horns, and we had plenty of spares to swap for them. We were short of mudguards, but we weren't bothered about that – they were for little kids and old people.

We borrowed some Duraglit from Ronny and sat on my Gran's doorstep cleaning and polishing the chrome, winding yellow plastic tape round the handlebars and painting the frames with little pots of enamel.

We had bikes to be proud of, and for the rest of that long summer, while Ronny's dad was still fixing his bike, we escaped the East End and rode off to adventure in Epping Forest.

Rebecca's Secrets

PART 2: LOST BABIES

In the Forest

Once our bikes were roadworthy we set off at the weekends to explore the world. Our first destination was Epping Forest – the far east of the Central Line, and Theydon Bois – the most intriguing name on the underground map.

On our first trip Larry, Davy, Errol, and I stuffed our saddlebags with any food we could sneak from our kitchens. I took half a packet of cornflakes in a brown paper bag, a half loaf of white bread and a quarter pound of New Zealand butter. The others brought jars of Robinsons strawberry jam, fish paste and Marmite, a tin of corned beef and some sardines in olive oil. We filled our water bottles with Tizer and milk. Larry brought a puncture repair kit. We were ready for anything.

It was a lovely sunny morning so we stripped down to shorts and vests and dumped our jumpers at Davy's house. We rode up Eric Street, dismounted and walked across Mile End Road, which was busy with Saturday traffic.

"Hi ho Silver!" Larry shouted.

"Awaaay!" we chorused, mounted up and set off four abreast. We dodged round a blond woman in a blue coat who stepped into the road in front of us. We dashed off as fast as we could at first but soon settled to a slower pace as we passed Brokesley Street where Uncle Solly and Aunt Marlene lived.

We could hear the honking of car horns, but ignored it, until we were past the hospital, when Larry looked back over his shoulder.

"Blimey! It's a bloody procession!"

We twisted round in turn to see a long queue of cars behind us, with drivers waving their arms and yelling.

"Must be a protest about something." Errol shouted above the din.

"Perhaps its Mosley." Davy shouted back. He covered his nose with one hand and shouted, "Down with the Jews!"

"My Granddad threw an egg at him." I yelled.

We rode in close formation in front of the procession for another mile. Davy waved at passers by who had stopped to see what it was all about. As we approached Bow Church, a big, angry policeman stepped out in front of me, held his arm up out and shouted, "STOP you boys!"

We all braked hard, but Errol's brakes were useless and he went sailing straight ahead. I pulled too hard on my front brake. The back wheel lifted. My feet left the pedals and I took off, head first over the cow horns. The copper raised his arms to protect himself from the bike and me. In mid flight I released the brakes, and the back wheel fell to the road. I landed on the crossbar on my crotch. I yelled in pain and fell to the ground, skinning my knees and the bike fell on top of me.

The copper's anger was immediately replaced with concern. "You all right, Son?" He asked.

"No! I'm bloody not!" I yelled through tears. The pain in my crotch was intense. I was shaky and weak and couldn't move the bike.

He lifted the bike and helped me to my feet and I became aware of the pandemonium around us. The drivers at the head of the procession were out of their cars, shouting at me.

"Come on, get out the bloody way!"

"We've been crawling behind you lot for 'alf an hour."

"Bloody stupid kids, holding up the bloody traffic!"

"Get off out of it! Sling yer bleedin' 'ook"

Passers by were shouting at the copper.

"What'd you do that for?"

"Knocked him off his bike."

"Kid didn't stand a bloody chance."

"You're big and ugly enough to know better!"

The copper looked bewildered.

"You'd better come with me" he said. He took the bike in one hand and me in the other and dragged both to the kerb. The crowd broke up and the traffic moved on and he pulled me up the steps of Bow Police Station. I thought I'd been arrested and started to cry again.

The copper asked, "What's your name, son?"

I thought about giving a false name, but I was too scared. He'd find me out later. "Angel" I spluttered.

"Good. I'm PC Blake, but my mum calls me Tony. What does you mum call you?" he asked gently.

"Haven't got a mum!"

"Oh, sorry about that, Son. So what does your dad call you then?"

"Haven't got a dad neither!"

"No mum, no dad… what about brothers and sisters?"

"Ain't got none." I said.

"All on your own then. So where do you live, Mr. Angel?"

"It's Thomas."

"All right, Thomas, where do you live?"

I dared not tell him Eric Street; He'd be round there telling my Gran I'd been arrested and our trip to the forest would be over.

"Wales." I said.

"Wales? Well you *have* come a long way haven't you! Whereabouts in Wales, then?"

"Up in the mountains, in the North... by the sea."

"I see." He stroked his chin, "Would that be near Swansea?"

"About three miles away."

"I think we'd better get this lot sorted out, Son. Wait here a minute."

He sat me on a bench in the corridor and went to another room. I could run, but my knees hurt and I'd be too slow carrying the bike. I could leave the bike and run faster, but I'd worked hard for months to build it. Hell! I'll run with the bike! I stood, grabbed the bike and turned to the door. Davy, Larry and Errol were there, peeking round the doorway with their heads one above the other, grinning, like the Marx Brothers.

"What's up, Tommy?" Larry asked.

"I've been arrested."

"What for?"

"I don't know, obstructing traffic, driving dangerously, badly adjusted brakes, no mudguards, swearing at a copper, er... lying about where I live."

"Blimey! Let's escape." Davy said and they charged in to help me with the bike.

As we scrambled for the door, a lady called, "Hello, Thomas. Nice of your friends to come and help."

She was very young for a policewoman and quite pretty. As she walked towards me, she took off her hat. She had short curly red hair and a big smile.

"PC Blake has to get on with other things. He asked me to help. Now lets get you sorted." She said softly.

She sat me down and placed a metal bowl with warm water on the floor beside me. As the gang crowded round, she gently cleaned my wounded knees and elbows with cotton wool and water, dried them with a towel and rubbed in some ointment. The boys stared open-mouthed. Then she checked the bike over, spun the wheels, tested the brakes, and checked the chain and gears. The boys were impressed with her know-how.

"Everything's in good condition." She said, "You and your bike. Here, you can share these later."

She pressed a bag of gob stoppers into my hands. The boys were very impressed.

"Off you go then." she said with a big grin, "PC Blake says single file from now on, OK. Oh, and he says give his regards to your Gran."

Oh no! He must have checked me out. He knows where I live. He knows about my Gran. I told him lies about Wales. Now I'm done for. The police know I'm a liar. He'll write it in a book. I'll have a police record. I avoided her eyes and made for the door.

"Oi, Davy." I shouted, as I cycled behind him, "Race you to the bottom of the hill."

We made our way, in the searing heat, through Stratford High Street busy with shopping ladies, on to Leyton and Forest Gate, out through leafy Woodford Wells to Epping New Road. The trees on either side gave welcome shade and we were glad to stop outside the Robin Hood pub, in the heart of the forest, to rest our aching legs.

After a short breather and a swig of Tizer, Davy said, "Let's get lost!" and we struck off randomly into the forest, cycling where we could and pushing or carrying our bikes when the bracken and brambles were too thick. It was wonderful to be surrounded completely by green and not to see or hear a car or another human. On every side the forest continued endlessly. Apart from each other, all we could see or hear or smell were trees. At first we were noisy – joking, laughing, teasing each other, but the deeper we penetrated into the shadows, the quieter we became.

"Look!" Larry pointed ahead to a pool of water glinting through the gloom. We broke through a ring of tall bushes into a sunny open perimeter. We dropped our bikes and ran whooping through the thigh-high grass to the hard-baked clay banks of a small lake. It was almost circular, perhaps fifty yards across, covered with a scummy film of algae and pondweed. A fallen Beech tree angled into the lake. We scrambled up and balanced along its trunk until it dipped below the water.

"Who's for a swim?" Larry said. We ran back to the long grass, threw off our sweaty clothes and raced each other along the fallen trunk. Davy leaped off, curled knees to chest and did a bomb, throwing up a huge corona of scummy water. We quickly followed.

We played like four dolphins, diving and surfacing, ducking each other, racing from one side to the other. We swam underwater as far as we could and broke the surface gagging for air. We plastered our hair with weeds and mud to see who made the scariest swamp monster. When we'd spent our energy we floated motionless in the pondweed like dead things staring at the hot blue sky.

We climbed out and ran into the long grass.

"Watch this", Davy said and half sat, half rolled and half fell backwards, flattening a channel in the grass where he lay looking up at the sunny sky.

"Make a cross." Larry copied Davy, flattening a channel for himself, diagonally opposite, so their heads were close together, feet pointing in opposite directions. Errol and I completed the cross, rolling back at right angles to the other two.

We lay on our backs in the long grass drying in the blazing sun. Although our heads were close, our bodies radiated like spokes, each in its private channel, separated from the others by the high walls of grass. Little white clouds raced across the sky and blue butterflies hovered over our heads. Unseen insects hummed around us. Little chestnut brown soldier beetles climbed up the grass stems and, when they reached they top they took flight.

"Who's got bedbugs?" I asked, and everybody raised their hands and shouted "Me!"

"I catch ' em with soap."

Larry said he took a bar of soap, made it wet, threw back the bedclothes and patted the soap down quickly on the bugs. The bugs stuck to the soap. He always left the soap bugs-down in the scullery sink so his mum didn't notice them until halfway through her morning wash and she screamed the house down.

"My Dad burns 'em with a candle", Errol said. "He comes down in the middle of the night and runs the candle round the end of the bed and they fizz in the flames. What do you do, Tommy?"

"Oh, I keep them as pets." I said and everyone laughed.

I ran back to my bike, dug for my gobstoppers in the saddlebag, returned to my channel of grass and shared them out and we all sucked seriously.

"What colour?" Larry asked now and then and we all extracted the sticky sweets and held them up at arm's length so the others could see.

"Pink."

"Green"

"Blue"

"Blue"

"SNAP!"

We laughed and joked and sang.

"Well since my baby left me."

"Bo Bom!"

"I found a new place to dwell."

"Bo Bom!"

"It's down at the end of Lonely Street to... Heartbreak Hotel. Oh well-a... it makes you so lonely baby, e-ever so lonely. You'll be so lonely you could die."

"And don't you step on my blue suede shoes. A-you can do anything but lay off-a-ma blue suede shoes."

"See you later Alligator."

"In a while crocodile."

"I-I'll be home, my-y-y darlin'. Please wa-a-ait for me-ee. I'll walk you home in the moo-oo-oo-oon-light. Once more our love will be free."

We argued about whether Pat Boone was better than Elvis for vocals or Winifred Atwell was better than Eddie Calvert for instrumentals.

Larry said his mate, Nathan told him this new singer, Buddy Holly, was going to be better than Elvis and Pat Boone put together, and he started singing, "Uh-blue days, uh-black nights, uh-blue tears keep on a-falling for you, dear, now you're gone..."

"Oh, that's rubbish. How about this?" Davy sang Alma Cogan's hit, "Willie can, Willie can Willie can Fair Lady, if Willy takes a shine to you."

"Oi, Errol," Davy said, "Your willy's different to ours."

"What do you mean?" Errol laughed.

"Yours is sort of floppy at the end." Davy said.

Larry, Davy and I were all circumcised.

"It's not floppy now." Errol said.

We all sat up and twisted round to have a look. Sure enough, Errol had a stiffy.

"Oh, I can do that!" Davy started fiddling with his willy. Larry and I looked at each other and shrugged, laid back into our privacy and copied him, looking up at the hot blue sky. We four boys lay in the forest, like some twitching starfish, almost joined at the head but with our cruciform bodies separated in the long grass.

It was the first time I'd done it deliberately. Before that it was a secret thing that mostly happened involuntarily. Sometimes while I was dreaming I got a stiffy and woke up. It felt nice, but that was it. I didn't know there was any more to it. Lying there naked, fiddling in the forest was embarrassing and pleasant at the same time. It felt totally wrong and absolutely right. It was an internal feeling, private from the other boys and at the same time public to the world above me, the grass, the trees the forest, the sky and the blazing sun.

"Tell you something dirty." Davy said.

Over the past year, Davy had been telling us stories about his mate, Ethan Rosenberg. Everyone called him Rosy. He and his younger sister, Frieda shared a bedroom. They could peek through a small crack in the back of a cupboard between their room and their parents'. They used to watch their mum and dad doing it on Sunday afternoons. Rosy told all his mates what happened and they told their mates and that's how we all learned about sex. Mr. and Mrs. Rosenberg had no idea about the contribution they made to the education of hundreds of East End kids.

Lying there under the hot sun, Davy told us how one Sunday afternoon Rosy asked him round to play. When he arrived the family had just finished dinner and cleared away. Mr. and Mrs. Rosenberg said they were going up for a rest and disappeared upstairs.

Rosy and Frieda took Davy up to their room. Rosy showed Davy the crack in the cupboard and let him peek through. He could see the parents' bed on the far side of the room. Mrs. Rosy was on her back with her pinny and frock pulled up to her knees. Mr. Rosy appeared at the bottom of the bed. He only had his shirt and socks on.

Davy said, He climbed on top of Mrs. Rosy and she lifted her knees and opened her legs just like a frog. He lay on top of her and they bounced up and down.

"What for?" Errol asked.

"They were doing it, stupid." said Davy, and he started making little grunting and panting noises, like he was having trouble breathing. Larry and Errol joined in. The pace of their panting quickened until Davy shouted, "Hi ho Silver!"

Larry and Errol responded in quick succession,

"Awaaay!"

"Awaaaaaaay!"

The strangest feelings welled up from below and took over my whole mind and body. It was like being at the end of a long underwater dive, when you are aching and aching to breathe and then finally burst through the surface and suck in a huge lungful of air and then you take flight and soar like a swan.

"Ahhhhh!" I cried uncontrollably, as my willy twitched and warm stuff splashed on to my belly.

"Hi ho, Tommy!" Davy shouted, and Errol and Larry chanted, "Awaaaaaaay!"

I didn't fully understand what had happened, but I thought it was secret and unique to me. I was elated and ashamed at the same time. Something mysterious had happened inside my body and my brain. It gave me the most amazing feeling – light-headed, flying, like an angel, straight from this world up into the blue sky.

I grabbed a handful of grass and wiped myself over and over, hoping the boys didn't look at me. The boys sat up and grinned at each other. I jumped up and ran to my bike and leaped into my pants and shorts. The others followed.

"Who's hungry?" Larry asked. We flattened a space in the grass near the pool and emptied the food from our saddlebags. The butter had melted in mine, soaked into the bread and covered everything else. The milk in my water bottle had congealed into one big lump of butter. The cornflakes had been bounced into crumbs.

We realized we had no way of cutting the bread, so we broke it into lumps. Davy opened the corned beef can with the little key thing attached. Errol did the same with his sardines. Larry sifted through his puncture repair kit and found a couple of tyre levers. We broke the bread into handfuls and used the tyre levers to spread a mixture of mackerel paste, marmite and strawberry jam. Davy carved out hunks of corned beef and handed them round and we fished in Errol's can for a couple of sardines, sprinkled cornflake crumbs on top and folded the lot into misshapen sandwiches.

We were so hungry that the mixture, swilled down with Tizer, tasted just wonderful. After the first course we came back for more and more until we'd emptied every tin, jar and package. We had a burping competition, which Davy won easily and then packed our saddlebags and set off to explore deeper into the woods.

It was good to be in the shade again and we walked and wheeled our bikes for twenty minutes, through dense shadow, until we came to a clearing. Shafts of sunlight conjured pools of gold in the leaf litter.

Larry suggested a game of fifty-fifty. Errol was to stay by the big log in the centre of the clearing. The others had to run into the woods, then sneak back to touch the log. If Errol saw us, he could shout "Fifty-fifty I see Davy!" or whoever, and the person he caught was on his side. The winner was the one to sneak to the log unseen. Errol sat on the log and counted to a hundred. We fanned out into the bracken. For a while we made Red Indian whooping noises, or hooted like owls. Later we settled into serious sneaking – crawling through the bracken and darting between tree trunks.

Errol spotted me, even though I was crawling. "Fifty-fifty. I see Tommy's bum!" he shouted and I reluctantly gave up. Later I saw Larry peeking from behind a tree and called him in. That left Davy.

We sat on the log, back to back straining into the gloom at the edge of the clearing. No Davy. Ten, fifteen minutes passed and we were getting bored, when we heard Davy shouting some way off. Then he came crashing wildly out of the brambles, blood slashed from his calves and knees, screaming at the top of his voice, "It's a murder! It's a bloody murder!"

"What? What's happened?"

Davy fell flat on his face at our feet, panting wildly. He looked up and cried, "Someone's dead!"

Davy was in a state and it took a while to get the whole story. He had run too far into the forest, thought he was lost and climbed a little way up a tree to take a look around. Through the leaves he saw a naked body, stuffed between the exposed roots of a Beech tree. He was so shocked he fell off the branch.

At first we didn't believe him. It was just like Davy to make up wild stories, but he was really scared, so maybe it was true. We agreed to investigate. Davy led us to the tree he climbed, and from there we carefully padded along a dried up stream with cracked mud banks. Davy stopped and crouched down, pointing silently ahead. Twenty yards further up the stream stood a big Beech. The soil had been deeply eroded by the winter floods, exposing a tangle of roots, and yes, we could see part of a naked body among them.

My heart beat loud enough to hear. After a few seconds I noticed Errol was gripping my forearm so tight it should have hurt, although I felt nothing.

"What is it?" Larry whispered.

"It's a leg."

"No, an arm."

"It's a baby." I said, "It's a dead baby."

Errol said, "It couldn't be. No one would leave a baby in a forest."

"People do leave their babies." Larry said, "My Dad left me. Your Mum left you, Tommy!"

"What do you know!" I protested.

"OK, where is she then?" Larry teased.

"I dunno, do I!" I said.

"Keep your 'air on, Keep your 'air on," Larry joked, "at least she didn't leave you with no clothes on. To die in a forest."

"Perhaps it's not dead." I said, "Perhaps it's just lost."

"How can you lose a baby?" Larry said, "It's been murdered and left."

We decided we had to do something. Larry was the best runner, so he should run, find the road, stop a car and get the police. Davy should go with him because he discovered it. Errol and I would stay and hide and keep our eyes open in case the baby's mother or its murderer returned.

Davy and Larry ran back up the gully. Errol and I scrambled up the bank and hid in a bush.

"What if it's really been killed and the murderer comes back?" Errol whispered, "What'll we do?"

He was scared, but so was I. "Keep quiet."

We sat in silence for some minutes, not daring to look towards the body.

"What's that?" Errol whispered.

There was a rustle close to our hideout. We turned expecting the murderer. Towering above us was a young stag. He stood as still as a statue, not a hair on his brown flanks moved. His broad antlers were ringed around with a fine halo of sunlight. He looked directly at us. I'd never seen anything so beautiful. His big brown eyes were deep and dark. Nothing moved. The whole world froze. We just stared at the stag and then at each other. For a moment it felt like we were all one, all in the same body.

There was something else – understanding. It was something complete, without beginning or end, without reason or condition. We completely knew and understood and accepted each other and everything and everyone in the whole world. In fact it felt like we *were* everything and everyone in the whole world. There was no you and me, no here and there, no before and after. It was all *us*, *here* and *now*.

I don't know how long we were frozen out of time, but the stag suddenly twitched, grunted, turned and was gone. Errol and I looked at each other. Neither wanted to say a word. We never spoke of it, not then and not ever afterwards.

When Davy and Larry came back a long time had passed. They brought four uniformed bobbies and a man in a crumpled brown suit. Inspector Mendel introduced himself and asked if we'd been near the body. We told him we stayed in the bush.

"Good. You boys sit tight and don't move a muscle."

They walked very slowly up the stream bed in single file, scrutinizing the ground ahead and to right and left – perhaps looking for footprints or clues. It took a long time, long enough for Davy and Larry to tell us how they ran to the road, tearing through brambles and leaping over fallen branches. They waved at a few cars, until a lady stopped. They tried to explain they'd found a body in the woods, but she thought they were having her on and drove off.

Larry stood in the road in front of a lorry, so the driver had to stop. They asked for a lift to the police station, but this time didn't say why. They climbed into the cab and he dropped them off in Epping village. They asked passers-by for directions to the police station. They were tired, hot, sweaty and scratched to pieces, so the desk sergeant had no trouble believing their story. They were bundled into a police car with the detective and had to direct the driver. Two more cars followed with the coppers.

Although the episode was frightening and serious, Davy and Larry couldn't help being excited about riding in a cop car, and Errol and I couldn't help being impressed.

While we'd been talking, the police had completed their slow march to the body and returned, more quickly.

"Well," said Inspector Mendel, "You have led us a merry chase."

"What is it?" Larry asked.

"Well, I'm pleased to say it's not a dead body."

"Still alive then?" I asked.

"In a manner of speaking, Son."

The detective was playing with us and a couple of the coppers were smirking behind him. He kept us on the hook, asking how we came to be in the forest and what we'd been up to before the discovery. We were worried. Had we done something wrong? Were we in trouble?

"It's all right, boys," he said at last "it's just a root – just a tree root. It's been eaten away by the deer. They eat the bark and leave the bare roots, and from a way off it looks just like human flesh."

I thought we'd surely cop it now, for wasting police time and raising a false alarm.

"It had us fooled from a distance," he said, sensing my concern, "It's OK. You did the right thing. Better safe than sorry."

"Now, boys, it's getting late. You'd better be on you way. I noticed you've no lights on your bikes."

"Elementary, my dear Watson." I whispered to Larry, who stifled a giggle.

They walked us back to our bikes and then to the road, and drove off, bells ringing for our entertainment.

In the woods, we hadn't noticed the sun was getting lower, and it was already cooler. We were tired from the excitement and mounted our bikes and set off slowly.

I suggested we go see my Aunt Hannah. No one was keen until I said we could have tea with her. The pace quickened a little and we took the road towards Loughton.

As we rode in the fading light we retold the story of the murdered Beech root a dozen times, rehearsing it for when we got home and could tell Vivien and Ronny. We arrived in Loughton, and found Aunt Hannah's street, Parkmead, on a mature suburban estate of red-brick council houses all pretty much the same, scattered around well-mowed greens. Number 57 had a neat front garden with rows of standard rose bushes either side of the straight concrete path cut between two small lawns.

We dropped our bikes on the lawn and I knocked on the door. Aunt Hannah was surprised to see us, but pleased all the same. She invited us in. Aunt Hannah's living room was the neatest room I'd ever seen. She had a red oriental-style rug in the middle of the floor with a settee and two armchairs around it. The furniture looked brand new, although I guess it was just clean. Everything was focused on the fireplace, with its modern tiled surround, a brass mesh fireguard, a brass coal scuttle and a brass firedog with a lion's head and an array of brass tools, all with lion's heads.

We so revered this pristine place that we spoke in whispers, like in the library or the synagogue. Davy walked to the sideboard. On top of the polished mahogany, Aunt Hannah had arranged clean white lace doilies, and on them, Uncle Sid's collection of silverware. At the back, a row of ornate silver picture frames with family photos – some I recognized – her son, big Louis, his namesake, Uncle Louis who died in the war, Gran and Granddad on the front doorstep – she in her pinny and Granddad wearing his cap. Others I didn't recognize – probably Uncle Sid's relatives. In the centre, a huge silver dish surrounded by smaller silver plates, jugs, bowls and tiny salt and pepper pots and rows of tiny spoons. Davy carefully opened one silver box, lined inside with deep blue glass. He looked at me mouthed a silent "Cor!"

Uncle Harry was in an armchair reading the News Chronicle. He peered over the top to beam at us. He said, "Very expensive that lot. Don't leave any finger prints will you." and returned to his reading.

Aunt Hannah wanted to know everything. Why were we here, where had we been, what happened in the woods, where were our jumpers?

"I expect you'd like a cup of tea, boys? Or some juice? A piece of cake? You must be famished."

"Not 'arf!" We followed her into the kitchen. No sign of food or drink, no bottles, no plates, cups or saucers – just lots of cupboards. The floor was polished pink-patterned lino, and she had a red Formica-topped drop-leaf table in the middle.

We rattled off various simultaneous versions of the murder in the forest and she smiled that smile that adults do to kids when they don't believe you, but don't want to upset you by saying so.

Soon we were slurping tea and gulping orange juice and attacking a huge three-coloured sponge cake. Aunt Hannah enjoyed feeding us, and brought more cake – a delicious but heavy fruitcake and then a bowl of plums from the trees in her back garden. We scoffed them all and Errol asked if she had lots of plums.

"Would you like some more?" she asked.

After another bowl of fruit and another pot of tea, she invited us to the front room and we sat on mahogany chairs around the mahogany dining table.

Aunt Hannah asked how Gran and Granddad were and told us how well her Louis was doing. In fact she went on and on about Louis and his jewelry business, and much as I liked him and looked up to him as a hero, I lost interest. My eyes wandered around the walls, idly browsing the family photos.

Suddenly I sat bolt upright.

"What's the matter, Tommy?" Aunt Hannah asked, and although I looked away immediately and pretended to be interested in her tales of Louis, she peered in the direction I'd been looking. On the sideboard, amongst the silver-framed family photos was a small copy of the photo of the little blonde girl in the red velvet dress – just like the one I'd found in our airee. In moments her expression flashed through shock, guilt, sadness and then returned to composure and her grown-up smile.

"Time you boys were on your way." She said, bustling into the kitchen, "It'll be dark soon. I hope you've got lights." She returned with a whole packet of Nice biscuits to share on the way home. We said goodbye to Uncle Harry and she gently ushered us to the door.

"Come back and see me again, Tommy. We could have a talk. Phone me next time so I can put the kettle on. Loughton 5280."

We saddled up and rode off in the evening gloom, suddenly hit by the cold after the warmth of Aunt Hannah's living room.

"Nice house." Larry said as we pedaled down Loughton High Street. Davy went on about all the silver and how rich they must be. Errol reminded us of every mouthful of cake. He didn't need to remind me of the plums. We'd all eaten too much. The pedaling motion churned the tea, orange juice, cake and plums into a gurgling mass, heavy in my stomach. As our conversation died away, I could tell the others were in similar discomfort.

It began to rain. With only shorts and vests, we were quickly soaked. Now we realized why girls. old people and Ronny Needleman had mudguards. Larry rode ahead of me with a dirty line of mud up his back, and soon my shorts were sodden with spray from my front wheel.

In half an hour it was dark. We had no lights. We were soaking wet and freezing cold and just as uncomfortable on the inside as on the outside. It was looking like a long slow journey home.

We only had one mishap, when freewheeling downhill at Wanstead. I rode too close to the kerb. My wheels locked flat against it so I couldn't turn. I squeezed the brakes, but they were useless in the rain. I shouted to warn Larry and Davy, who had slowed down ahead, but it was too late for avoiding action and I crashed into them. There was a tangle of pedals and spokes, legs and arms and we fell in a bundle at the roadside. Luckily our bodies and bikes escaped unharmed, apart from Larry's front wheel, which was a bit wobbly for the rest of the trip, and my saddle, which had twisted forty-five degrees sideways and which refused to twist back, even with all four of us trying. So I had to ride the rest of the way standing up in the pedals.

We took a diversion at Bow to avoid the police station – just in case PC Blake was still around, and finally we saw the welcome lights of Mile End Station. We freewheeled down Eric Street and stopped at Davy's to collect our jumpers. Too tired to stay and talk, we all started for home.

"Wanna go back tomorrow?" I shouted back over my shoulder.

I'd never heard so much swearing in such a short time.

"OK, guess not! See you!"

When I got home Gran made a big fuss. She said it was really late and she didn't know where I was. She was worried sick and thought about calling the police, but she didn't want them coming to the door and the neighbours talking. She'd sent Vinny out to look for me, but he was tired and had to go to bed. There would be trouble in the morning.

"Sorry." I was in no mood to explain. I walked away as she nagged on. I parked my bike in the passage, jumped down the stairs, opened the put-u-up and fell straight into bed.

That night I hardly slept. My legs were throbbing and cramping. My bum was sore from the saddle. My crotch was raw from friction with my wet shorts and pants. I thought about that little girl with the red frock on Aunt Hannah's sideboard. Why did she have that picture? Why did no one else have it? Why did she look upset when I nailed it to Gran's wall? Was she my Carol, my sister? Where is she? Where is my mother? Where is my father? Where did I come from? Who am I? Who is Sylvie? Why is it all a secret?

Hannah's Secrets

The next morning I woke early. I sneaked into Vinny's room to look for his bike spanners. As I expected he lay snoring in the corner, but the room was nothing like I'd expected. The whole room had been swept and scrubbed. Even the windows were shiny clean with fresh curtains. No more piles of old papers and magazines. No more medical apparatus. Vinny's junk had been tidied away in neat piles. It even smelled nice. Perhaps he'd found a good woman to sort him out.

It was such a shock I forgot why I'd come in. Oh yes, I needed something for my bike. Luckily he'd kept all his car and bike parts and carefully laid them out on newspapers to catch any dripping oil. I found his spanners.

I left the room and quietly wheeled my bike into the street, where I straightened the seat and tightened the brake cables. I came back and tiptoed down to the kitchen and took some bread pudding. I filled my bike bottle with tap water and took all my pocket money; 1s 6d.

I found a blue Basildon Bond pad and a Biro and scribbled a note. I left it on the floor outside Gran and Granddad's room.

"Sorry, but I have gone to live with Aunt Hannah."

The saddle hurt my bum and my sore groin grated against my shorts, but the pain subsided as I dashed past Bow police station. I was focused on one thing – the little girl in the photo. I was going to find out once and for all. Aunt Hannah would tell me everything. We would have that talk she promised.

I stopped at a telephone box on Stratford High Street to call Aunt Hannah. She was the first person I'd ever phoned. It was about nine o'clock. I stuffed sixpence into the slot and dialed LOU 5280. When she answered I pressed button A. I told her I was coming for lunch. I didn't say I was going live with her.

My legs were pretty weak after the previous day's ride and it took three hours to reach number 57. Throughout the journey I'd been rehearsing what to say.

I opened the iron gate, ran up the path and pressed her doorbell. But when she opened the door, a shock wave of emotion overtook me. I forgot my carefully rehearsed script. Tears flooded my eyes. I pushed past her and blurted out, "You've got to tell me everything, Aunt Hannah."

I hadn't meant to be so blunt. It wasn't at all what I'd rehearsed. I was embarrassed and scared she might be angry. But Aunt Hannah was calm. She followed me into the kitchen, then turned her back to me and put the kettle on. She said nothing. I knew she was embarrassed too and was wondering what to say.

"I want to know about that girl in the picture and about my real mum and my dad." I looked down at the red Formica table top, "No one says anything. I want you to tell me. Please, Aunt Hannah. I want you to tell me. Please." I fought back the tears. I wasn't going to cry any more, in case she thought it would upset me to hear the truth.

"All right, all right. No need to get upset. It's about time you knew." She plopped a knitted cozy over the teapot, placed three cork table mats and set the pot and cups between us. She brought a little silver bowl with sugar cubes and little silver tongs and a bowl of Nice biscuits.

I hated Nice biscuits. "I don't like them." I said and immediately felt ashamed that my greed had taken over from deeper emotions. She went to a cupboard and brought a packet of chocolate digestives, which she spilled into the bowl. I blushed. I thought she'd be angry with a boy who put chocolate biscuits before the mysteries of his parenting, but she just smiled and sat opposite me. She reached over and took my hands gently in hers. No one had ever done that to me, not like that, so gently. Here hands were thin and wrinkled, but her skin was soft and clean and her nails were perfectly rounded with perfect new-moon cuticles.

"The girl is your sister, Carol." She said and before she could take a breath. I burst into tears. I tried so hard not to cry. I felt stupid. I was too old to cry like a baby, but I couldn't help it. I felt a great wailing come from deep inside my body, from an old emptiness I'd felt many times before. I tried to hold it back but it was beyond my control. I uttered a loud cry like a dog wailing for it's dead master and I buried my face in her hands.

Uncle Harry opened the door. "Any tea?" He looked at us, froze and backed out quickly. I was shaking and breathing in tiny breaths. Even with my eyes shut tight I could see red everywhere. I stifled my cries and looked up through tears to see Aunt Hannah silently weeping too.

She reached across, stroked my hair and kissed my forehead and I remembered Mrs. Green's Purim kiss. She sat down and stroked the tears from my cheeks with the back of her hand.

"Oh Tommy! I am so, so sorry. I should have told you before. So many times I wanted to tell you. But Mum said we shouldn't. I didn't know what to do for the best."

Tears rolled down her cheeks and although I felt it was disrespectful, and I feared it might make her angry, I reached across with one hand

and stroked her cheek. She angled her head into my hand for a moment and looked so sad. but then she drew back, sat up, wiped her face and composed herself. She spun round, took a big box of Kleenex and pulled some tissues for both of us.

"Blow your nose, Tommy."

"I'm sorry, Aunt Hannah. I didn't mean to upset you. Something came out of me."

She poured the tea, and using the tongs, not her fingers, she plopped two sugar cubes in mine and slid it across the table smearing a sprinkle of teardrops across the Formica. She dropped another cube in "Just for luck." and looked straight into my eyes and smiled. I knew there were things that she couldn't say that day or ever – not about my sister, my real mum and dad, but about her. I felt her love flood over me – more love than an Aunt has for a nephew.

And it suddenly struck me. Aunt Hannah was Carol's mother! That's why she was the only one with the picture. That's why she was upset when she saw it at Gran's house. So Aunt Hannah was my mother! That's why she was angry with Aunt Stella for calling me a bastard. That's why it's a secret – my Aunt is my mother. But... Uncle Harry's not my father. That's why it's such a big secret.

"I have to tell you about a young girl at the end of the war." she said. "You have to understand, Tommy, your mother was not really to blame. She was so young and we're modern now, but it was all very different then."

She talked quietly, like she was telling a story about a stranger. I listened intently not daring to interrupt in case she stopped. She told me how this sweet girl had grown up the apple of my Granddad's eye. Among all his children, she was his delight. She was pretty, affectionate and fun, always into mischief, always laughing. She was generous, innocent and trusted everyone.

"It was in the last year of the war. We'd been evacuated to East Hanney – a little village near Wantage. The house was about two miles from the American Army base at Grove Airdrome.

"Just one month before her sixteenth birthday there was a dance at the base. Your mother asked if she could go. Other girls her age in the village had been to dances before, and she thought she was old enough.

"That was January 1944 and most of our boys were overseas. Solly, Sammy and Louis were away with the Eighth Army, fighting Rommel in Tobruk. The Americans had come over to end the war and save us. The ordinary soldiers were called GIs." She smiled as she remembered.

"They were big tall handsome boys, Tommy. When they came round courting they made a big fuss. They brought us nylons and oranges and cigarettes for Mum and Dad and chocolate for Stella and the other kids in the street. Everyone liked them.

"Your Gran said your mother was too young to go dancing, but Granddad said she could. So she set off down the lane on her bike with her sisters and the other village girls. They had a great time at the camp. The yanks loved swing music and wild dancing and the girls had too much to drink. I have to say she loved all the attention and when one of the boys asked, she didn't hesitate to get up on stage with the band and sing Sentimental Journey. People danced while she sang and when she stopped everyone clapped.

"Well, as the night wore on the GIs paired off with the village girls for a kiss and cuddle, but she was frightened and wanted to go home. She was blind drunk. She couldn't find any of her friends. So she went alone, found her bike and pedaled off down the lane.

"She'd only gone a little way and out of the dark came this man on a bike. He crashed straight into her at top speed and they both fell into the brambles. She screamed but no one could hear out there. Then this big airman was on top of her pulling at her clothes.

"She had no idea what was happening, Tommy. She struggled and he elbowed her in the face. After a few minutes, he pulled away and rode off shouting back that he was sorry. She hurt all over. She lay there for a while and then dragged herself out of the brambles. She was covered in blood. Her face was scratched, arms and legs. Her frock was ripped. She hurt everywhere. She shouted for help, but no one came, so she climbed on her bike and pedaled home. When she got back she hid the bike in the bushes in the garden.

"Your Gran was very angry with her, for getting into a fight and spoiling her clothes. She tried to explain that a Yank had beaten her up, but Gran would hear no more about it. Granddad didn't make a fuss, but he was very quiet. He told her to get cleaned up and go to bed.

"When the other girls got home, Granddad gave them the third degree, but no one knew anything about the incident. Everyone assumed that she'd got into an argument and it had led to a fight, which she'd probably exaggerated. She wasn't allowed to go back to the camp.

"A few days later an airman called at the house to see her. He was a good-looking boy. He said he was called Jackson and he was the one who crashed into her in the dark. He said he didn't see her. She had no lights. He was sorry about the bike and wanted to make up for it. He'd bought her a new bike with dynamo lights. Gran told him to 'Bugger off' at first, but Johnny Jackson was the best looking boy on the base. He looked like a film star. He also had a lazy Louisiana drawl and southern good manners that left women weak at the knees – young and old alike. Mum decided she'd keep the bike, and she let them both go off for a walk."

Aunt Hannah poured herself another cup of tea.

"Spring went, then Summer, and the war ended in Autumn. There were celebrations in the streets, parties and dances but your mother didn't go to them. She'd fallen sick. She'd been having dizzy spells and fainting. Gran said she was making a fuss over nothing and was just after attention. She'd also put on weight – though no more than to be expected – girls do fill out when they get to sixteen or seventeen.

"Christmas came, and it was very special. We'd all come through the Blitz alive and Dad and the boys came home from the war. Sammy had lost a finger. Solly was fine, but Louis was missing. So Christmas was happy and sad at the same time. But she, your mother, felt ill and stayed away from the celebrations.

"Just after Christmas, Dad went to work for a couple of days on a local farm, and Gran was helping a neighbour with some cleaning. When dad came home he heard someone screaming – from half a mile away. When he got to the house, he found your mother slumped on the doorstep jammed half in and half out the street door. She was screaming with a pain in her stomach.

"Dad thought it was appendicitis. He pulled her inside then ran for help. He came back with the doctor. They bundled her into the doctor's car and drove to the hospital. In a few minutes they had her ready for an operation and they put her to sleep.

"It was only when they were about to cut her belly open that a nurse noticed blood between her legs and told the doctor 'I think she's having a baby.' The doctor told the porter to take her to maternity. On the maternity ward she had a baby." Aunt Hannah said, looking down, stirring her tea, "and that was your sister, Carol."

"Your mother was half asleep through the birth, with the anesthetic and when she came round and found a baby in a cot beside her, she asked whose it was. The nurse said it was hers, but she couldn't believe it. She thought it was a joke. She still didn't understand what had happened. In fact it took weeks to convince her that the baby was hers."

I knew, from Davy's reports about Rosy and his parents and from talking to other kids in the street and at school, a bit about how babies were started.

I had seen plenty of pregnant women and by eavesdropping on my aunts' whisperings in Gran's kitchen I knew what happened during pregnancy and how babies came out – not much of the detail, but enough to suppose that a woman would notice it. Although it was embarrassing I couldn't resist asking, "How could she have a baby and not know about it?"

"She was innocent, Tommy, she didn't know about the facts of life and she didn't know what happened that night after the dance. She didn't know she was..."

"Raped?" I said.

I felt guilty admitting I knew the word. I knew from the other kids that rape was when a man forced himself into a woman when she didn't want it. I didn't understand how it could happen or why anyone would want to do it, and I never thought about the consequences. Now it all came together.

"Yes," Aunt Hannah, fiddled with her teaspoon.

"And then she had a baby and it was my sister."

"Yes." Aunt Hannah looked into my eyes with sadness and perhaps guilt.

"It wasn't her fault," I said, wanting to reassure her, "You... she was made to do it."

"Yes," she said, "That time."

"What do you mean?"

Aunt Hannah went on to say that shortly after Carol was born, my mother recovered and asked if she could go out to the base. Gran and Granddad refused permission, but she sneaked out at night. They couldn't stop her. She was there every night flirting with the boys. She loved the attention, and now she knew how to get it. She knew what they wanted. Word went round when she was on the base and there was always an airman keen to take her in the bushes, and give her a pair of nylons.

The whole family knew about it. The whole village knew about it. Gran was ashamed and threw her out of the house many times. She called her a slut. Granddad always argued with Gran and let her back in.

Before long she was pregnant again, and this time she knew perfectly well how it happened.

"She had another baby, and that was you, Tommy." Aunt Hannah stopped and looked into my eyes.

I was shocked – not only at what I'd heard, but that Aunt Hannah would confess all this to me – so openly. I didn't know what to think of her. She had been forced to have my sister, but then she became... like a prostitute and she had me.

"Does Uncle Harry know about this?" I asked.

"Oh, he's not interested in old family history."

My head was spinning. A cacophony of voices rehearsed hundreds of responses to Aunt Hannah. Some were incredulous that this intelligent dignified woman could behave like that; some voices were angry, raging against her stupidity; some were sympathetic, forgiving and reassuring. I hated her. I loved her. I wanted to scream at her. I wanted to hold her. What could I do? What could I say? What do I call her – mummy, mother?

"I still love you, Aunt Hannah."

"Of course you do and I love you too Tommy. I'm sorry I didn't tell you all this sooner."

There were so many things I could say, but I couldn't decide what was appropriate so I kept silent.

"You know, when your mother left you behind and went to America, I asked Gran if you could live with me, and she let me bring you up when you were little."

What? What was she saying? Did I hear that right? It didn't make sense. I sat up so fast I nearly fell over the back of the chair.

"What? My mother left me and you asked Gran... It wasn't about you then! It's not... you?" I said, "You're not my mother?"

"Oh my God!" Aunt Hannah stood up and her chair screeched across the floor. Her eyes were wide. She slapped her hand over her open mouth. "What have you been thinking? No! I'm not your mother! I'm not that... stupid whore!"

My mouth dropped. I stood, threw the chair aside and backed away across the room.

"I wasn't me!" she shouted, shaking her head, "It was Sylvie!"

What have I done? What have I said? I thought it was her. How could I be so stupid? Aunt Hannah's not my mother. She doesn't love me. She hates me. I'm not her son, I'm the son of a whore! I pushed my way past her, threw the kitchen door open and ran into the front room.

"Hello Tommy." Uncle Harry beamed, looking over the top of his paper.

I fumbled with the latch, flung the street door open and ran headlong down the garden. I grabbed my bike, clattered through the gate

"Tommy! Tommy!" Aunt Hannah ran out after me. "Don't go now, please!"

My rage made my head throb and my hands were clumsy and I struggled to get on the bike. I shouted back,

"Where is she?"

"Your mother?" she asked.

"No! My sister!" I shouted.

"I… we don't know, Tommy – somewhere in London. Wait!"

I jumped on the bike put my head down and pumped at the pedals as hard as I could repeating, "Somewhere in London. Somewhere in London".

Hours later, when I got back to Eric Street, for the first time I noticed the dirt and litter. Everything was grey – no grass, no trees, no roses. Gran's house was dark and small inside and smelled of damp.

Gran didn't ask me where I'd been. She didn't mention the note I'd left by her door. She just said, "You've got an interview – at the Grammar."

Best and Borrowed Clothes

The morning of the interview I woke to find a bar of Five Boys balanced on the arm of my put-u-up. Granddad had left it.

I didn't wear my normal school things that day. I dressed top to bottom in my best clothes. My shoes were polished black, although they were too scuffed to shine.

I ironed crisp creases into my best grey flannel shorts. I struggled with my white shirt – the whalebones were missing from the collar, so no matter how hard I pressed, or how hot the iron, the wings curled up like Salvador Dali's moustache. Although a few stains survived the wash, I covered them with a blue tie and an old navy blazer I borrowed from Ronny Needleman. With hair Brylcreemed neatly to one side, I was as shiny and clean as I could be.

Gran gave me a brown envelope and asked me to run it round to Mr. Levy's. I protested, but ran off across the street, past a woman in a blue coat who was staring at Gran's house. She turned away as I ran past her across the bomb site. I dodged abandoned bedsteads, jumped over walls and kicked a few cans on the way.

For a while now, Gran's envelopes carried notes rather than change. This one was fatter than usual.

When I returned from Mr. Levy's. Gran and I walked up the street to the bus. My socks had slipped down my skinny legs and bunched at my ankles, my collar and Ronny's tie were twisted and my shoes were scuffed and scruffy.

We caught a trolley bus, which was slower than the new diesel Routemasters. At the big junction at Gardiner's Corner the power arms fell off the overhead cables. It took the conductor five minutes to hook them up with his long pole.

I watched a dog, caught in the middle of the traffic – a small black mongrel surrounded by buses, cars, taxis and bikes. Drivers shouted at the poor thing, which was spinning in tight circles desperately searching for a way out of its nightmare. It finally panicked and shot off randomly at top speed. A man on a bike swerved out of its way and fell, swearing. The crazed dog ran in front of two cars. The drivers braked hard to avoid it, but a third car drove straight into the dog. Headlight hit skull and they both shattered with a loud crack. As our bus drove away, a small crowd gathered round.

By the time we got off at Old Street, we were fifteen minutes late for the interview. I jumped to the kerb without looking and bumped into a girl, knocking her back into her mother's arms. I only had a glimpse.

She was blond, about 13. She was with a tall dark-haired Jewish lady. They had nice clothes. I thought the girl would shout at me or even hit me, but she just smiled. I turned away quickly to help Gran down from the bus and, as fast as Gran's arthritis would allow, we rushed off down Singer Street. I glanced back and the girl was still smiling.

We turned into Tabernacle Street, through the big gates into the playground of the Central Foundation Grammar School for Boys.

We were enclosed on three sides by a terrifyingly huge building. Three imposing blocks of brown brick containing a wild confusion of boys – hundreds of them in navy blue blazers. Some tore around the playground linked in strings of three or four playing chain-he, others chased tennis balls in small dusty crowds, pushing and clawing each other off the ball. Others stood in heaving bundles, shouting and tussling.

The noise was tremendous – trapped and amplified by the tall buildings. Gran froze, her eyes wide and darting all over like the dog at Gardiner's Corner. I was frightened. We heard a long loud whistle. Every boy froze in mid flight and the playground was momentarily silent and full of statues. A tennis ball rolled to a stop by my feet.

Gran and I picked our way through the frozen boys towards the building on the right.

Another whistle and the kids unfroze and shuffled into long lines by the doors of each building.

We walked along the railings, up the wide steps and took the door labeled *B Block*. Inside it was like a prison. Above us a towering square stair well with glinting concrete steps spiraled up forever, enclosed by black railings. Everything was hard – polished parquet corridors, blue glossy walls, and cold black iron rails.

Gran steadied herself with one hand on the wall.

A door behind us burst open and a rush of boys spilled into the corridor, they tumbled noisily past us, like a sack full of coal thundering into our cellar.

"QUI-ET!" screamed a teacher at the top of his voice. He was standing right beside us.

The jostling mass streamed up the stairs and disappeared into the echoing corridors above.

"Hello, there, come for the interviews?" the screaming teacher asked softly.

Gran and I stared at him.

"Down there, to the right," he said. "Headmaster's Office."

We walked where he pointed.

"Good luck." He said as we turned into the corridor.

"I said, QUI-ET!" He bellowed up the stair well.

A dozen well-scrubbed boys and their Sunday-best mothers sat on a row of benches outside the Headmaster's study. We were all there because we'd passed the eleven-plus and were applying for a place at this famous grammar school in the heart of the City of London. Everyone was nervous. The boys were fidgeting, swinging legs, biting nails and picking noses. The mothers were fussing with ties and shoelaces and cuffing the nose pickers with whispered threats that echoed along the corridor.

"Benjamin Jacobs!" a lady called and I spun round with relief to see Benny, my best friend from Stepney Jewish and his Mum.

"Hiya, Benny!"

He smiled as he walked past and held up crossed fingers for luck as he entered the Headmaster's study.

The rest of us sat looking at each other until Benny and his Mum emerged five minutes later. They walked away to the far end of the corridor. Benny twisted round and gave me a thumbs-up before they turned out of sight.

"Thomas Angel!" the secretary called.

My stomach fell to the floor. The few yards walk to the Headmaster's door was like a journey to the gallows. Every step took conscious effort. My legs had forgotten how to work. I thought about the frightened dog.

In the centre of the room was a big dark table. Five men sat behind it. They looked very severe and wore black academic gowns that looked like Batman capes. Gran and I sat on chairs in the big open space before them.

The Headmaster, Mr. Cowan, was a soft rounded man with pale skin and gentle eyes. He introduced himself and the rest of the 'Panel', which included Mr. Spencer the Deputy Head – an angular man with rocky cheekbones and a smile that kept trying to creep up one side of his face. At the end of the table sat someone he called the "Guvnor", who must have been the real boss, and two others whose names I didn't catch.

"We pride ourselves on our very high standards of behaviour and academic attainment." said Mr. Spencer very quickly, as if he had said it a hundred times before, "Do you think you are capable of living up to them, Angel? With a name like that you should find it no problem!"

He smiled on the left side and raised his eyebrows.

No one ever called me Angel. I was Tommy, to my family and mates. Obviously I was in trouble, deep trouble – perhaps because we were late, or because my collar was curled up. My mouth went dry and my tongue doubled in size. It took huge effort to control.

"Er... what'sat, Sir?" It came out like a drunken drawl. It felt like talking with a gobstopper in my mouth.

Gran glared at me.

"Do you think, Angel," Mr. Cowan said, slowly emphasizing every word, as if he was talking to an imbecile, "that you embody the social, moral and intellectual qualities that are required to make a significant contribution to the life of this great institution?"

"Don't know, Sir." I said – partly because I really had no idea what he was talking about and partly because I'd always found, when in serious trouble at school, that trying to explain or argue your way out always made things worse. If, on the other hand, you kept saying 'I don't know' long enough, the teachers eventually gave up and let you off.

"Did you understand the Headmaster's question, Boy?" the Guvnor spluttered.

"Don't know, Sir."

All five of the Panel stared at me like I was something repulsive – I felt like a three-headed slug. Then they stared at Gran, who said,

"Sorry, Headmaster. He's a bit of a *luftmensh* and a bit... well, slow, but he's fine when he catches on."

Nothing could redeem my situation. I was grateful to Gran for having a go, but I was sure it was exactly the wrong thing to say. The Grammar was for kids who were quick. Slow kids went to the Secondary Modern.

Ever since I found out Vinny had a hole-in-the-heart and a colostomy because he didn't pay attention to his schooling, I believed that education would be my escape from poverty, crime, sickness, squalor and boredom. Now I'd messed up my best and only chance. I was done, finished, sunk. My potential would wither unrealized and my life would be a dead end street.

The Panel looked at each other, shrugged and raised eyes to the sky. "Well, Angel," Mr. Spencer, mocked, offering me one last chance to redeem myself "dooo pleeease. If you would be sooo kind, tell the Panel why have you have chosen to apply to this school?"

"I like the uniform, Sir." I chirped and smiled weakly.

They smirked at each other and gave me pitying 'hopeless case' looks.

I protested "But I do like the uniform, Sir. It's really smart!"

They looked on in silent shock.

At Central Foundation Grammar School for Boys you wear long grey trousers in the second year, a dark blue tie, a smart navy blazer with a beautifully embroidered badge with the school coat of arms – not like the daft maroon blazer with green piping they got at Ben Johnson Secondary Modern.

"Thank you, Mrs. Angel" Mr. Cowan sighed. He didn't look at me "You'll hear in a couple of weeks. Next!"

We left the building in silence and said nothing on the bus all the way home. Gran stared in front of her. I stared out the window, looking for the girl I'd bumped into. Perhaps she was my sister somewhere in London. By the time we got to Mile End I'd seen three other blond girls, some a bit older some younger. Any of them could be my sister. I decided to find out more about her.

Outside the station, Gran bought the Evening News. On the front page was a big headline *Suez – War in Egypt*? But Gran wasn't worried about impending war. She turned to the racing pages. She couldn't make out the small writing and made me read the results of the 3:35 at Wetherby. I don't remember which horse won, but it wasn't Gran's and we walked down Eric Street in silence.

During the next few weeks I stayed in. I listened to the radio, drew pictures, wrote poems, sorted my picture cards into ordered stacks. I arranged the 400 free sample stamps I got from Stanley Gibbons to replace my swapped collection, by country, then by theme (animals, transport, people), then by colour – all in a useless effort to stop thinking about the rough kids I'd be with at the secondary modern. The Grammar kids were scary, but the secondary mods were like Donkin and worse. They'd kill me.

After three weeks Gran got a letter. Despite my pathetic interview performance I had been offered a place at Central Foundation Grammar School for Boys. I thought they had taken pity on me because we were poor, but Vinny said it was because they hadn't filled their quota of idiots.

All Our Fathers

Through the Summer I kept seeing girls on the street who could be my sister and women who could be my mother. I had to know more.

I called round to see Aunt Marlene. She was very kind and answered my questions – hundreds of them. I wanted to know what Sylvie was like, why she left me behind, where she went, what she did, but mostly I wanted to know about my sister.

Each answer spawned a dozen new questions. Aunt Marlene must have felt my interrogations would never end, but she patiently helped me construct Sylvie's story.

I told Aunt Marlene what Aunt Hannah had said. At first she was shocked. She listened in silence, eyes down, fiddling with her pinny.

I had to tell her everything. Aunt Marlene wouldn't want to be the first to open that box of dark secrets. I used the words Aunt Hannah used about Sylvie – rape, pregnant, whore, even though I didn't entirely appreciate their meanings. I recounted the birth of my sister in as much detail as I could. I wanted Aunt Marlene to think that she could talk to me like I was an adult. She had to know I wouldn't get upset whatever she said. I made out it was just a story and I didn't care about it. I was just curious. I just wanted to know – why was she like that, why did she leave me, why did she go to America, what happened?

Eventually she looked up. Her face was soft, her eyes wet. She sniffed, forced a smile and said, "I suppose you have a right to know… Everything."

I spent the afternoon with her, listening and storing away every detail.

"You mustn't be too hard on her, Tommy, It wasn't all her fault. You see, she was always the baby of the family. Your Granddad doted on her – so much that your Gran was jealous.

"But when Sylvie was three, Stella was born and Sylvie wasn't the baby anymore. She hated Stella. She resented the attention she got. As Stella grew up Sylvie thought Dad was pushing her away. She tried everything to win his love, fussing around him all the time, but she just irritated him. If you ask me, that's where it all started and she's been after the attention of men ever since."

Aunt Marlene held nothing back. It seemed to be a relief to let it go. "When she was a teenager, she fell in with a bad lot. She went for rough boys. They preyed on her, Tommy, used up her innocence. And then she wasn't so innocent anymore. She was always running home to Mum and Dad saying the boys had done something rude, you know what I mean?"

I said I did. But I didn't really.

"She knew it upset Dad. I think that's what she wanted. It was as if she was saying – 'You don't love me so I'll waste myself on bad boys and then you'll be sorry.' Who knows what went on in her mind?

"Once she came back from a dance. Dad told her off for sneaking out and flirting with the men. She said she wasn't flirting. Said she was... attacked. I don't know if it was true – she'd become a real teaser and led the boys on something rotten. She'd certainly been up to mischief. Later she had Carol it was like she was... spoiled. Mum and Dad and all her brothers and sisters, they treated her as if she was... contagious – all except me, and Vinny, bless him.

"I felt sorry for her. We all make mistakes. No one's perfect. That's no reason to hurt people. And Vinny, he was only young and he'd missed a lot because of his illness. He didn't understand what was going on.

"Mum and Dad took her in, but not for Sylvie's sake – it was to protect the baby and keep Sylvie off the streets. And to keep her away from Stella – she was only thirteen and she looked up to Sylvie. They didn't want Stella following her."

Aunt Marlene told me how Sylvie was locked up in the house all day, but would sneak out at night and go to the base. She went from man to man. "They used her, Tommy, and they left her... threw her away."

"You mean like a sweet paper when you finish the sweet."

"Exactly. Yes."

"It happened over and over – she wouldn't learn. None of those boys loved her, but they held her for a while, Tommy, and made promises and it felt like love. I know about that."

Her eyes were soft again.

"Did she marry them?"

"Those boys weren't looking for a wife. They promised everything of course – they'd get married live in a beautiful house have lots of kids and a Cadillac – but it was all promises. Sylvie was like a child. She fell for it every time. She even convinced Mum.

"She came out with a story that this Airman Jackson wanted to marry her. Of course Mum jumped at the chance of getting rid of Sylvie and started planning a wedding. She even bought Sylvie a wedding veil to put by and promised to get her the dress when a date was sorted.

"But a few days later when Sylvie went to the base to meet Jackson, his mates said he'd been flown back to America. She asked if he'd left a message. They said he told them to tell her he would write.

"Mum was livid. She chased Sylvie round the house, calling her a stupid cow. She'd have beaten Sylvie black and blue if she'd caught her. But Sylvie ran out screaming down the road.

"When she came back Mum had calmed down. She told Sylvie her wedding veil was in the rubbish where it belonged and for all she cared Sylvie could go and join it."

That's *Sylv Angel 44*. I thought.

"None of them loved her, Tommy. Only Dad loved her. He tried to protect her and in return she made his life a misery."

"Thanks for telling me, Aunt Marlene."

"Look, Tommy, if you really want to know more about all this, you should ask your Aunt Hannah. She knows more than I do. She's always looked out for you.

I thanked her again and told her I was off to play with my mates. But I wasn't. I jumped on my bike and headed off for Aunt Hannah's.

As soon as Aunt Hannah opened her door I apologized for my outburst the last time we talked. She put her arm on my shoulder and said it didn't matter, it was a lot for a boy to take in. She led me through to the back garden where we sat at her outdoor table and chairs.

We wasted no time. She knew what I wanted.

I asked why Sylvie went away and left me behind. "How can a mother leave a child behind, a baby?"

"I'll tell you," she said, "but it's not nice."

I nodded.

"I told you about the GI called Jackson – the one who crashed bikes with Sylvie after the dance at the base and then gave her a new bike. Well he asked Dad's permission to take Sylvie for a walk and they ended up in the bushes.

"Sylvie had plenty of boyfriends after that. But ten months later after she had baby Carol she got fed up with the pointed fingers and the whispers in the village and she told your Aunt Miriam and me that Jackson had raped her and that he was the father. We didn't know whether to believe her. Sometimes she said it was when he crashed into her bike, sometimes it was when they went walking afterwards. Anyway Miriam told Mum and Mum told Dad.

"So Dad and Mum dragged Sylvie down to the Airdrome and demanded to see Jackson. For some reason he was in the brig – he liked to drink hard and play hard and was often in trouble. His commanding officer had him brought out and asked him if he was the father. Jackson denied it and listed half a dozen other GIs it could have been.

"Sylvie maintained she hadn't had sex with anyone else and the military believed her. They didn't charge him with rape, but from that day Jackson had to pay a monthly allowance for his child. The money came straight out of his pay, but I don't think Sylvie got a penny of it – your Gran took care of that."

"What happened to the baby?"

"Well, as soon as Sylvie got out of hospital, the baby was taken back to London to live with your Aunt Miriam. She named her Carol Ann and Sylvie wanted the child to have the name Angel to punish Johnny for saying he wasn't the father. Johnny wasn't bothered – he'd gone back to Louisiana.

"Months went by, and Sylvie heard nothing from him. No – tell a lie... He did write one letter, promising he'd send for her, but only one and he didn't write again. But Sylvie didn't care anymore. She was having too much fun.

"Miriam wasn't very well – never has been really, so Mum got Carol back from her and told Sylvie she had to look after her own baby. But Sylvie had no feelings for the poor mite and left her with Mum while she sneaked out to the base. Even before Jackson left, she had taken up with another boy, Billy, who told her he was General Patton's son and she believed him, silly cow! She believed anything the boys told her. Patton is a very famous American General."

"I know. I read about him in the Eagle."

"Well, son of a general or not, he got her pregnant and six months after Jackson left she had another baby – you."

"So was my father really General Patton's son?" I asked. "Is General Patton my real Granddad?"

"Who knows? Billy went back to America before you were born – never set eyes on you. Mum said she wrote to General Patton's wife, telling her about the baby. She thought she might get some money out of them. But Mum heard nothing for ages and then she got a letter from Mrs. Patton saying her son had mumps as a child and couldn't have babies, so it couldn't have been him.

"Did Sylvie go to America to look for my dad?"

"No," Aunt Hannah sighed, "Mum thought it would be a waste of time with the family claiming their son couldn't have babies. That meant either they were lying or your father lied to Sylvie and wasn't the general's son. Either way it was obvious that Patton (if that was his name) didn't want anything to do with the girl he left behind in England, or her baby."

I know my Granddad loved me. It didn't matter that he wasn't my real dad. He always smiled when he saw me. He looked after me. He talked to me. He treated me the same as his sons. For years I half-believed he was my father. My aunts and uncles called him "Dad" and so did I. But I couldn't pretend anymore. He wasn't my father. My father was a man who went away.

"Anyway, Sylvie started messing around with other men at the base. There was a Ukranian Yankee from Philadelphia called Frank – had a very long surname – can't remember it. He was a well-built boy with a blonde crewcut. He said he loved her and wanted to take her home to the States to get married.

"Sylvie didn't love him, but by this time, Mum was cheesed off with Sylvie. She couldn't afford to look after two children.

"Frank told Mum he had a good job with Yale the lock company and he showed Mum a picture of his house, said he was going to make it into a fine home for Sylvie and baby Carol. It was a beautiful large house by the sea.

"Mum was convinced that Sylvie and Carol would have a good life with Frank. But Dad wasn't sure of him. Lots of the Yankie boys had pictures of grand houses. They cut them from magazines and pretended they were their own to make out they were rich and impress the girls.

"Mum told Sylvie she was lucky to have someone who really loved her. She should go to America and marry him and he could be a good father to Carol. So Sylvie agreed.

"As soon as Frank got back to Philadelphia he sent money to pay for tickets for Sylvie and the baby, and wrote that he'd send for them when he'd arranged the proper permissions. Mum told Sylvie she'd look after the money.

"Later Frank wrote back with a date for travel and told Sylvie if anyone asked she was to say that Carol was his baby. But Mum had spent the money."

"Like she spent my social money?" I asked.

"Yes, Tommy. I'm afraid so. Sylvie was so ashamed, but she wrote to Frank and asked him to send more money. He did and she set off to find a new life.

"She didn't really want to take your sister, who was three then, but Mum said the baby was the reason the Yanks would let her in and she'd have to take her. Dad said it wasn't fair on Carol and it was dangerous and she should stay here, but Mum made a big fuss and she won. Sylvie left with Carol and a suitcase.

"That's the last they heard of her until she came back six months later. Out of the blue one night. She phoned Solly from a phone box in Southampton and asked him to come and get her. He drove down in the Austin and brought her back home to Mum.

"She wouldn't say a word about what had happened over there, but she was in a terrible state and so was the baby. They were weak, exhausted and thin and their clothes were in a terrible mess. And Sylvie was pregnant again.

"Mum didn't want to take her in, but she was worried about Carol. She quizzed Sylvie for hours, trying to find out what happened, but all she said was Frank was wicked. He didn't really want her, but he tried to steal Carol for his sister who couldn't have babies of her own."

"And the new baby?"

"That was Frank's. She was already pregnant with his baby before she went away. Three months after she got home, she had a little girl – called her Jacqueline. Mum let Sylvie stay until the baby was three months old and on the bottle.

"Sylvie had already taken up with another man.. She was staying out all hours again, coming home in a state – usually drunk and sometimes beaten up. Mum was having no more of it. She kicked Sylvie out and told her not to come back. This time Dad didn't stop her – no one did. Everyone had had enough of Sylvie."

"And the baby. Is she my sister?" I knew it was a stupid question, but I had never heard the name Jacqueline mentioned in the family.

"She is. Well, half sister, I suppose."

"Where is she?" I asked.

"South Africa."

"What?"

"They had her adopted when she was four months old. Dad tried to stop it, said the family should keep her, but Mum put her foot down – she wasn't looking after three little bastards... Oh sorry!"

"It's OK,"

I'd got over the bastard thing when I learned it only meant being born to parents who weren't married. I worked out that wasn't any of my doing, just something that happened. I wasn't to blame. Being a bastard wasn't something for a child to be ashamed of. "I don't mind being a bastard." I said.

"Well, Mum said she wanted little Jacqui to go to a good home and be close, so the family could keep an eye on her and make sure she was all right. The Jewish Board of Guardians promised she would go to a family in London.

"Later Solly went up to the office and asked where the baby was and they said they weren't allowed to say. But the adoption lady had Jacqui's file open on her desk. Her phone rang and she turned away to take the call. Solly grabbed the file and read it. He saw Johannesburg written there. He demanded to know if the baby had been sent to South Africa, but she denied it and said it was a South African Jewish family living in London, but she couldn't say where.

"We heard later they were sending thousands of babies out to South Africa and Australia. The people there wanted kids so they had workers for their farms and sheep stations. But it was supposed to be a secret. In fact a few years later, we heard all the adoption files were 'accidentally' burned. Solly said it was to cover up what happened."

"So do I have a sister in South Africa?"

"Maybe – we don't know. We didn't hear anything and the JBG wouldn't tell."

"So I've got two sisters." I said. "What happened to Carol?"

"She was adopted too."

"To South Africa?"

"No she went to The Jewish Board of Guardians orphanage near Sydenham in Kent."

"Every Saturday they had an open day and people came around looking for kids to adopt. Each kid would put on a little show or do a party trick – one would sing, one would dance. Carol was pretty and knew how to get attention. Lots of visitors were interested in her.

"One day the Board lady called round to say a couple wanted Carol. After what happened to Jacqueline, Dad insisted that he and Mum met the new parents. The JBG didn't want to do it, but he said 'no meeting no adoption' and they made an exception."

"Who took her?"

"We don't know. Mum and Dad met them – said they were a nice couple. They were Jewish, nicely spoken, well off. They fell in love with Carol as soon as they set eyes on her. Well who wouldn't – she was so pretty – five years old with beautiful blue eyes and lovely blond curls."

"And a red velvet dress." I said, "I found her picture."

"Yes. You put it on the wall."

"Nobody said anything." I said.

"I know. I'm sorry, Tommy." She turned to look in my eyes, "It made everyone feel bad."

"Why?"

"That was her last picture. The Board had it taken so they could show it to parents who might want to adopt her." She stopped. She looked down and wept quietly.

"Those beautiful babies." She stared ahead into her garden – neat lawns and pretty flower beds. "We let them go, both of them. We could have stopped her, Tommy. She didn't have to send them away. Oh, I know Mum was too old to look after three of you, and she needed the money. But we could have taken you in, between us – me and Harry, Sammy and Nina, Solly and Marlene."

"What money?" I asked.

"The couples who took the girls paid for the adoption." She said. "It was a lot of money." She paused. "We let those babies go. That was the last we ever saw of them. Lost them, both of them."

"So... she sold them?" I asked.

"Well, not just like that. It's just that they paid for the adoption and Gran needed the money."

"She sold them." I said. "Does Carol still live in London somewhere?"

"Yes. But they didn't get any name or address. That was the rule. Sammy said he thought he saw her once when he was driving his lorry. She was skipping in the street with other kids. He couldn't stop, and anyway he couldn't be sure."

"Where was that?"

"Somewhere in North London, a part he didn't know very well. No one's seen her since. I don't suppose we'd recognize her now. She must be... twelve, thirteen."

A wild, thought exploded in my head. I heard a voice escape from my mouth. "I've seen her!"

"What? Where?" Aunt Hannah sat upright and stared at me. "You saw her. Where?"

"I mean... I see her everywhere. Well I think I do... on the train, on the bus, when we're playing out. But it's not really her. They can't all be her can they."

I felt a sourness in the back of my mouth. I tried to hold back, but my face crumpled and tears streamed. My mouth opened wide by itself and let out a huge wail that came from a deep unknowable darkness and filled the summer garden with loss and anguish.

Aunt Hannah put her arm around me and hugged me tight. I wailed without inhibition for a long time. Aunt Hannah held me tighter, and just kept repeating "Oh Tommy, Oh Tommy."

"Why did she sell my sisters? Why did she keep me?" I sobbed, "Why was I the only one?"

"Oh, Tommy. You are so young. How can you understand what grown ups do? Mum said you should have been adopted too, but I convinced her to let you live with Harry and me for a while. Then Mum had you home again and the Welfare came. They said you were failing to thrive."

"Uh?"

"Like... a flower that doesn't get enough sunshine." She said.

"They said you had to go to a home to build your strength. They took you to the Muller. You were there for four years. Dad made them bring you back. He tried to adopt you properly, but they said he and Mum were too old and they wouldn't have it. But the social lady suggested Dad applied to foster you. It took months of to-ing and fro-ing but they agreed. You know your Granddad loves you and he would never let you go."

"Thanks, Aunt Hannah" I said, "Thanks for telling me."

"You're a good boy, Tommy" she said, "Don't let it turn you. And please don't blame your mother, she was young and didn't know any better."

"Why is it all such a secret?"

"Your Gran didn't want any of it to get out. She's not proud of what she did. But Tommy she did what she could. It was difficult. She was old. She couldn't cope with three babies. She needed the money."

"She sold my sisters."

For many nights after that, I lay awake thinking about my lost sisters. I took Carol's picture from the wall and stared at it for hours, stroked her hair, touched her rosy cheeks, stared into her watery-blue eyes. Then one night her face smiled back at me – not the photo, but her real face. I saw her kneeling beside me, on the armchair by the window. We were looking up through the airee railings, waiting for Granddad. She sang a song and I clapped.

Clap you hands 'til Daddy gets home.

Then he'll bring a cake-e.

One for you, and one for me.

One for all the family.

It was real, not imagination. It was a memory – my only memory. It was just five minutes of our short time together, back when I was three years old – just before they took the money and sent her away. In that one moment of memory I had a real sister. I could see her, smell her, and feel her warmth beside me.

I felt overwhelming and complete love for her and joy in her being. She was sunshine and laughter... and acceptance. She loved me, for who I was – no matter what I was – no matter what I did, good or bad, clever or stupid – she loved me. I didn't have to deserve her – she was part of me and I was part of her. She didn't choose me. I didn't choose her. We just belonged with each other – brother and sister.

I replayed that moment every night until I knew I'd remember it for the rest of my life.

Sylvia's Secrets

Aunt Hannah said no one heard from Sylvie while she was in America. But when I next visited Aunt Marlene, I asked her if Sylvie ever said anything about the trip.

At first she said no, but I pressed her.

"She must have said something."

Aunt Marlene didn't reply. She looked at me for a while and then made a decision. She walked to her sideboard and opened a drawer. She rummaged around and pulled out a small bundle of blue papers, rolled up in an elastic band.

She sat by me holding the papers in her lap, eyes down.

"She did write." There was something in her voice like she'd been caught doing something bad. "I promised not to tell a soul."

She fiddled with the rubber band round the papers. "Your mother wasn't stupid, like they all said – only with men. She had a good brain. She was good with words – always reading and scribbling. If your Gran wanted a letter written, she'd get Sylvie to do it. She loved to write.

"Before she left for Southampton, I asked her to write to me. There was nothing for a couple of weeks and then she sent me an airmail. It was short. She said things were bad, but I wasn't to tell anyone in the family, not even Solly. I had to hide the letter away and she'd send more. She said she trusted me because I didn't turn against her.

"I got seven all together. I kept them all this time. I've only read the first one. It was, well, not nice. I didn't dare to open the rest. I thought there might be more bad stuff in them and I didn't want to keep her dirty secrets. If Solly got hold of them or Mum or Dad they'd go mad! I thought about burning them, but that was like burning her life, and it wasn't for me to do that, so I hid them away." She waved the bundle. "You're too young for all this, Tommy. I was going to keep them until you were grown up. But then she is your mother and I suppose you have a right to know... whatever. If you want them now, you can take them. Or you can throw them on the fire. It's up to you."

She reached out to hand me the letters. I stared at them. I didn't want to touch them. I didn't want Sylvie's life in my hands. I was frightened, I might catch it – whatever she had that made her bad. Perhaps I had it anyway – she was my mother, I came from her body. Perhaps I was already contaminated.

Aunt Marlene's hand was trembling. I could see she didn't want to give me the letters, but she didn't want to keep them either.

I didn't know what to do. Take them. Leave them. Leave them. Take them. No I'm too young. Leave them! Burn them!

"I don't want…"

She pressed them into my palms, wrapped my fingers tight around them and snatched her hands away.

"She's your mother." She said.

She reached over and kissed me on the cheek. Her face was a mixture of relief and guilt like someone who'd passed on a curse. Perhaps she had. I didn't look at the letters. I stuffed them in my pocket. I couldn't think of anything to say other than "Thank you" and I stood to leave. At the door I turned back to say goodbye, but she was sobbing. I left quietly.

I had to read the letters in private. I dared not take them into Gran's house, in case someone found them, so when I got home, I hid them in the air raid shelter, under a pile of boxes.

I didn't go near them for days. I remembered how bad I felt reading Tommy Isaac's letter to Rachael. Tommy's letters weren't meant for me and neither were these. I was also reluctant to release her secrets into the world. I didn't want to read her words and think her thoughts. But at the same time, to my deep shame, I was curious. I had to know – not just for me, but for Carol and Jacqueline. I had to know what happened over there. So one evening, I stuffed them in my shorts and ran across to the camp. I thought it would be empty, but Larry and Vivien were there, playing gobs.

"Hiya Tommy. Wanna play?"

"Nah."

"What's up?" Vivien asked.

"What?" I snapped.

"Something wrong?" She persisted.

"Oh no." I said, "It's just…"

I hesitated. Should I tell them – let her secrets out? If I told, they might tell others and soon the whole East End would know and it would get back to Gran and Granddad and then all the aunts and uncles. If there was anything bad in there, it would bring the guilt back into the family and it would spread like a disease, and from then on, I'd be blamed for bringing back Sylvie's shame. But Viv and Larry were good friends and they never told on me before. It would be good to share the secrecy with a couple of mates, who wouldn't care too much, who wouldn't feel responsible. But then they might be disgusted. Aunt Marlene said it was bad stuff. Or they might make fun of my mother, or me. Or, they might be really impressed with some real grown up secrets.

"OK I'll tell you, but you have to promise to keep it a secret… from everybody."

"What?" they chorused, with eager expectation.

"No, it's serious," I said, "and you really must keep it secret."

"OK, OK" Larry said, "close the door."

Vivien pulled a scrap of tarpaulin over the entrance and Larry lit some candles in the gloom.

"I've got some letters from my mother." I said.

"What your Nan?" Vivien asked.

"No my real mother."

"You haven't got a real mother." Said Vivien, "You live with your Nan."

"Everyone's got a mother, stupid." Larry said.

"But she's dead, isn't she!" Vivien said. "I thought you always lived with your Nan… Yea, you did. You've always been here, 'cept when they put you in the home. You never had no mother."

"Well, I just found out I do have a mother."

I told them how I went to my aunts and made them tell me all their secrets. I told them how Sylvie went with the Americans at the base and got pregnant three times and was kicked out and had three babies – me and two sisters. My Gran sold them – one to South Africans and one to a rich family who lived in a secret location somewhere in London and she was blond like me with blue eyes, and beautiful and clever and could sing and dance and I had seen her everywhere.

"Blimey!" Vivien said, "What about your dad? Who is he? Where is he?"

I told them he was the son of General Patton the great American general, who helped to win the war and had a story written about him in the Eagle. I said my real name was Thomas William Patton and one day I was going to find him.

"Is that where she went, your Mum… to America, to find your dad?" Vivien asked.

"Yes. She went all the way to America with my oldest sister on a ship. But, to see my youngest sister's father, not mine."

"What happened? Did she stay with him?" Larry asked.

"Yes, but bad things happened out there and it's a secret that no one knows about. I think it's in these letters."

"From your Mum?"

"Yea, to my Aunt Marlene. She just gave them to me. No one's read them, only her, and she's only read one and she wouldn't say what was in it – just that it was bad."

"Wow! Let's read 'em!" Larry said.

"Yea, go on." Vivien said.

I looked them in the eyes. "Secret?"

"Cross my heart."

"Pain-of-death!"

"I dunno." I said. I remembered the dread in Aunt Marlene's eyes when she handed them to me.

"Come on!"

"OK," I carefully slipped the elastic band and spread the envelopes on the floor between us. "Which one?"

"First one. You can tell by the postmarks." Vivien grabbed them sorted them into date order.

"Not sure about these last two. Both in December, but these four are right. This one's been opened already it must be the first."

She handed me the envelope. It felt empty.

"You read it," she said, "It's your Mum"

"Here. Have a gobstopper." Larry popped a bright orange golf ball in his mouth and handed a green one to Viv.

"No thanks." I couldn't read and suck a gobstopper at the same time.

"Goonreaditthen." Viv gurgled, passing me a candle.

The blue envelope was addressed in neat sloping, joined-up handwriting to Mrs. M Angel, 37 Brokesley Street, London E3, England. I'd only seen one letter with England written on it before. It was Tommy Isaacs' airmail to Rachael. This one was thin and delicate. I unfolded it very carefully. There was no separate letter paper inside. The writing was on the inside of the envelope, in neat joined–up Biro script.

10th July 1947
Ocean Haven, Pennsylvania
Dear Marly,
I said I'd write, and I want to keep my promise. You are the only one I can trust. You stood by me when the others turned away. I don't have a family anymore, only you.
Promise me you'll keep my letters secret and never tell a soul. I don't want Mum and Dad to know about me. They

> *kicked me out, so this is my life now. You must never tell Stella, Hannah or Nina. Please tell <u>NO ONE</u>, not even Solly. I know it's unfair to ask you to keep secrets from your husband and he is a good man, but you must promise. You can't write back. I don't have a fixed address. If you promise to keep our secret I'll write again. I trust you, Marly.*
>
> *Well, the sea crossing was hard. No one wants to talk to an unmarried mother. I told them I was going to get married, but they treated us like they treat niggers over here – at best like we didn't exist, at worst like animals.*

"Is she an unmarried mother?" Viv asked.
"Course she is," Larry said, "So's mine. Go on, Tommy."

> *A few of the crew boys were nice. They gave me nylons, and chocolate for the baby, but it was awkward having them in the cabin with the baby there on the bed.*

"Did she have crew boys in her cabin?" Viv asked.
"Shuddup" Larry said. "Listen."
I read on.

> *New York was hot and sweaty and people were rude. We rode the Greyhound all the way out to Philadelphia.*
> *I was so looking forward to finding Ocean Haven. What a wonderful name for a town. But, Marly, what a let down! It's just a trailer park. Frank's house is just a busted up old caravan.*
> *And Frank is a down-and-out bastard. You remember how smart he used to look in his uniform? Well now he looks like a tramp, or a bum as they say over here.*
> *He lives with his sister, and she is a right nasty cow. When she saw me with the baby, she told him to send me away, but I pleaded with him – we were so tired from traveling. He said he sent for both of us and he let us in.*
> *Oh Marly, how I regret crossing that threshold! I am like a prisoner. I'm only allowed out of the van for the toilet. They treat me like a slave. I have to wash and cook. I*

> serve all their meals like a waitress, scrub the pans. They make me do everything. I even have to empty their piss pots in the morning and clean the toilet.

"Eeeeyukkk!" Vivien said.
"Shuttup! Go on." Larry said.

> They have proper beds, but I have to sleep on the floor with the baby. It's terrible Marly. I have to get out of here. I can write to you when they are asleep. I'll post this when I can sneak out. I'll write more next time.
> I trust you, Marly. Please don't tell a soul.
> If you see Tommy, give him a kiss for me, but don't tell him where it came from.
> Love
> Sylv."

"So she's a slave in America?" Viv asked.

"She *was*. This was years ago. Nineteen Forty Seven, right?" I said, with a touch of annoyance.

"How did she get away?" Viv asked.

"I dunno, do I? Might be in another letter."

"Let's see." Said Viv.

"Not now. Another time. I gotta get back… for tea."

"Awww!" Larry complained, "When then?"

"Tomorrow." I grabbed the letters, snapped the elastic band round them, stuffed them back in my pocket and crawled out.

"Oi Tommy," Viv called after me,

"What?"

"Just… I'm sorry." She said.

She knew I felt bad. I'd just violated something. The letter wasn't meant for entertaining a bunch of kids. I didn't like reading swear words and stuff about piss pots. There were things I didn't understand, and found disturbing – that stuff about crew boys in the cabin with the baby on the bed? I suspected it was something bad.

I hid the letters and left them for days. I felt dirty and ashamed. I shouldn't have read them to Larry and Viv. I shouldn't have read them at all. I shouldn't have let those things out into the world and into my head. I should have thrown them straight in the fire.

Viv and Larry kept the secret. They never said anything when the others were around. For a few days they asked when we'd read some more. I lied – I said I'd had read them all and they were boring. They soon stopped asking.

But over the weeks that followed I found myself drawn to Sylvie's letters. I'd go to the shelter when no one was around and read one. When I put it down, I'd be overwhelmed with shame and promise myself I'd leave the rest alone. A few days later I'd find myself reading the next. It was a compulsion – a curse.

I read her second letter in the shelter by myself, one night after tea.

> 29th July 1947
> Ocean Haven, Pennsylvania
> Dear Marly,
> I hope you got my letter. I gave it to a women to post for me. I saw her walking past when I went down to the toilet. She promised she'd post it and take more if I wanted.
> Remember I told you about Frank's sister? She's called Rosie. I think she's about thirty but she looks much older. She's dead thin, smokes like a chimney and her face is grey like fag-ash. She bleaches her hair and walks around in a pinafore like Mum, and she's an arsehole!
> She hates me. If the baby makes the slightest noise, she screams at me, Fucking shut it up! As if I could stop a baby crying if it wants to!
> I've been feeling sick in the mornings. I've had to run out in the yard to throw up. That fucking cow screamed at me for disturbing her sleep.

I put the letter down. I didn't want to read anymore. She used bad swearwords – and in a letter, to my Aunt Marlene! What would she think if she'd read this? She'd never have given them to me. What if someone caught *me* reading it? It made me feel dirty and ashamed. Aunt Marlene was right. I was too young for this. I was frightened that the words I read would take the filth in her mind and glue it to the inside of my brain and it would stay there like a disease and I'd become like her.

I was glad Viv and Larry weren't here. I'd be too ashamed to read it aloud. I closed my eyes and took a long deep breath and continued.

> But lately things have changed. I think Rosie's taken a liking to the baby. She's had no kids of her own. Her husband left her. Her mum and dad kicked her out and she had nowhere to go. That's why she lives in the trailer with Frank.
> She started playing with the baby. Just for a few minutes at first, and then longer. She told me the baby should sleep in her bed where she could be warm. She didn't care about me. I have to sleep like a bloody dog, by the door.
> Rosie was asleep one night and Frank came and dragged me into his bed. I hated it, Marly. There was no love in it. He just did it to me and never said a word. Afterwards he kicked me out. The next day he never mentioned it. But at least he didn't hit me. God forgive me, I even hoped that he might grow to love me properly.

I didn't want to imagine Frank doing it with Sylvie, but it reminded me of when Davy did it with Leah Goldberg under the bushes in the cemetery. He said he must have been in love with her because it was all over in a few seconds – it happens like that when you're in love, he said. But he fell out of love as soon as it was over and felt dirty and ashamed.

> One afternoon Rosie went to see someone in another trailer. I was alone with Frank. I tried to talk to him about the baby, but he wouldn't listen. I asked him for money. But he called me a thieving bitch and slapped my face – really hard. I hate him, the bastard.
> The next day I put the baby out in the yard to play and I tried to get Frank to talk to me. I told him he was handsome. I touched him. He pretended he wasn't interested, but the thing in my hand said otherwise. I said we could live together in England. He said things like Sure, Honey that would be so nice. I said there was plenty of work and they were giving away council houses. I said we could get married and have babies and live somewhere nice, like Dagenham.
> I thought I was getting somewhere, but he wasn't listening. The bastard pushed my head down to make me do it with my mouth. I had to do what he wanted.

There was much that I only partly understood. Why did she flirt with a man she hated? What did she do with her mouth?

A while ago I knew nothing about my mother, but now I knew more than I did about anybody and more than I wanted to know. I felt dirty reading this stuff, but compelled to read on.

> It didn't make any difference. I still had to do all the work. There was no rest except for Saturday nights. They went to the bar with their buddies and left me and the baby. We could sleep in Rosie's bed until they came back blind drunk.
> It's been seven weeks and things haven't changed. Rosie is more attached to the baby. It's not like she wants to be her mother, it's more like she's found a real live baby doll.
> I'm getting nowhere with Frank. My belly's getting bigger. I must be expecting. I've got to get away from here.
> God Bless, Marly. Please don't tell anyone about all this. If you see Tommy, give him a kiss for me, but don't tell him where it came from.
> Love
> Sylv."

I felt like tearing the letter into little pieces. I didn't want her kiss.

The next day, when I saw Davy in the street I asked him, "What do women do with their mouths."

"Er... dunno. Is it a joke?"

"No. I mean when they do it with a man."

"Oh, well they moan, like this," He put on a posh ladies voice, "'Ohhhh darling, it's lovely. Ohhhh. Do it again. Ohhhh!' – That's what Mrs. Rosenberg does, anyway."

I wondered if that was what Sylvie did with Frank. It didn't sound right – it must be something else, but I still couldn't imagine what.

But school started next week and I'd have other things to distract me for a while.

Malinski's Alphabet

On my first day at the Grammar, I jumped off the bus and marched proudly to the school in my elegant new uniform. In my anxiety not to be late on the first day, I'd left home ridiculously early and was one of the first new boys to arrive – mistake!

A small gang of boys hung around the playground gate. They turned as I arrived. They must have detected my ironed collar with its new whalebones and the untarnished glint of gold silk in my school badge. I grinned at them.

The biggest boy, swept the others behind him. "Welcome to Central Foundation Grandma's School for Boys!" he said with fine diction and an exaggerated sweeping bow. "And what might your name be, most honoured guest?"

"Tommy." I said, "Tommy Angel."

"Oh, we're so honoured to have a real Angel come from heaven to walk amongst us! And what's your middle name. Every one important has a middle name."

"Er... Thomas. Er... William"

"Interesting. Well, welcome, Tommy Er Thomas Er William, I am The Great Malinski. Let me introduce you to my friends..."

He gestured towards his mates, "Maurice, Abe, Jacob and Jeff." I nodded to each in turn. They grinned.

"So, Tommy Thomas Willy, let us help you settle into your new school. The most important thing you need to know is your alphabet. Do you know your ABCs?"

"Oh yes."

"Excellent" said Malinski, "A is for..."

"Er... apple." I was a bit puzzled by the childishness of this game.

"A good try, but no. Not here."

"A is for Arsehole my boy!" He said, "At Central Foundation, we use the Malinski Alphabet. So... A is for Arsehole, get it, Tommy?"

"Oh... Er... Yes."

"OK, let's see how clever you are. Spell Arsehole."

I'd seen the word in Sylvie's letter, so I spelled it as she did.

"Very Good. Most people miss out the 'e'. And B is for...?" Malinski raised his eyebrows.

"Er... Bus?"

171

"Well, no, Tommy-Boy, not quite. You can do better than that. Try again." Then he cuffed me so hard I went flying into the railings my head spinning. His mates cheered him on.

I was in serious trouble. This lot were turning mean and there were five of them – all bigger than me. I lifted my arms to protect my head as he came for me again. My face glowed red hot with anger and fear. He raised his hand. I screamed at him, "Bastard!"

He stopped. His fist froze in mid air. He slowly opened his fist and lightly slapped my cheek, took a step back and smiled.

"We've got a good 'un here, boys," he crowed. "B is for Bastard! At Central Foundation Grammar School for Boys, B is for Bastard! Now spell Bastard."

Again I visualized the word in Sylvie's letter "B... a... s... t... a... r... d."

"Ex-cellent! He's very good! Most people add an extra 'r'. So, let's try once more. C is for…?"

"C is for… Cock!" I blurted out, with finality, gripping the railings behind my back for strength. I prayed, "God let me pass the test. Let me into the playground to start my education."

"No!" Malinski bellowed.

I had misjudged the game. I had made a terrible mistake and had uttered a word too obscene. I was so embarrassed.

"No!" He cuffed me so hard I could hear a church bell ringing loudly in my ears.

"Cunt!" He shouted.

"Cunt cunt cunt!" the gang jeered.

"After me… C is for cunt!" Malinski chanted.

"C is for… c… can't." I said. A trickle of blood ran down from my right eyebrow.

"Spell it!"

"Er… C… a… n… t?"

"No that's 'can't' you cunt. You can't spell cunt!"

"Can't spell cunt! Can't spell cunt!" they jeered.

"OK Tommy Thomas Willy Wanker. We'll give you another chance. D is for…?"

"Er… Dog shit?" I wiped the blood from my eye. It smeared over the back of my hand.

"Mmmm not bad." He said, "How about E?"

"E is for…" I had no idea. I couldn't think of a swearword beginning with E. "Emphysema!"

"What's that?" Malinski asked.
"It's something my Aunt Miriam got." I said.
"Is it filthy?" he asked.
"I'm sure it is." I said.
"OK, boys, add that to the list."
"Alright Tommy, one more and you can enter. F is for...?"

I wasn't used to swearing. Even though Granddad and my uncles all had hard jobs and worked with tough men, they never swore properly in the family. 'Bloody, Bugger, Sod, Cow' – that was the most I heard at home. I'd heard worse from kids on the street but I'd never used strong swearwords willingly. My active swearing vocabulary was limited, but after reading Sylvie's letter I thought if she could use bad words, it was all right for me.

"Fucking." I said. "F... u... c... k... i... n... g."
"Oh you *dirty* little boy." Malinski whispered, "Where did you learn a bad word like that?"
"My mother." I said, defiantly.
"Blimey!" Malinski turned and shouted loud enough for dozens of kids nearby to hear, "Tommy said FUCKING!" All of his mates turned and pointed at me and chanted, "FUCKING, FUCKING, FUCKING, Tommy said FUCKING!"

They surrounded me, punched and cuffed me, but I was numb to pain now, and the humiliation hurt more than their blows. I ducked low, wriggled under their arms into the playground and ran through the crowd of boys to the far end.

I swore I'd get Malinski.

From a safe distance I cleaned up the blood with one of Granddad's hankies and watched them snare another three victims. As each was released or escaped, I weaved my way to them, introduced myself and asked if they wanted to get back at the bullies. They all agreed. I took a scrap of paper from my satchel and between us we listed the swearing alphabet. For each letter we agreed the most disgusting word and a few alternatives and we resolved to circulate the list to all the first years so they could learn the words and get past Malinski without being beaten. We got as far as P is for prick, piss and pox and the bell rang for class. Louis Nyman had the list in his hands as we shuffled into a line by entrance A.

Once in class, our new teacher, Mr. Walker, impressed upon us what a great privilege it was to be selected for Central Foundation Grammar School for Boys. What history, what excellence, what nobility had preceded us through those courtyard gates. He told us about the great

Dr. Jacob Bronowski, distinguished scientist, author of the *Ascent of Man*, famous science expert for the British Broadcasting Corporation.

I knew about him I'd seen him on The Brains Trust at Uncle Solly's and I thought he looked funny with his shiny bald head and funny eyebrows and he was boring, but Mr Walker said he was a shining example of what we CFGS boys could be if we just put our minds to it and knuckle down to work.

While he lectured, he walked up and down between the desks. Mr. Walker was tall and thin, with a trim moustache. Only his black academic gown differentiated him from Terry-Thomas. He talked with affected superiority.

"There's a nasty smell of boy in here!" he said for the first of many times.

"What's this, Nyman?" He pounced on Louis and grabbed the scrap of paper he clutched in his fist. He opened it carefully as if it was booby-trapped.

"A is for Arsehole?" He read aloud.

Every boy giggled.

"Cease!" He yelled, and we did.

"B is for Bastard and Bum?" We all look suitably shocked.

"Well! Is that the kind of *filth* you brought with you from Stepney, boy?" His face was an inch from Louis's and he sprayed him as he spat out "*filth*".

"No sir." said Louis.

"What do you mean?" Walker bellowed.

"Sir. He gave it to me this morning, sir. A boy called Malinski, Sir."

"Malinski gave you this?" Walker hissed.

I nodded vigorously at Louis.

"Er... yes, Sir, Malinski, Sir, at the gate, Sir." Louis spluttered. "He said all the first years have to learn it, Sir."

"We'll see about that!" Walker stuffed the paper in his pocket.

"All right, boys, let's get to know each other a little. Er..." He slowly waved his arm across the mass of faces and then stopped and pointed. You boy!"

"Yes sir?" Terry Willard snapped upright in his desk.

"Relax boy. I won't bite your head off. Tell us about your first life-changing day at Central Foundation Grammar School for Boys. Speak slowly and clearly with good pronunciation and tell us about your morning – before you came to school."

Willard took a deep breath.

"Well, Sir, I goddup…"

"Got up, boy, got up."

"Yessir, I goddup and took me gran for a walk." Willard continued.

"Your Gran, Willard? You take her for a walk every morning?"

"Yessir, that's my job. An' I 'ave to brush her down and feed 'er sir."

"Feed her, Willard? What do you feed you Gran – cornflakes? Porridge? Kippers?"

Walker was playing to the gallery. We laughed and jeered at Willard.

"Gawd no Sir. She has proper dog meat, Sir."

"Dog meat, Willard? You feed you Gran on dog meat? Poor wretch!"

The whole class collapsed into giggles.

"Can't feed 'er on leftovers, Sir, she'd get too fat to run."

"Run? Run what? Does your grandmother run in races, Willard?"

"Oh no sir, she couldn't run to catch a bus. She's got half-right-arse and bellicose veins, Sir."

"Arthritis, Um… So what kind of races does she go in for? Knitting races?"

"What Sir?"

"Pardon, Sir!"

"Doanunderstand, Sir." Willard was confused. He scanned every face in the room for a clue.

Walker took a long deep breath and said very slowly, as if he were talking to an infant, "All right Willard, let's get to the bottom of this. What kind of races does your Grandmother take part in?"

"Not me Granny, Sir me gran!"

"I am confused, Willard. I'm sure we all are. Please enlighten us. Tell us about your Gran."

"She's beautiful, Sir – long pointed snout, lovely short sleek grey coat. Dad said we could have shown her, but you have to treat 'em different if you want to race 'em. She's won us six races this season, Sir. If you like, Sir, I can let you know when she's running and you can put a bet on 'er. You won't lose Sir."

Throughout this monologue, Walker appeared completely bemused, until something dawned on him.

"Willard, will you come out and write Gran on the blackboard. Can you spell it?"

"Oh yessir," Willard chirped and he strode to the front of the class, grabbing the offered chalk as he passed and wrote. *"GREYHOUND"*.

"I think you boys might be in need of a little um... elocution." Walker said.

"Electrocution Sir?" Willard grinned widely.

"Now don't push your luck, Willard. Sit boy!"

Willard sat.

"Lets do the register. When I call you name, you say 'Yes, Sir!' if you're here."

"Whaddwe say if we're not here sir?" Willard chirped.

Walker just sighed and began the first of hundreds of weary recitals of the class register.

"Benson, Bower, Carne, Cheney, Cohen, Coleman..."

"Yes Sir." "Yes Sir." "Yes Sir." "Yes Sir."

"Cosgrove, Drewitt, Emerson, Frankenstein..."

"Frankenstein?" Walker sat upright and glared at a big boy who was in mid response. "Doctor Frankenstein I presume!" Kids stifled their giggles.

The boy stood up. He was big and soft – shaped like a pear, his mouth still hung open with a frozen "Yes..."

He composed himself. "Abraham Solomon Frankenstein, Sir." The boy said, with measured dignity. "I *would* like to be a doctor, Sir. When I grow up."

"Better change your name then, Boy, or you'll have no patients." Walker laughed. "And patients will have no patience with doctors who have no patients!" he scanned the room inviting our laughter. I laughed with the rest, but I felt manipulated and ashamed because I was joining in making fun of other boys.

He used registration as daily exercise for his sarcasm. No one escaped Walker's wit and there were no boundaries. When he got to "Pollock", a small timid boy stood up and said "Y...Y...Y...Y..." Walker checked the boy's name in the register and his moustache curled up both sides of his grin.

"Mmm" he said, "What's your full name boy?"

"P... P... P... P... P..." he spluttered as his face blushed bright red. "P... P... Peter... P... P..."

As Peter struggled we willed him on.

Walker raised his eyes theatrically to the ceiling. "Hurry up, Pollock, we've only got twenty minutes." He laughed, and despite our empathy for Peter we laughed too. To Peter's credit he didn't give in and after dozens of attempts he managed "P... P... Peter... P... P... Pollock Sir!" He smiled triumphantly and we all clapped and cheered.

Walker sank into his seat behind the huge teachers desk, which was elevated on the teacher's plinth and separated from the front row of kids by two yards of no-boys-land. He slowly scanned his assembled victims with a look between pity and disgust. He stopped when he saw me.

"You boy!" he roared, "What's that... blood?"

"Blood, Sir?" I spluttered.

"Blood boy. You're dripping on your books."

I hadn't noticed the splashes of brown on the blue cover of my pristine exercise book.

"Won't do boy. Won't do at all! Fighting on your first day! Not the thing at all. Have to keep my eye on you. Name?"

"Angel, Sir."

"From the Realms of Glory?"

"Pardon, Sir?"

"Never mind. Not an appropriate name for a boy who exercises his fists before his brain."

I vowed to show Malinski no mercy.

After register Walker spent an hour dictating the timetable. He drew a grid on the blackboard with a t-shaped ruler. We had to copy it into the back of our "general" book and fill in the teachers names, room numbers, subjects and times. I misjudged the width of the grid and only managed to get the morning lessons from Mon to Wed on the page. But Benny, who sat next to me, drew a perfect grid and we were in the same sets for everything, so I just followed him around the rest of the day – and for the rest of my school career.

When I got home, Gran asked me what I did. I knew it wouldn't be useful to say I was beaten, humiliated and manipulated by some of the kids and my form teacher. "Er... Science and Geomorphology – that's part of Geography." I said, thinking she wouldn't be interested.

"That's nice." She said.

After tea I told Gran I had to do my homework, it would take an hour and Mr. Walker said I had to concentrate and I was not to be disturbed. I ran down to the basement, opened half the dining table and spread out my exercise books. I felt important and grown up and had a real excuse to be left alone and excused from running errands.

Being the first day, I didn't have any proper homework. I just had to finish the timetable, draw margins with pencil and ruler in all my books and write what I thought light, heat and sound were, for General Science. I thought about it for a while and wrote, "We all need light to make day come from night. We all need heat when we've got cold feet. We all love the sound when the record spins around."

I'd finished in ten minutes. I thought science was easy and I wondered what to do next. I crept out to the air raid shelter to look through my treasures and found Sylvie's letters. I slipped them from the elastic and thought about reading another one. I remembered how ashamed I felt when I'd read the last one – like I'd done something really bad and dirty. I decided I definitely wouldn't read any more.

> 10th September 1947
> Ocean Haven, Pennsylvania
> Dear Marly,
> I hope you and Solly and the kids are well.
> I wonder all the time what it's like in London. I pray to God to get me away from here. Yesterday I tried to run. I'll tell you from the beginning.
> Frank has started sending me out to run errands – get a packet of fags or a bottle of beer from the park store.

For the first time, I thought we had something in common – we both hated running errands so much we would run away.

> On Monday night, when I came back, Rosie and the baby were gone. I asked Frank where they were and he said, "They've just gone for a walk. And you can talk a fucking walk too you little tramp!" He grabbed his fags and slammed the door in my face. I banged on the door but he wouldn't let me in.
> I sat in the yard and waited for Rosie and the baby to come back. It was hours, Marly, and it got really cold. I only had my frock on. I crawled under the van, under the door, so I could see them. I pulled rubbish round me to make a shelter.
> It must have been about two in the morning and a car came. Rosie got out with the baby. I was stiff with cold, but I ran out and grabbed Rosie round the throat and shook her. I was wild. I wanted to know where she had been with my baby. I wanted to kill her, Marly, but she spat in my face and pushed me away. Frank opened the door, took Rosie and the baby in and slammed it shut.

I had never known adults to be violent. They slapped kids and kicked dogs sometimes, and my uncles killed people in the war, but no grown-up I'd known in ordinary life ever hit anybody. No woman in my family would try to strangle someone and no man would punch a woman in the face. I was afraid to read on. What if she killed Rosie? What if my mother turned out to be a murderer? I said aloud "I'm not reading anymore."

> I stayed under the van all night, but I didn't sleep. I knew they wanted to keep the baby and get rid of me. All night I thought about getting away.
>
> The baby hates being shut up in the van all day, and by nine in the morning, she makes a fuss so they let her out in the yard. So I decided to stay quiet and grab her when she came out.
>
> In the morning I heard them moving in the van and talking. I could hear the baby crying. They put her out in the yard and slammed the door. I waited to be sure Frank and Rosie didn't come out. I called the baby and asked her to go for a walk with Mummy.
>
> We crawled to the end of the van under Frank's bed. He always keeps the curtains closed so I thought he wouldn't see us. I ran off with the baby.
>
> I was terrified, Marly. I didn't dare look back. I ran through the park and up the dirt track to the highway. It was a couple of miles and when I got there I was exhausted. I sat down by the road and cried.
>
> But then I heard a car coming up the track. I grabbed the baby and jumped into the ditch. I didn't dare peek out. I waited half an hour. When I was sure it was safe, I crawled up the bank. But when I looked up, Frank was standing there!
>
> He grabbed me by my hair and slapped me hard, both sides of my face. There was blood in my eyes. He punched me in the chest and belly with his full strength, the bastard. I felt the wind driven out of me and I fell down. He called me a "fucking whore" and kicked me in the back and round my head. I couldn't breathe. I could hear the baby screaming. Frank took her.

I'm going to destroy Malinski. I'm going to kill him before he grows into a man like Frank. I'm going to kick his head and make blood run down his face and I'm going to punch him in the belly.

> *I must have passed out. I don't know how long it was. I woke up with lights in my eyes. Two cops stood over me, shining torches in my face. They jeered at me. One of them said some trailer trash had washed up on his nice clean highway. They asked if I had a rough night and said I gotta pick 'em more careful. Bastards!*
>
> *They didn't help me, just made fun. The big one, Earl, said "It's illegal to dump refuse by the roadside, Honey. Just get your sorry ass off home."*
>
> *I said I didn't have a home. He asked if I was talking back. He said he could find me a nice room at the station with a few friends who might like company. I knew what he meant, dirty bastard. I didn't want to go to a cell.*
>
> *I dragged myself back to the trailer park. My nose and mouth were bleeding and my head was spinning. My belly was sore. I thought the baby inside me might be hurt. When I got to the trailer, I heard voices inside. I slept in the garbage bay.*
>
> *I'm going to do it again. I'm going to get away. I'll write to you when I can. God Bless, Marly.*
>
> *If you see Tommy, give him a kiss for me, but don't tell him where it came from.*
>
> *Love*
>
> *Sylv."*

When I got to the end of the letter, I started to open the next one to find out if she escaped, but Granddad came to the door of the shelter.

"What you doing, Tommy?"

I must have gone bright red in the dark, I felt so ashamed that he'd caught me reading this dirty stuff. I crammed the letters up my jumper, grabbed my duffle bag and held it in front of me.

"Nothing, Dad, just some homework."

"Homework, eh? Why don't you do it in the house?"

"Just looking for something. Coming." I popped my head out.

"Good day at the Grammar?"

"Oh yes, It was good fun."

"Did you learn anything?"

"Yes. We did geometry." I thought he would be as ignorant as Gran about all the new subjects I was learning.

"That'll come in handy. If you want to be a builder or a draftsman or an architect."

I felt ashamed for assuming he was ignorant.

"So… what are you doing in there?" he asked.

"Oh… it's only geometry. I'm looking for rectangles." I held up one of my cardboard boxes.

"Oh, right." He said and turned to go back in the house.

"Dad," I asked, "What… What was Sylvie like?"

He froze for a moment and then turned back to me.

"I know you've been asking about her, Tommy, and it's only natural but you don't want to worry about her. She made her own decisions in life and she got everything she asked for."

"What do you mean?"

"I mean you've got your own life to lead. You're not like her. You're a good boy and you've got a good education ahead of you. You'll make something of yourself. You don't want to be like her. Let her go, my boy. Let her go. Concentrate on rectangles."

He didn't want to say any more. He went into the house.

He was right. She might have got herself into trouble, but it was through her own choices. I'd spent enough time thinking about her. It was time to think about my own life. I ran over to the bomb site and hid the letters away in the cellar under the camp. I put them in the drawer with Tommy's letters to Rachael and for a couple of months I forgot about them and got on with my education.

Getting an Education

I loved my first few months at the grammar school. Everything was fresh and new – new teachers, new subjects. I particularly liked General Science, Algebra and Geometry – subjects we hadn't done at Stepney Jewish. I loved Geography with its magical phrases like *hanging valley* and *oxbow lake*, mysterious sounding words like *moraine* and my favourite "ology" – *geomorphology*.

I loved the newness and I threw myself into learning, which was easy for me because I was curious about everything. I had a million questions. I wanted to know and to understand. I wanted to test everything to the limit, including the teachers.

My job in class was to interrogate teachers and keep them talking and, if possible, distract them from the serious content of the lesson. So when Mr. Trelevan-Thomas talked about the Indus Valley, I'd ask a dozen questions, "What was life like there, Sir?" "What did they do for a living?" What did they eat and drink? How did they travel?"

Sir would think I was really interested and soften his guard. Then I'd go for the distraction.

"Have you ever been there, Sir?"

"No, Angel, I have not."

"Have you ever been to other countries, Sir?"

"Oh yes, Angel, many times."

"Where have you been, Sir?"

"Well I once went to the Amazon jungle."

"Wow, Sir, that must have been fascinating. What was it like?"

Then Sir would launch into ten minutes of reminiscence and we could forget about the boring Indus Valley. With luck, I could keep him talking until the bell rang and he'd forget to set homework before we escaped. My mates rewarded my most heroic achievements with little gifts – extra afters at lunchtime, fluffy sweets from the bottom of their pockets, comics they'd done reading.

If I couldn't distract Sir with interrogation, my second technique was to get the class to fall about laughing. When Trelevan-Thomas gave a lesson about erosion and asked what we call a collection of screes, I called out, "An alluvial fan club, Sir!" and the whole class exploded into exaggerated giggles and guffaws.

My witticisms didn't need to be very funny – in fact, it was more fun if they weren't. The class would laugh uncontrollably for three minutes while the teacher stretched his mind to the limit to comprehend the joke.

All this sparring with the teachers forced me to be alert through every lesson, while my mates were doodling, playing battleships or snoozing. Consequently, and to my great surprise, I scored high on every end of term test, coming top of the class in lots of subjects. I gained the reputation for being a mad genius and I played it for all it was worth.

While other first years were getting baited and beaten in the playground, I'd learned to joke my way out of trouble and make the bullies laugh. Failing that, I was wiry in build and flexible in movement and I could dodge out of harm's way. On the rare occasion I failed to escape a good kicking, my mates were always ready to help me concoct some exquisite revenge.

So when Malinski, who was already marked out for death for baiting first-years and for what Frank did to my mother, deliberately tripped me during a game of chain-he and sent me sprawling across the concrete yard, grazing knees and elbows almost to the bone, I first considered strangling him like my Mother did to Rosie. I then remembered how she'd failed. So I got this big boy Harvey Mendel, who I'd helped out with geography homework and Benny Jacobs and we plotted revenge.

One of our specialties was forgery and our opportunity to apply it came in Mr. Lacey's French lesson. Malinski was useless at French and had been left far behind the other kids in his year. His father blamed Lacey's teaching and insisted that his son must pass his French O'Level, so Malinski was sent down to our first-year French lessons. Of course Malinski, being a third year, found this humiliating. He would sulk at the back of the class and grab every opportunity to disrupt the lesson or hit any kid unlucky enough to be within reach. Lacey was equally embarrassed to confront the living evidence of his failure every day. Hence he detested Malinski.

During the lesson, we passed a sheet of paper between us and drew pictures of Lacey with no clothes.

Now Lacey was a tall elegant man. He looked a bit like Sir Anthony Eden, and perhaps he knew it, because he behaved like a Prime Minister – haughty and pompous. So stripping Lacey naked, giving him big tits and drawing farts exploding from his bum, was a common distraction from the boredom of Je suis, Tu es, Il est.

While Lacey turned to write a long translation passage on the board, Benny passed me the drawing and I laughed loud enough for Malinski to hear, but not enough for Lacey to notice. Eventually Malinski's curiosity got the better of him and he reached over and snatched the paper from me. He triumphantly added his own details – a long willy that dangled to the ground into a pool of pee.

We had him!

With a big grin, Malinski passed the paper back to Benny for his approval, and Benny, while pretending to be impressed at Malinski's wit, wrote beneath the picture

"M. Lacey, je t'adore. Baiser moi, s'il vous plait – Mal."

At the end of the lesson, Lacey asked, for a volunteer to collect the exercise books. Harvey Mendel shot up his hand. As he passed Benny he took the paper. Once he had Malinski's book, he slipped the paper between its pages. He handed the pile to Mr. Lacey and we all ran off to our next lesson.

By the end of the day, Lacey had reported Malinski. He was dragged in to the Headmaster's study, given six of the best and threatened with expulsion should he set one foot wrong ever again.

Benny, Harvey and I met him at the gate at home time.

"Misher Lacey, je t'adore." we chanted, until he turned and slunk away. After that Malinski left us alone.

Now and then I thought about my mother and her letters, but I'd made up my mind to get an education. I was finding school a lot of fun and I wouldn't let her spoil it for me.

I had a reputation for being a rebel. Benny said I was even braver than Derek Ararer, who would do anything for a dare, and was known around the East End as Ararer the Darer. Being a hero went to my head. I launched a crusade to protect my mates from violence from any quarter.

Bullying was not only the pastime of the bigger boys. Some of the teachers were too handy with the slipper or the cane, like Mr. Stammers our woodwork teacher.

It started well, when Stammers announced, in our first lesson that we were going to make our own boats. Wow! We all cheered, grinned at each other and we looked up with awe at the beautifully varnished real rowing skiff that hung on the wall at one end of the workshop.

Benny said it probably wouldn't be a real boat, more likely a model. I thought of the exquisite model boats that Ronny made with his Dad – working steamers with real engines and full rig sailing boats that he sailed in the park. I thought I'd love woodwork. It would be like making cardboard models with Mr. Balkin at Stepney Jewish.

That night after school I went to Barry's flat and we searched through his Children's Encyclopedia, old Eagle Annuals and his Dad's collection of National Geographic magazines. We found lots of pictures of boats and African ladies with bare breasts. We spread them across his bedroom floor in two rows in order of our favourites – first the boats, then the breasts. When Benny's dad popped his head round the door to ask what we were doing, I quickly rolled on top of the breasts grabbed a boat picture and held it up. "Picking the nicest ones, Mr. Jacobs."

"Very good, boys." He smiled and closed the door.

We made our final decisions. We weren't just going to build little boats – we'd build ships! Benny was going to make the Cutty Sark – a tea clipper with lots of masts, ropes, pulleys and sails. I wanted to do a working scale model of the Titanic, with a real engine, like Ronny's boats, so we could sail it and then sink it. We agreed the lady from Togoland had the nicest tits.

We planned to keep our boats secret from the kids on the street until they were finished and then we'd invite Ronny to a boat competition in the park and show them off.

For the first four weeks in woodwork we didn't touch a piece of wood. Stammers gave lectures about tools.

We had to draw them and label all the parts, including a close up diagram of the way the teeth of the tenon saw alternated left and right along the blade. We took the wooden planes and metal planes to bits and put them back together a dozen times. We learned about the different grades of sandpaper and the order you had to use them.

None of us found this at all fascinating, but we went along with it and feigned interest – it was better than double maths and in the most boring bits, Benny and I swapped the latest drawings of our boats.

We started to suspect something was amiss when Stammers told us we had to "love your tools like they were your little babies". That raised a few giggles around class. Later he started giving the tools names – Tommy Tenon, Peter Plane and Billy Brace. We suspected Stammers was a bit mad.

Most of the kids lost interest and played up – nothing serious – making farting noises when he turned his back, throwing paper aeroplanes round the workshop, drilling holes in each others' shoes.

One day he lost his temper and shouted, "Why don't you boys behave yourselves? Do I have to get Mr. Piggy out?"

We thought this was a unique new way to keep our attention and so encouraged him.

"Yes please, Sir. Show us your little piggy."
"Go on, Sir, let's see it."
"Show us yours, Sir, and we'll show you ours."

185

Stammers bent down behind his desk, while we tried to stifle our giggles. He seemed to be searching for something.

"Can't you find it sir?"

"Is it too small, sir?"

Benson unbuttoned his flies and pretended to look for his willy. "Can't find mine neither, Sir. Shrinks in the cold."

A dozen kids followed Benson's lead and rummaged in their pants for lost willies.

"Mine's gone! Who's pinched my little piggy?"

The class was in uproar. I laughed so much the muscles under my chin went into cramp and I had to lean right back and look at the ceiling to stretch out of it.

Suddenly a wild roar filled the room and Stammers rose up from behind his desk screaming and waving a bamboo cane a yard long. He whacked it hard on the desk and the loud crack brought instant silence. Our mouths dropped open.

"Meet Mr. Piggy!" He whacked the desk again. "Mr. Piggy bites!" His grin turned to a grimace. He whacked again, faster and faster. He stared wildly. He broke into a sweat. "Bite, Piggy, bite!" he screamed. His face was bright red.

We all cheered. This was better than Saturday morning pictures. We chanted "Bite, Piggy, bite! Bite, Piggy, bite!"

It was amazing. We'd heard of his temper outbreaks from other kids, but we'd never witnessed one. He was dangerous – out of control. He rushed from behind his desk screaming and swinging the cane wildly in front of him. Benson leaped out of his way, but too late as the cane cut across his forearm.

We scurried to the back of the room behind the workbenches. Stammers was left alone at the front surrounded by scattered satchels, exercise books and pencils.

He suddenly stopped shouting, dropped his hands and stared at the empty desks in front of him. He walked back around his desk and slumped down breathing heavily. After a few seconds he looked up, smiled broadly at us and said, "Sit."

We did and the lesson continued as if nothing had happened.

The next lesson we started building our boats. Each of us had 18 inches of what he called "two b' one". We had to use a metal ruler and a square to make cutting marks at one inch, two inches and six inches. Stammers inspected our marks and cuffed the kids who got it wrong.

We spent the next lesson learning how to hold a tenon saw and we mimed cutting a piece of wood. Those who demonstrated the required level of skill in air-sawing were allowed to make real cuts.

Then we had lectures about the various properties of different species of wood – it's colour, density, most importantly its grain. After a wood identification test where Stammers held up some scraps of wood and we had to shout "Oak, Pine, Beech, Ash", we were allowed to plane and sand our four chunks of wood, paying careful attention to the direction of the grain. Stammers then let us practice piling them up to resemble some kind of boat.

Next week we heated little cauldrons of stinky brown glue and stuck the pieces together, and the week after we were allowed to drill a hole through the top of the cabins with a brace and bit and insert a piece of dowel for a funnel. The clever kids sloped theirs slightly like the funnel on the Queen Mary.

At the end of term we could take our boats home, but Benny and I decided their resemblance to the Cutty Sark and the Titanic was too remote to impress Ronny or any of our mates, so we jumped off the bus at the Regents Canal. We climbed down to the edge of the cut and set the boats afloat – hoping for a little race. To our dismay they both capsized and floated upside down. They didn't sail anywhere. They just bobbed in the still dark water with the orange peel and dog turds. So we bombed them with stones until we got bored and sat together with elbows on knees, chins in hands staring into the cut, stirring the oily rainbows with sticks.

"What you gonna do when you grow up?" I asked Benny.

"Civil Engineer", he said, "Building roads and bridges."

"Blimey – how'd you know about that stuff?"

"My uncle told me. It's good work and good money and you can go all round the world. What're you gonna do – be a writer?"

"No, I can't write."

"You did a good job with Carne's note!"

Once I'd done Charlie Carne a favour. He hated maths, and we had double maths with Mr. Walker every Tuesday afternoon. I forged a note from his mum, showed it to Benny and we put it in an envelope addressed to Mr. Walker and dropped it on his desk at the start of double maths. When we were all sitting down copying a "problem" from the board about a man with three sheep, a dog and a boat, Walker opened the note.

I'd written, "Dear Mr. Walker, I regret to inform you that Charles has head lice. You can imagine we are horrified, but the boy refused to go for treatment this afternoon because he didn't want to miss his favourite double maths. Will you please be so kind as to send him straight home from school, so I can take him to clinic and get him cleaned up."

Mr. Walker believed the note and sent Carne home with a flea in his ear, for disobeying his mother. Carne spent the day hanging round Spitalfields market. He paid me two bob, last year's Eagle Annual and half a packet of sherbet for getting him out of maths.

"Even I believed it was true when I read it." Benny said, "You wrote it like it really was his mum. How do you do that?"

"I just pretended I was his mum and I thought what she would think and what she would say and then I wrote it." I said.

"Oooyuck!" Benny feigned a puke, "Imagine being Carne's mum!"

"So, you gonna be a writer then?" Benny asked.

"No," I said, "Gonna be a geomorphologist"

"No such thing,"

"OK I'll run an alluvial fan club!"

That night I had little homework, so after tea, I went over to the debris. No one was about. I crawled into the camp, lit a candle in a jam jar and settled down to read the Eagle. But I was distracted – thinking about Carne's mum – how I had put my head into hers to imagine what she'd think. It felt like that when I was reading Sylvie's letters. Even though I hated what she was writing – the swearing and everything, I could imagine what she felt. And even though she got herself into bad situations, I felt sorry for her. I wanted to believe she wasn't a bad person, but a good person who had bad luck.

I poked my head out to make sure none of the kids was around. I closed the entrance, took two candles and climbed down Viv's ladder into Tommy Iassac's cellar. I slid the trapdoor closed above me to mask the light. I set the jam jars on the arm of the sofa. Then I rummaged in the sideboard drawer where I'd hidden Sylvie's letters.

I felt like an intruder sitting on Rachael's sofa, where she cuddled her two babies. I opened the last letter I'd read and I skimmed through it in case I'd forgotten, but I knew every single word, as if I had written it myself. I wanted to know how she escaped from Frank. I opened the fourth letter.

13th September 1947
Greyhound Bus, Pennsylvania
Dear Marly

She's on a bus. That means she got away from him, I thought.

> *I got that lady to take the last letter. I do hope you're getting them. I know you can't reply, but it makes me feel that I'm not alone if I've one friend in this cruel world.*
> *Well, things are better now. I've left Frank.*
> *After I ran away they made me sleep outside. It was so cold. When I made a big fuss they threw me a blanket. I ate scraps they threw from the table. I lived like a dog. They didn't let me near the baby. I stayed in the garbage bay for two days, watching them come and go. I thought about leaving them all. I could run without the baby. It would be easier. I could thumb a lift on the highway and get to Philly and then get a bus. They wouldn't care. They wouldn't care if I died out there – none of them. But I thought about what Dad would say, Marly if I got home without the baby and then I couldn't do it.*

I threw the letter down on the settee. She'd have left Carol behind with Frank in that horrible place, like she left me behind. How could she do that? Didn't she care about her baby? Disgusted but still fascinated I picked it up and read on.

> *On Saturday Frank and Rosie went to the bar. I knew they'd be out most of the night. I waited two hours. I went round the back, where the neighbours couldn't see and looked in through the windows. It was too dark. I called out Carol, are you there, darling? It's Mummy, but she didn't answer. So I went round the other side of the van and pushed the door. It was open. I crept inside and listened. Nothing. They had taken the baby to the bar. So I hid under the van and waited.*
> *Hours later they came back with friends. They were talking and singing. I could see the baby behind them. They went in and closed the door. I heard them – singing, and moving about. Later it went quiet. I knew she'd be pissed and she'd be fast asleep for three hours, before he woke up wanting a piddle. I waited an hour and then I sneaked in.*

Frank was on his bed. Rosie had collapsed beside him. The baby was on Rosie's bed, rocking and sucking her thumb like she does sometimes. I grabbed her and stuffed some of our things in a carrier bag. I knew Frank kept money in a cookie jar. I grabbed it, but dropped it and it spilled over the floor. I thought they'd wake up but they didn't. I took a few dollars. I ran as fast as I could.

Would you believe it, Marly, I'd only gone fifty yards and I ran into Earl and Wayne. Wayne asked who I had with me and I said it's my daughter. He said she was pretty and Earl said "Yea, just like her Mommy."

They asked where I was going so late and I didn't know what to say. I said to see my aunt in Philly. I said she was ill. I was going to stay a few days. I said I was going to thumb a ride. Wayne said No need, and offered me a lift. I was scared, but what could I do? I looked back to see if Frank was following but there were no cars. Earl asked where my aunt lived and I said near the Greyhound depot and he said he'd drop me there.

It was a long way to Philly. They kept talking all the way about sports. They weren't bad boys really.

Earl put his hand on my knee. I was frightened, but it was nice that he liked me – considering the state I was in. At least when a man is touching you up, Marly, he isn't beating you up! I didn't dare move or say anything or they might throw me out on the highway. I guess Earl thought that meant he could do what he liked. He put his hands up my skirt. I shut my legs tight, but he pulled free and started stroking me up top. All I could do was stare straight ahead and pretend nothing was happening. Then he put my hand on his trousers and I pulled away.

He started joking with Wayne. He said I was lucky they found me tonight because there were nasty folk about and I wouldn't want to walk all the way to Philly. He pulled my hand back. I did what he wanted.

I hated reading about her doing things with men. It made me feel so ashamed. I thought that was only for people who loved each other and got married, but she did it with anybody.

I was so happy when Wayne said, Here you are, Honey, Philly Greyhound. I grabbed the baby and the bags and we fell out of the car. Earl called out after me, See you when you come back. When I was far enough away I shouted, No way you dirty bastard!

I ran to the ticket office and emptied the money on the counter. I asked where I could get to. The booking clerk asked if I was English. She said she loved the way I talked. She wanted a conversation, but I just wanted a ticket to anywhere. I said New York and she gave me a ticket and some change. The bus was already loading, so I got on before the cops or Frank turned up. And that's where I'm writing to you now, Marly. We're on the road. The baby's sleeping. We're going to New York. I'll post this when we get there.

God Bless, Marly.

If you see Tommy, give him a kiss for me, but don't tell him where it came from.

Love
Sylv."

She lied and she did something rude to the policemen. But I couldn't help but admire her courage. Perhaps she really was a good person who had to do bad things – like Granddad, Uncle Sammy and Solly had to kill people to beat Hitler, liberate France and free the Jews from the concentration camps.

Perhaps she was doing a good thing saving her baby. But why did she think about leaving her to save herself? Did she only take Carol because she was scared of what Granddad would say? Didn't she love her? Why did she always call her the baby when she was three years old? Why didn't she call her Carol? I read the next letter.

20th September 1947
New York
Dear Marly
I hope you are well.
Just a quick note this time.

> *You'll be pleased to hear that I have nothing to complain about in this letter. God is smiling on me again. I am staying with the kindest people.*
>
> *It's Harry. He was the bus driver who brought us from Philly. He's ever so nice. After Dad, he's the nicest man I ever met. In fact he's just like Dad – same age.*
>
> *When we got to New York, I was asleep. Everyone had got off the bus. Harry woke us up. He said he liked the baby. He gave us some chocolate. He asked what I was doing in New York and I said I wanted to get a boat to England. He asked if I had somewhere to stay and said he and his wife would put me up in their apartment. He walked us up Broadway. Imagine Marly – Broadway! It was so busy – thousands of people rushing everywhere. We took a side street and stopped at one of those big brownstone buildings with ziggy-zaggy fire escapes. When we got up to his apartment he touched the mezuzah on the doorpost and kissed his fingers. They are good Jews, Marly.*
>
> *I was worried whether his wife would want us there, but when she came to the door, she was so nice. She said she was Rivka, and she put her arm round me straight away. She said I looked done in and she sat the baby and me on the settee and brought me a coffee and bagels and some soda water and chocolate for the baby. She brought Harry a beer and they both said L'chaim.*

We didn't use many Yiddish words in our family. Gran collected insults and my Uncles sometimes said *l'chaim* when they lifted their beer and *mosultov* to wish each other luck. These words gave me comfort whenever I heard them. I had always felt like a stranger in my Gran's house, but also like a foreigner in my own country and Jewish words and Jewish things meant safety in a foreign land. I understood how the *mezuzah* by the door gave Sylvie confidence.

> *Afterwards I had my first shower – they don't have baths here. It was good to be warm and clean. She had soft towels. She took us to her spare room. Marly, it was like a princesses' room – so pretty. She said it was their*

daughter's room, but she'd gone away and it would do for the baby and me for a while.
In the morning, she brought me coffee in bed. She wanted to know all about me, so I told her everything – leaving home, finding Frank, running away from him and his sister, and getting the bus back to New York.
Rivka was so understanding! She said, Why you poor honey. You must feel this is a terrible country when all that happens to you is bad news. Well. I tell you it ain't. There's good folks here too.
Harry said they'd take care of us. She said we could stay as long as we needed and Harry would help us get a boat because he knows everyone and can arrange anything. Harry said he would find me a passage if I could work my way. I said I've worked my passage before and I'll do it again.
Rivka is a wonderful cook, Marly. She does delicious meals – lots of Jewish things that Mum didn't cook anymore. She has friends in the garment factories and she brings clothes home for the baby. She brought a pretty white dress and a pink bonnet with white ribbons, white socks and pink shoes.
She bought me a blue cotton frock, some underwear and a pair of bright blue shoes. Best of all, Marly, she brought me a beautiful blue coat ready for the winter. It's such fun when she brings us clothes. I always dress the baby up straight away and she does a little dance to show off and Rivka claps her hands and says A shayna maidel!
Marly. I am happy at last and we are safe here. I wonder if Mum and Dad ever ask about me? God Bless, Marly.
If you see Tommy, give him a kiss for me, but don't tell him where it came from.
Love
Sylv."

I thought, if Harry and Rivka, like her, then she can't be so bad.

Why did she always write: "Give Tommy a kiss, but don't tell him where it came from?" Did Aunt Marlene kiss me? No. She said she didn't read the letters, and that must be true, because they were unopened, until tonight. Except one – she read the first one. And she did kiss me, when she gave me the letters. That was Sylvie's kiss!

But I don't want her kisses! She left me. I was just two years old and she left me behind. And where is she now? Aunt Hannah said she came back – that was years ago – nine years ago. She didn't come back for me. She never wanted me. She never wanted any of us. She hated her babies. I hate her. I hate her letters. I wish I'd burned them. I wish Aunt Marlene had burned them. I stood up quickly and stuffed the letters in the drawer.

When I looked around the sofa was on fire. It started with just a wisp of smoke coming from under one arm, but within seconds it burst into flame. I tried to smother the flame with one of the cushions but it was no use. The smoke was choking. I ran up the ladder, slid the trapdoor open and scrambled out of the camp, just as Davy, Ronny and Viv were running in.

"What's up, Tommy?" Davy asked.

"Fire! In the cellar!"

"Blimey and it ain't bonfire night yet." Ronny laughed.

"It's not funny. We'll lose the camp." Viv said. "What we gonna do?"

"Piss on it." Ronny said.

"Don't be stupid" I said, "that won't put it out."

"Well there's four of us", Davy said. "Come on."

"No good – too much smoke."

I thought about Sylvie's letters and Tommy and Rachel's things.

"Call the fire brigade." I said.

"We'll get in trouble." Ronny said.

"No need" said Davy, "They're here!"

Without consultation, we scattered in different directions..

It was the beginning of November and kids were building bonfires on bomb sites all over the East End. One of our favourite tricks was to sneak up to a rival street's fire and set it alight before bonfire night. We'd tried Ropery Street a few nights before but they caught us. I guess this made the neighbours nervous and those few who had telephones would call the fire brigade at the first sign of smoke. Mrs. Bresslaw was the only one in our street with a phone. Her son Bernie had it put in.

We ran off round the block and then strolled nonchalantly back down Eric Street. We regrouped on my doorstep, with a grandstand view of the action across the road. We perched two by two on the walls on either side of the steps, like four gargoyles – miserable faces resting on knees.

A gang of kids had gathered from the streets around to cheer the firemen. There were no flames – just a cloud of thick black smoke. The firemen tore our camp apart scattering the doors, boxes, carpets and chairs that we'd taken so long to collect, until they exposed the trapdoor. Two men unreeled a hose and then drenched the cellar for five minutes. When they were satisfied there was no fresh smoke, they threw a pile of doors over the hole to stop people falling in and packed their hoses. They told the cheering kids to bugger off, jumped in their fire engine and left.

"Took us bloody years, that." Davy was fed up.

"Yea, I know. I had a candle in the cellar. It fell over."

"Bloody stupid!" Davy said.

"Not his fault." Ronny defended me.

"Yes it was" I said, "I was stupid. Sorry."

Those bloody letters. There were two I hadn't read and I wanted to know what happened next, but now I was sure Aunt Marlene was right. They belonged in the fire and now the fire's come for them and that's the end of it.

"Oh well, Tommy." Vivien said, "never mind it's getting winter. We won't be playing out so much. We'll make a new camp next year.

Old William Walking

One freezing evening, in mid December, I was coming home from school. It had been snowing for a week and snow was falling now – big soft flakes drifting like feathers in the light of the street lamps. I took a short cut across the bomb site. Covered in snow it was beautiful – the mounds of rubble like little mountains covered in soft untrodden snow.

Over where our camp used to be, I noticed smoke first, then a small fire, and someone squatting in its glow.

I wandered over, thinking it was one of the boys.

As I came close I saw it was an adult. He wore a big overcoat. He had a snow-capped scarf draped over his head, putting his face in shadow.

He had taken over our fireplace – a square of bricks, topped by the grill Davy nicked from his Mum's electric oven.

He was cooking something in a can, poking it with a stick.

He looked up at me and his face caught the firelight. I knew him. He was the tramp I'd seen on the street. Old William – that's what we called him, but I am not sure if he was old or just looked old, or if his name was really William.

Kids told stories about him – said he was a dangerous robber and took small children away and they were never seen again. That was rubbish. He never hurt anyone.

"Hello. Who are you?" I asked.

"William", he said, "and who are you, young man?"

His voice was soft and cultured with no East End accent.

"Tommy. Tommy Angel."

"Ah, Angel – Engel. You Ashkenazi?"

"Er. I don't know."

"Or perhaps you're a marauding Angle, come over from Jutland to rape and murder and give England it's name?

"Sorry?"

"You know in Holland they'd call you Angel if you had the sign of an angel on your door? Do you have an angel on your door."

"Er, no, we've got a knocker."

"I'm Mankowitz. We came in from Russia."

"Pleased to meet you."

He pulled back his scarf. He had long hair, like a woman, but matted and dirty. He had a dark weathered face, deeply wrinkled with sad-lined eyes and a big nose. He had a beard – mostly white like Father Christmas, but brown around his mouth. His lips were cracked with the cold and scabby.

"You live here," he said, "I've seen you."

"Over there, with my Gran."

"Brothers and sisters?"

"No." I said, feeling guilty, because it was a lie. But it would do for now. I thought he didn't really want to know about my family.

"Why are you here?" I asked.

"How long you got?" He shrugged, raised his bushy brows and smiled. His coat dropped open a little and I saw he was wearing a suit with a fob watch on a chain. I thought it strange that a tramp would wear a suit.

"You gonna sleep here?"

"Oh yes."

"But it's freezing!"

"I'm OK," he said. "You know what keeps me warm?"

I shrugged.

"Well this week it's the price of coal, the Suez Crisis and the threat of more smog." He took a newspaper from a pile in front of him, opened it and stuffed it under his arms.

"And then there's the horses." he said stuffing more pages, "and the small ads and my favourite – the obituaries." He chuckled as he wrapped his coat around him.

He poked at his dinner with a stick.

"Want some sardines?"

"Hate sardines"

"Everybody does. That's why they give them to me."

"Who does?"

"People."

"People give you food?"

"From where I am," he said, "you see the best and worst of people. Once I sat on a woman's doorstep for a rest. She saw me there and brought me a full plate of dinner and a cup of tea. Another time I just leaned against the railings outside a house and a woman poked her head out her bedroom window and told me to piss off. I didn't move fast enough and she emptied a full piss pot over my head."

"Errrghh!" I groaned, "What did you do?"

"Nothing. Just walked away."

"But weren't you angry?"

"In the end it's down to intelligence."

"What do you mean?"

"Stupid people live in fear and clever people live in love," he said. "But they're not good or bad – they're just people, and you can't blame people for being people anymore than you can blame dogs for being dogs; cats for being cats; rats for being rats. You can't change them either – you have to accept them for what they are and forgive them."

"Forgive them for what?"

"For everything. For living, for dying, for getting in your way and making you miserable, for making promises and breaking them, or for making you happy and leaving you."

"Why are you here?" I asked again.

"Somewhere to rest for the night." He smiled and looked away at the fire. He spoke with finality, as if the conversation was finished and he expected me to walk away. But I was curious and I thought if I had secret stories of lost sisters and letters from my mother, then perhaps he had more to him than just being a tramp.

"But... why are you here... sleeping on the debris? Why don't you go to the Sally Army or go home to your family?"

"I went to the Sally once." he said, "But they make you sing hymns before you get your breakfast and it's full of smelly old tramps."

He smiled again and nodded towards the vacant orange box by the fire. I was a bit frightened to sit with him in the darkness, but I dropped my satchel, brushed the snow from the box and squatted opposite him, close enough to see his pitted teeth and smell the stale urine and sweat wafting from under his big coat whenever he moved.

"And I don't have a home." he said.

"Why not?"

"My family's gone."

"Where did they go?"

He searched my face, to see if I really wanted to know. I must have passed the test. He smiled a little. I nodded and shifted position, sitting square in front of him, leaning forward elbows on knees, hands warming over the fire, so I could hear every word.

"I wasn't always like this." he said, "When I was young I was a teacher at London University."

I sat up, half amazed half incredulous.

"My subject was philosophy. I gave lectures about Wittgenstein, Aristotle and Descartes – 'I think, therefore I am.'" He said, "That means we make our own world and everything that happens in it. Do you believe that, Tommy?"

How can that be? I thought, Did Poor Dead Katy make herself fall ill and die? Did Uncle Louis make the Germans kill him? Did Uncle Sammy and Uncle Solly make the war happen? Did I bring Carol's photo to me? Did my mother rape herself? Did she make Frank beat her? Did my sisters make Gran send them for adoption? Did I decide to be born in this family?

"Don't know." I said. "What happened to you?"

He told me he was very successful. He was respected in the university and he did very well. He became a full professor when he was thirty-nine and earned good money. He said at the end of the war, he bought a big house in Woodford Green, with a lovely garden and antique furniture and paintings in every room. He had a lovely wife called Ruth who was a classical pianist.

I'd seen the big houses in Woodford Green when I'd cycled into the Forest. They were beautiful. They were painted white with beams criss-crossing the walls. They stood in gardens so big they had whole trees – lots of them and ponds big enough to swim in. Granddad said you'd have to collect the rent from everyone in Eric Street to pay the rent for one of those houses. William said he bought his house. I didn't know you could buy a house.

He dug under his coat, into his suit and brought out a tiny photograph. He offered it to me. It was one and a half inches square, cracked and faded and out of focus, but in the light from the fire I could make out a man, a woman and a girl – about fifteen.

"That's her." he said, "Naomi. Like in the bible – Ruth and Naomi. They were so close – not like mother and daughter – more like sisters.

I knew the story of Ruth. I'd made it into a paper plane.

"*A shayna maidel.*" He said.

"What is that?" I asked.

"Naomi – a pretty girl." He said, "But I lost her. I lost them both."

He told me Naomi had her father's intelligence and her mother's artistic talent and good looks. He said she was beautiful and full of life.

"But, you know, Tommy, you can have everything and then life can change in a heartbeat." he said. "Do you understand that?"

I thought how life at Gran's had been exactly the same for years. Gran, Granddad and Vinny had always lived at 90 Eric Street. The house had never changed – it was always old and damp and dirty. All the men in the family had the same jobs all their lives. Granddad and Vinny went to work and I went to school every day and had the same teachers for the same lessons. Weekends were the same with Saturday morning pictures and the family round in the evening, with the same jokes, stories and rows every week. Sundays we always had the big dinner and Granddad slept on the sofa. Nothing had changed for years. And then...

"Well?" he asked

Suddenly every heartbeat moment popped into my head "Yes" I gabbled, "I've had lots of heartbeats. Like when the sun cut the street in half and Mrs. Levy said God would punish me and I knew he wouldn't and when I found the photo in the airee and when I saw Poor Dead Katy and when I found out I had a sister – two sisters, and when I found Aunt Hannah was my mother and then she wasn't and when Aunt Marlene put the letters in my hand and when I burned down the camp!"

William smiled. "Oh my! I see you do understand. Do you want to tell me about it?

But I didn't want to tell my story. I was more interested in him. "Did you have a heartbeat?" I asked.

"Yes." He said, "My Naomi had been complaining of headaches. Ruth had known about it for some time, but they were so close, those two, they kept it between them. It was their secret. One day I went up to her room to see if she wanted help with her homework and she was sitting on the edge of the bed, with her head in her hands, crying with the pain.

"She said she didn't want to bother me about it – me being so busy at work. She said I'd have made a big fuss and dragged her off to the doctors and it was really nothing just a headache.

"We were sitting together a few evenings later. Naomi asked if I'd walk her to her friend Sarah's birthday party and walk her home when it finished. I knew she was scared of the dark, and I teased her. I said she was a big girl now and should walk by herself. Sarah only lived around the corner. She knew I was joking.

"I asked if she had a present for Sarah and she began to tell me 'I've got her...' In the middle of the sentence, she just stopped and stared straight ahead. I looked to see what she was staring at. It was the clock on the mantelpiece."

"She stared without blinking. Ruth and I spoke to her. She just stared. I touched her and she didn't move."

He looked into the fire.

"She was gone" he said, "It was like she had been switched off. Nothing. We found out later it was a brain tumor, but at the time we didn't understand. Ruth screamed and screamed and didn't stop until the ambulance turned up."

William fell silent. I stared at him. No one had ever told me something real about themselves before. My Aunts told me about Sylvie, but not about anything that happened to them. My Uncles told stories about the war, but they didn't say what really happened. Gran and Granddad never spoke about their lives – no one did. It was awesome, frightening, exciting and at the same time embarrassing because I didn't know what to say.

The snow had melted through my trousers and pants. My bum was freezing.

"Are they done?" he asked.

"What?"

"The sardines. They smell right, but I can't see so well. Cataracts. It's all like... fog. Gets worse every day. I'm going to need a white stick."

"Yes. Yes – they look done." I said. He slid the can out of the flames and continued.

"They took Naomi to hospital, but it was too late. She was gone – just her body left there like an empty house with no one home. They said they could have done something if we'd caught it sooner. They kept her alive, but she didn't come back. In ten days we buried her."

I couldn't imagine what it would be like to lose someone you loved so much. I had never lost anyone. I had no sisters, mother or father, but I didn't lose them – I never had them in the first place.

"After that, Ruth was quiet. She stopped talking – to everyone, including me. I think it was the guilt. I told her if she hadn't kept it a secret, I'd have called the doctors sooner and we might have saved her.

I went back to work at the university. Life goes on – that's what I thought, but one night I came home from work and she wasn't there. I called her but there was no reply. I ran upstairs and there she was on the bed – pills all over the counterpane and a bottle of gin – nearly empty. She was gone."

I looked at the tiny photo. The man was William when he was a teacher. The woman was dead and so was the girl. I gave it back.

"You know, Tommy, it wasn't the tumour or the pills that killed them", he said.

"What was it?"

"It was the secret. It killed them both, don't you see?"

"Yes." I could see – sort-of.

"Secrets are dangerous." he said, looking straight into my eyes, like he knew my life was full of secrets. I was too scared to say anything.

"Every family has secrets, Tommy." he said, and he lightened up a little and put on a spooky voice like Boris Karloff,

> *"There's places where no one should be and photos that no one must see. Names that should never be said and letters that mustn't be read. Feelings that no one will show and secrets a boy mustn't know.*

"There! A Poem for Tommy by Prof. William Mankowitz, 1956."

He ended with a half-bow and a smile.

I was embarrassed. It was as if he knew everything that had been happening to me, everything I was thinking. Suddenly I felt terribly guilty and, for the first time, a bit frightened of this strange old man.

"What did you do next?"

"Well. I had nothing, Tommy. No wife, no daughter. Nothing. No matter how much I cried, Tommy, I couldn't bring them back."

That was the first time I had heard a man talk about crying. He stared ahead, focused on something far away.

"So I put on my coat and my boots and I walked." He said.

Like Tommy Isaacs, I thought.

"I walked away from my empty house and my meaningless work. I walked out, Tommy, and after eleven years I'm still walking."

Eleven years – that's all my life – he's been walking all my life.

"Do you know Tommy Isaacs?" I asked. The question popped out too fast for me to stop it. Immediately I felt stupid – why would he know him – why would he care?

"Tommy? Used to live right here on this very spot where we're having our little picnic."

"Yes," I said, "He went walking."

"I know – lost his wife and babies. But he's not walking anymore."

"What's he doing now?"

"Nothing. He's dead. God rest his soul."

I stared into the fire. I wanted to ask about Tommy – how he died, but I didn't want to distract William.

"They pulled him out of the canal a couple of weeks ago. No one knows what happened, but there are only three possibilities. Either he fell, he was pushed or he jumped. Anyway he's dead.

"How do you live?" I asked.

"That's easy." He smiled, "All a man needs to do is eat and drink and find somewhere warm to sleep, like my room here!" He gestured towards the makeshift tent he'd made from two of our doors.

"I eat what people don't want. They throw it away – the markets, Billingsgate, Spitalfields, Roman Road – there's plenty to eat – good stuff. What I drink comes free from taps. I sleep in places other people have left."

"What will you do?" I asked.

"I'll keep on walking... until I find it."

"Find what?"

"What every philosopher has searched for since the beginning of time, Tommy... The reason... The reason why."

I said I didn't understand. Did he mean the reason why his daughter died or why his wife took the pills or why he was going blind? Did he want to know why, if God existed, He allowed bad things to happen – like mothers leaving and babies dying and people going to war?

"Oh no, Tommy." he said, "I spent years trying to find the reason why bad things happened and why they happened to me. At first I blamed myself for thinking it and making it happen – Descartes, remember? But now I know there's no reason behind anything. It just happens and it happens in a moment. One minute you have a family. The next minute you don't. That's just life.

Yes, one minute I didn't have a family and now I do.

"I want to find another reason. When you have nothing – no family, no home, no work, no philosophy, nothing that matters, nothing to justify your existence or reward your efforts – what is the reason to carry on?"

I was afraid he might stop walking and die like Tommy Isaacs. Although I knew it wasn't appropriate – I could think of nothing else to say or do – I reached in my pocket for what was left of my spending money. "Can I give you something?" I asked, holding the coins in my palm.

"Not that. I wouldn't know what to do with it."

"What can I give you then?"

"You gave it already"

"What?"

"The only other thing a man needs in this life," he said, "after food, water and a warm fire."

"What's that?"

"A friend to talk to now and then."

"You must talk to lots of people, when you're walking."

"God bless you, Tommy." He chuckled. "No one ever comes close enough!" He gave me a big grin and winked.

Under the long hair and the stained beard, the muck and the smell, he was like my Granddad – only William lived on the debris and Granddad lived across the street in a proper house.

"Teatime." I said, "See you around." and I left.

Gran was cooking sausage and chips. When she wasn't looking I pinched a sausage and wrapped it in newspaper. I tiptoed out the door. When I reached the camp, William was gone. I peeped in his tent and he was there – wrapped in his coat and newspapers.

"William!" I whispered.

"Who is it?"

"It's me, Tommy. I got you something."

He popped his head out.

"A sausage."

"Oh heaven" he crooned "Sweeeeeet heaven!"

Sylvie's Last Letters

The next day, I couldn't concentrate on anything at school. I was thinking about William. He said that we make our own world and everything that happens in it. I understood that, but I needed to think about it.

During Music, Mr. Cameron played a record – Tchaikovsky's Swan Lake and said we should listen and be improved. He leaned back in his chair, put his feet up on the desk and opened the paper. On the front page was a picture of a bus with its headlights diffusing through the fog and the conductor walking ahead – the headline "Eden Act Fails to Clear the Air."

Things were happening in my head. I was seeing the world outside differently and the world itself was changing. God was different, my family was different and school was different.

Today I felt I could make my own world. My grandparents had low expectations of life but I wanted to do something glorious. They had no education, but I was ravenous, gorging on every particle of learning. My mother did bad things and neglected her children, but when I grew up I was determined to love my children and do good things for them, and for other children too.

But William said there was no reason behind anything. It just happens and it happens in a moment. So how do you deal with that – like when your camp blazes up in a second? Did I make it happen? I did light the candle. Or did it happen by itself? I was confused. He said you have to forgive people for being what they were, but I couldn't forgive my mother – for leaving me and giving my sisters away, for doing bad things with bad men. I couldn't forgive my grandmother for selling the babies. I couldn't forgive my father for leaving.

When I got home from school, I dumped my duffle bag in the passage and ran over to the debris. It was a month since I burned down the camp – and not just the camp. I'd burned Tommy's house and everything inside – his babies' pictures and Sylvie's letters.

There was no trace of William. His tent lay flat, covered with fresh snow. Our main camp was just a few feet away – under the snow, under the doors. I tried to lift the corner of a door. It was too heavy with rubble and snow, but Errol and Larry were passing and saw I was up to something. We cleared the snow and rubbish away. We lifted one door, then another and exposed the floor of the camp and the cellar opening. Our ladder was still there – charred but intact. Errol ran home for a torch and when he returned we climbed down.

It was a mess. There were still puddles of water on the floor. It smelt pungent. It was hard to see anything – even in the torchlight. Everything was black.

"I'm invisible." Errol said.

I groped my way to the sideboard. Miraculously it was still there. Errol shone his torch and we could see it was charred, but intact. I opened the drawer, expecting to see nothing but ashes, but most of the contents were untouched. I grabbed the blue bundle of letters. I looked at the others.

"What is it?" Larry asked?

"The letters... from my Mum."

"What are they doing here?"

"I hid them, so Gran wouldn't find them."

"What did they say?" Errol asked.

Larry looked at me, remembering our secret pact.

"Oh, not much" I said, "Only that she went to America to live with my sister's father who was a bad man and he beat her up and did bad things to her and *his* sister tried to steal *my* sister and my mother ran away and was caught by the cops, so she ran away again and got to New York and found some nice Jewish people to stay with."

"Wow!" Errol said. "Is she still there?"

"No. She came back."

"Did you read them all?" Larry asked.

"Not all" I said – "two to go."

He looked at me, eyebrows raised.

"OK" I said, "but it's a secret."

"Pain-of-death." Larry said.

"Come on." I led them out of the cellar and across to Gran's house, into the shelter. We made ourselves comfortable between the boxes, I lit a candle and I read Sylvie's sixth letter aloud.

26th November 1947
New York
Dear Marly,

"That's my Aunt" I said, "she wrote to Aunt Marlene. But she hasn't read the letters. She thinks they're cursed or something. We're the first."

"Go on. Go on!" Errol said.

> *Why does God want to punish me?*
> *What did I do in my life to deserve such heartache?*
> *Why do I mess everything up?*

Do you deserve heartaches? I thought, or do they just happen to you? Do you mess things up, or is it all a mess anyway, whatever you do?

"Gilbert Harding has heartaches." Errol said.

"That's heartburn, and anyway he doesn't suffer from it." Larry said.

"My dad says I mess everything up." Errol said.

"Are you gonna shut up and listen or what?" Larry said.

> *Marly, it's all gone very, very wrong. You know I said Rivka was nice. Well it turns out that she's not and Harry is like every other man – just out for what he can get. I'd only been here three weeks and Rivka started complaining. She said I was untidy. She criticized me for everything like leaving wet towels around or underwear. She kept following me handing me Kleenex I'd just put down.*

"Eeyuk. I thought I was a slob." Errol said.

I wondered if this was a bad idea. I looked at Larry.

"Go on." Larry said, "Never mind him."

> *I thought I was a guest in her house, Marly, but she resented everything I did. She said I could go to the park and leave the baby with her, so I did and I met a few blokes who were happy to pay a few dollars for no more than most men take for free. But Rivka couldn't be happy for me that I was making a few bucks. She complained every time I came in. She wanted to know where I'd been and who with.*

"What's she talking about?" Errol asked

"She's doing it for money." Larry said.

I thought… this is a *really* bad idea!

"My Mum's told me about it – prostitutes do it for money." Larry said.

"Blimey!" Errol said.

"She's not a prostitute!" I said, feeling a great rush of shame, "She had to do something to get money to save her baby and get home."

"Keep your 'air on!" Larry said, "I didn't say *she* was one did I?"

"Well she's not!"

"Course not." Larry said, "Go on."

> *I offered her 10 dollars towards my keep, but she refused. Fucking cow! She said she wouldn't take money when she didn't know where it came from. I said I was working for it, and she wanted to know what work. I said I was doing a little bit here and there – to help out. And would you believe it – after she almost begged me to let her have the baby during the day, she had the cheek to say I was a bad mother leaving the baby alone so long.*
>
> *I told her right out – I had been through hell for that bleeding kid and I could have left her at the trailer but I didn't.*

I read out every word. I read *fucking* like it was a word in a foreign language. Errol and Larry looked at each other. Errol was about to say something, but Larry sensed my embarrassment and beat him to it.

"Good swearer, your mum." He said, grinning.

"What's a trailer?" Errol asked.

"What?"

"She said something about a trailer. Is it like at the Odeon, you get trailers for next week. Did she leave the baby in the pictures?"

"No – It's a kind of caravan," I said "She had to stay in a caravan with this Frank."

"Who's Frank?" Errol asked.

"My sister's father – I told you before!"

"Oh," he said.

Sylvie's last phrase stuck in my head – *I could have left her at the trailer but I didn't*. Aunt Hannah said Sylvie left all her babies. I didn't want to believe that. I thought maybe her babies were taken away from her and it wasn't her fault. But she called Carol a *bleeding kid* and said she could have left her, so did she lose all her babies or did she get rid of them?

> *I know she wants to get rid of me. She keeps making comments about the new baby and says she doesn't run a home for unmarried mothers and she doesn't want another screaming kid around. Well, who does? I don't, but I don't have a bloody choice do I?*

"What new baby?" Errol asked.
"She's pregnant." I said.
"Whose baby?" Larry asked.
"Not sure."
"So how many babies has she got then?" Errol asked.
"Carol my sister, then me, then Jacqueline – that's the one she's pregnant with." I said.
"And was Frank your dad? Errol asked.
"No. We all had different dads."
"Blimey!" Errol said, "Did she 'ave three 'usbands!"
"No." I said, "She didn't marry any of them."
"So how did she have babies if she didn't marry anyone?"
"Errol, you wouldn't understand. You're too young. Go on, Tommy." Larry said.

> *Well I don't care what Rivka thinks anymore. She keeps trying to chuck me out, but Harry won't let her. Harry looked after me ever since the Greyhound and he won't let me go now – not now he's getting what he wants. I suppose I should tell you what happened with Harry. I'm not proud of it, Marly. He's old enough to be my Dad, but these things happen. About a week ago. We were all sitting around the fire. Rivka had been critical all day. She'd had some Bourbon before bedtime, like always. I just made sure she had a bit more than usual.*

"What's Bourbon?" Errol asked.
"Biscuits" Larry said.
"I dunno." I said, "A drink… for bedtime, like Ovaltine."

> When she fell asleep, I said to Harry he must be happy with such a good job, a lovely home and a kind wife. He said, well – not so kind in every department.
>
> I said Rivka must know she has a husband in a million and he came over bashful like men do and said, You think so? I said, I know so and I can prove it. It didn't take much, Marly. I just looked towards the bedroom. He followed my eyes and then he followed me – easy as that! Poor old Harry – he'd never done it before – not since he married. He kept looking back out the door to Rivka. I put my hands on his trousers. And he gave in.

"Gave in what?" Errol asked.
"She's doing it again." Larry said.
I read faster to avoid Errol's questions.

> After that it was Harry who made sure Rivka had enough Bourbon to fall asleep and it was Harry who stuck up for me when we had a row. But I didn't want to stay there anymore. Rivka was a pain in the arse and Harry got more and more nervous. I knew she'd find out. I asked him to get me on a ship. He talked to his buddies and found a cargo boat leaving for Southampton in three days. They needed help in the kitchens – no money but free passage. Harry gave me a name and address. I have to go to the dock at six on the day of sailing – that's tomorrow. When I told Rivka I was going, she cheered up. Last night I heard them in the kitchen. Rivka said, "Harry, dear, won't you be glad to have the apartment to ourselves again?" Harry said, Yes, of course, Dear, but she must have noticed something in his voice. She said nothing. She knew!

"Knew what?" Errol asked.
"About her and Harry doing it." Larry said
"Doing what?" Errol asked.
"Oh blimey, Errol – having biscuits and cocoa!" Larry said.

Well, Marly, we're sailing back to England tomorrow, so today I've been out doing a bit of work for some spending money. I just got back to the apartment and I found two bags of clothes and a note that said I know what you have been doing with my husband. You are an ungrateful tramp. Get your child and get out on the street where you belong and never come back

Would you believe it, Marly, I was only doing what she didn't want to do, doing her a favour and it wasn't my fault. It takes two – or had she forgotten? But the men always win, don't they! No one's here except the baby, and me so I'll close now and we'll be out of here and on the boat tomorrow. Marly. I am so looking forward to seeing you again.

I didn't read the usual closing.
"Do you think she got the boat then?" Larry asked.
"There's one more letter." I said
"Go on then." Larry said.
I opened the last letter. It was short.

27th November 1947
New York
Dear Marly,
Just a quick note to say I'm setting off, at last, although it didn't go smooth, does it ever! Last night I came down to the docks. I found out where the ship was, and found a place under a bridge where we could sleep. It was bloody cold and uncomfortable, but at least I knew we would be out of here today. At 6 O'clock I went to the boat and I asked this young sailor where I'd find the galley master. He took me to a wooden hut on the dockside.
The galley master was a rough bastard, big round face, big beer belly. I said I'd come for the kitchen job. He said it was too late – the job was gone. I should have come earlier. I couldn't believe my luck, Marly. I pleaded with him. I even cried. I said, please have pity on me and my little girl. We have to get home to England. He just said,

> *Sorry, Honey. So I said, Do I have to get down on my bended knees? The, dirty bastard said, Now there's an idea, and he pulled me into this little store room. You know well enough what happened next without me telling you. I know it was wrong, but I wasn't going to miss this boat for anything.*

"What happened?" Errol asked, "Tell me what happened."
"She did it again." Larry said.
"Blimey!" Errol said, "She does it all the time."

> *Well, Marly, I got the job. He says I've got to work hard and help all the boys in the kitchen. Keep them happy. I can handle that. Marly, I don't know how Mum and Dad will treat me when I get back, but I just want to be home. I hope to see you soon, God willing. Thank you for being my friend. Remember, I trust you, Marly. Please don't tell a soul about any of this.*
> *I'm just so glad it's nearly over.*

I skipped the closing again.
"Then what?" Larry asked.
"My Aunt Hannah said she got the boat to Southampton and phoned my Uncle Solly to get her. She came home for a bit but went away again."
"Where is she now?" Errol asked.
"Dunno. Hasn't been seen for years. No one says anything about her now. She's gone."
"Blimey!" Errol said.
"Secret?" I said
"OK"
"Pain-of-death!"
"OK."
They left.
I was glad I'd read the last letters. Her words had hung around me like a bad smell and now they were gone and there wouldn't be any more.
I still didn't know whether she made the bad things happen or if it was bad luck and she was really a good person – perhaps a bit of both.

Whatever she was, was what she was. A dog's a dog, a cat's a cat, a rat's a rat and you can't change that. That's what William said.

He said you can forgive dogs for being dogs and people for being people, but even dogs don't leave their puppies and I couldn't forgive her for leaving her babies.

I folded the letters and stuffed them in a biscuit tin. I tied it tight with string. I spent an hour in the air raid shelter, digging a deep hole in the dirt floor. I buried the tin and replaced the dirt and dragged a flagstone over it. I left her there under the floor.

At last Sylvie was out of my head and out of my life.

Into The Smog

It was the last day of school before we broke up for Christmas. I woke in the dark, when I heard Granddad shut the street door as he left for work. I swung my feet over the bedside and padded into the kitchen. There was the familiar smell of cockroaches. I switched on the light, and a few scuttled away between the layers of brown lino, under the cooker and the cupboards.

It usually took me ten minutes to get out of the house on a school day, five minutes to run up Eric Street to Mile End Road, where I could jump on a bus or dive into the station to catch the tube.

My morning ritual was optimized for speed, so I could stay in bed in the warm as long as possible and still make it to school as the morning bell rang.

I filled a kettle and dropped it on the gas. I made a cup of tea for me (three sugars) and for Gran (no sugar because she had diabetes) and took her cup upstairs. I left it on top of the piano next to the jar with false teeth. Gran was snoring.

I drank my tea and had cornflakes and milk. I always shook the cornflakes box first so any mouse droppings fell to the bottom.

I poured the remaining hot water into my washing bowl. I found the bowl in the Isaacs' cellar. I expect Rachael washed her babies in it. We'd used it as a German helmet when we played war and then I brought it home. It was white enamel with a chipped blue rim – not much to look at, but it held water and it changed my life. Before then I used to wash upstairs in the scullery. It was icy in winter and we only had cold water. Now I could wash in the kitchen, which was near my room and a bit warmer and it saved me running up and down the stairs. I kept the bowl on top of the dresser – out of Gran's reach. She might have claimed it for other uses. I kept the soap in the bowl, away from the cockroaches.

I washed my face and hands, emptied and stashed the bowl and jumped into my pants and school uniform – grey socks, a white shirt, which could last about three days, short grey flannel trousers, black lace-up shoes, which I kept laced to save time, a blue and white stripy tie, which I kept knotted to save time, and my navy blue blazer

I quickly folded the put-u-up away, grabbed my duffle bag and blue Gabardine raincoat, and snatched my dinner money and bus fare, which Granddad had left on the sideboard. I ran upstairs, popped my head round Gran's door to say goodbye and rushed out into the street.

But the street had gone.

Where our doorstep ended there was nothing, just grey, stained yellow by the streetlight. It was dead quiet.

The smog usually started around November and came and went until January. The family talked a lot about the smog. Uncle Arthur told me about the first one, the Great Smog, in December, four years ago. He was down the docks driving a crane. He said it was a lovely day. He was supposed to be unloading timber from a Russian ship. The sky was blue above but when he looked down everything was covered in thick brown fog. He'd never seen anything like it. He had to stop work. When he came down he said it was like the blackout in the war – no light anywhere and you couldn't see further than the end of your nose. He could hear birds crashing into the buildings and falling to the ground.

Uncle Sammy said some of the cattle in Smithfield Market dropped dead with the fumes. He said so many people died of pneumonia the undertakers ran out of coffins, and the funeral cars got lost on their way to the cemeteries. He said a whole family died in Ropery Street and the police had to knock down the door and found eight of them dead in their beds. He said it lasted four days and killed twelve thousand people.

Uncle Solly said Mr. Eden's Clean Air Act was supposed to put a stop to it. No one was to use ordinary coal on the fire anymore. But he said it would take a long time, since no one could afford the smokeless.

I felt bad about all the death and suffering, but secretly I loved the smog. It meant I could legitimately get to school late.

This one wasn't as bad as the Great Smog, but it was the worst I'd ever seen. If I stretched out my arm I could see my hand, but nothing beyond. I eased my way down to the pavement and turned right to head up the street. I tapped my right shoe against our steps, and then Abe Cohen's steps Then I ran my hand along his railings.

That's how I made my way up the street – doorstep, railings, doorstep, railings, Ronny's, Mrs Yershon, Mr Levy's, until I came to the end of the terrace. I knew the pavement carried on past the snooker hall yard, but there were no railings or fences to mark the yard's boundary. It was a leap into nothingness.

Something came up behind me. I smelled it first – a disgusting shitty smell. I heard a stick tapping and then a grey mound appeared at my side.

"No problem for me, Tommy. It's all a fog anyway."

It was Old William.

"And the first shall be last and the last shall be first. Come on."

I followed him up the street.

"Remember Tommy. Everything can turn around in a minute – in a heartbeat."

You're right, I thought – one minute you're the smelly old tramp I felt sorry for, and next you're leading me through the smog. My blind philosopher led me safely to Mile End Road, and disappeared as we came into the glow of the station lights. A small crowd huddled under the station canopy. They stamped their feet and blew into their gloves to keep warm, and complained about the smog.

"Bloody 'opeless, I'll never get to work in this."

"Yea, and it's no bloody work – no bloody pay."

"They don't bloody care you got bloody mouths to feed."

Their voices were curiously flat and carried only a few feet in the muffling fog.

I found the bus stop and joined a long queue, peering into the gloom. No buses passed. One car came crawling out of the smog, guided by a passenger leaning out of the window, calling instructions, "Slow down. Left a bit... No right..." A few more cars passed very slowly and a man on a bike, with his scarf tied around his face, his breath steaming through it.

Most of the people in the queue were masked with scarves so you could only see their eyes. Some were coughing – from the smog or the cigarettes. A lady behind me was in distress. She was coughing her lungs out! It was a wet guttural cough that seemed to come from deep in her chest. She was fighting to inhale between the spasms and then inhaling too deeply so the smog irritated her lungs and threw her into more violent coughing. She was panicking. I guess she thought it would never stop.

The man standing with her took his flask from his lunch bag. "Come on, Peggy, have some nice hot tea." She drank a little and calmed down.

I wondered if she'd die today. I wondered if her kids would see her again. I wondered if they said goodbye when she walked out this morning.

I usually alternated between bus and tube – just for the fun of it, but this morning the roads were in chaos. It was freezing cold. The queue behind me disappeared into the gloom and people were getting irritated. I headed for the underground – no smog in the tube.

The tube was an adventure. Each time I tried to find a different route to Old Street. I had already found nine routes. I could take the Central Line to Bank or Liverpool Street, change to either the Northern Line, Hammersmith & City, the Metropolitan or the Circle Line to Moorgate and then take the Northern Line to Old Street. Or I could start on the

Hammersmith & City or District Line, opening up another six routes. These were all the most direct routes, and I believed there were many more to be discovered. Each route had it's own character. Some trains were strewn with litter and full of people who smoked and coughed. Some trains filled with city people in dark suits, or mums with push chairs, toddlers and bags. Today the trains were packed solid with people who couldn't get buses.

I went by the simplest route – Hammersmith & City to Moorgate. I had to squeeze my way in and stood holding the central pole between the doors. I fought my way off at Moorgate and was swept along by a wave of people in a hurry to get through the tunnels to the Northern Line. The train drew up as I reached the platform and although it was full, and the porter was letting no one on, a fat man at the door of the nearest carriage made a joke of sucking in his big gut to make room and pulled me in.

I wasn't happy being crushed against his belly and he gave me funny looks and moved strangely, so I wriggled my way to the central pole. Unfortunately when the doors opened at Old Street, I couldn't get across in time. I had to ride on to the next station, my station, Angel. Two working men had noticed my failure to cross the crowded carriage, and at Angel they each took one arm and lifted me off my feet. The other passengers thought this was great fun and passed me over their heads to the door. They cheered when I touched down on the platform. I turned and bowed deeply before running to get the return train to Old Street.

Outside the station the fog was just as thick as when I left Mile End. Luckily there was a stream of kids late for school. I joined the shuffling procession.

"Say you came on the bus." One boy advised me. "They've hardly been moving. Then you won't get into trouble."

I didn't think I'd get away without a detention, but I took his advice and it worked. In fact the teachers were pleased to see us for a change. They had the same trouble getting in as the boys.

The assembly hall was half empty, which created an unusual intimacy. Mr. Cowan launched into his usual morning rant reminding us we were all disgusting loafers skilled only in dropping litter, disobedience, insolence, fighting in the playground, stealing from cloakrooms, running in corridors and messing up the dining room. His words echoed harmlessly around the hall. Then he told us to behave over the holidays because wherever we went, in or out of uniform, we were always Central Foundation Grammar School Boys and must conduct ourselves in a way that would bring honour to the school.

The morning went as usual but a few afternoon classes were cancelled because teachers didn't turn up, so we were told to catch up on our homework and left to our own devices. That meant climbing on desks, bundling in the aisles and general mayhem.

When we heard Mr. Spenser's approaching footsteps in the corridor we dived back into our seats and pored over our books. He smiled through the classroom windows. We smiled sweetly back. He popped his head round the door and said "Happy Christmas boys." and we called back "Happy Chanukah, Sir."

When he'd gone, mayhem resumed.

Surprise in Wentworth Mews

In the afternoon the smog was even worse and they let us off school early. Benny and I grabbed the opportunity for adventure and rather than take the safety of the tube, we caught the bus. It was slow, but we didn't care. We had to talk about today's antics and plan our holiday adventures. By the time Benny jumped off at Stepney Green it was getting dark and the fog was thickening. It was impossible for the passengers to see where we were, but the Jamaican conductor gave a running commentary.

"Swimming baths coming up. Anyone want a dip with me? How about you Darlin'?" he teased a big lady, "Shall we do the breast stroke?" He mimed. She chuckled and the other passengers laughed.

"New Road... or is it Old Street?" he joked. "I think, ladies and gentleman we might be going round in circles!"

"Driver must have his head up his arse!" said a man near the front.

"Why I do believe you're right, Sir. That seems to be the normal position for the Routemaster driver." said the conductor, "This vehicle, Sir, is so modern with its light alloy body, independent front suspension, power steering, fully automatic gearbox and power hydraulic braking – that our drivers think they don't have to look where they're going anymore."

"Get on with you!"

"But don't you worry, Sir. My name is Jesus and I'm here to lead you out of this darkness and into the light. He who trusts in me shall be truly saved."

His name really was Jesus. I'd ridden with him before and he told me about coming over on a ship from Jamaica and how hard it was for a black man to get a good job.

Everyone laughed and a few responded.

"Bless you Jesus."

"Halleluiah!"

"Praise the Lord!"

"Mosultov!"

"Queen Mary College coming up." Jesus said in a posh voice, "Now who's going to university? How about you, Professor Brainbox?" He laughed and mussed my hair.

"Mile End, I think." He said, mysteriously "Or is it World's End? You never know where you'll end up in this fog!"

I was sorry to leave the bus. I said "Goodbye Jesus." as I hopped off and he shouted "Goodbye Professor!" and waved cheerily as he and the bus faded quickly into the fog.

The bus stop was on the wrong side of Mile End Road. There was nothing to guide me across and I could see only a few feet ahead, so I just had to strike out in the right direction and hope for the best.

The traffic was moving slowly so I started to dodge across. Unfortunately my dodging sent me off course and instead of the pavement I expected on the South side there was just more road. Now I could hear the cars coming from ahead and behind me as well as from each side. After a few seconds I realized I must be in the middle of the junction with Burdett Road. A bus appeared just two feet to my right and the driver shouted,

"Get out of the road, stupid!"

With traffic coming from every direction I got confused. I turned this way and that and spun round a few times until I'd completely lost my bearings and didn't know which way to turn.

I remembered the dog that died – how he got confused and ran off randomly. I had to choose a direction – any direction. I started walking into the smog in as straight a line as I could. I walked into the path of an oncoming car. Neither the car nor I were moving fast, but it was like walking into a wall that was walking into you. The bumper hit my front-most shin and the bonnet hit my chest. Knocked off my feet, I slid down the bonnet.

It's daft the things you think about when you're about to die. First I noticed it was an Austin 7. Then I saw tomorrow's paper "Stupid boy walks in front of car." I wondered who would tear up the toilet paper when I was dead. I wondered if my story would be on the toilet paper. I thought of all the questions I had left in my head about my sister, my father, my mother. I had plenty of time to think about all these things as I slid under the car.

But I didn't die. The car stopped with the front bumper over my chest. The driver jumped out grabbed me under the armpits and pulled me up. My shin hurt like hell but otherwise I was all right. He pointed towards the invisible kerb and I limped off in that direction until I reached the pavement.

I was at the entrance to Wentworth Mews, a small alley that joined Burdett Road to Eric Street. It was dark and unusually quiet as I walked away from the traffic. I thought I could hear footsteps behind me. I stopped and the footsteps stopped. I started and they started.

Images flashed through my head. I saw evil people with murder in their hearts. I imagined myself stabbed and bleeding in the gutter in the freezing night. I imagined being tied up and dragged away to some horrible torture. I dared not turn to look, in case that spurred my stalker into action. If I ran, he might run faster and catch me. I tried to walk as if I wasn't scared. It was just him and me and there was no escape in that alley. I imagined him strangling me from behind with a rope, stabbing me, splitting my head with an axe.

I felt a real hand on my shoulder.

"Ahhh!" I cried out and spun round with my fists raised.

It was a woman in a dark coat with curly blond hair. She glared at me, wide-eyed. Her mouth was open, snarled up at one corner, her nostrils flared. She bared her crooked teeth. Her breath was foul with cigarettes and drink. She raised her hands, in attack or defense, anger or fear – I couldn't tell.

She screamed, "I am your mother!"

My heart beat hard enough to jump out of my body.

We stared at each other in silence, our arms dropped, our breathing gradually subsiding. My fear gave way to disbelief. She forced a nervous smile. I stared.

"I'm Sylvie." she said.

Every word of every conversion with my aunts and every word of every letter she wrote and every thing she did came flooding into my head.

"What do you want?" I demanded.

She was hurt by my challenge, but she smiled again.

"Just to talk, Tommy." She said.

I hated to hear her use my name. It belonged to me, my friends and my family. She'd never spoken to me before. She had no right.

"Let's go to your Gran's" she said.

We walked in silence from one sodium light to another. I wished she would fade back into the fog. Why was she here? What did she want? My head swam with unpleasant possibilities.

When we got to Gran's, she climbed the steps before me. I was surprised that she knew the house. She knocked on the door. Gran opened up, looked at her and said nothing. I was surprised that Gran wasn't surprised.

Gran turned and walked down the passage. She followed Gran down to the basement. Gran went into the kitchen. She went into the front room – my room. I sloped in after her. She took off her blue coat. I wondered if it was the one Rivka gave her. She laid it over the back of a dining chair and sat down on my settee. She wore a print frock, pinched at the waist and flared – the kind a teenager would wear. It looked strange on a grownup woman.

I dropped my duffle bag on the table, threw my mac over another chair and walked to the far side of the room. I perched on the arm of Poor Dead Katy's chair. We sat in silence for a while. She stared at me. I turned and looked out the window at the airee. Gran brought some tea.

"You found him then?" Gran said.

She and Gran talked. I listened and picked up what had been going on. She had come to the house several times over the past weeks, when I was at school. Gran had kept her visits secret. They'd argued about whether she could see me. Eventually Gran gave in and told her she could meet me from the bus this evening.

"She wants to take you home with her." Gran said, turning to me. "It's up to you. You don't have to go."

"It's just for tonight." she said, "I'll bring you back tomorrow."

Gran didn't use her name, just called her "She". What would I call her? Not "Sylvie" because she was older, like my aunts. Not "Mum" because she had no right. "She" would have to do.

I didn't want to go. I hated her. She left me behind. She left her babies. She did bad things. She went with bad men. She probably lives in a caravan with someone like Frank. I'd never, ever go anywhere with her, never, NEVER!

"Will you go?" Gran asked.

"All right." I said.

Gran told me to get some things. I stuffed my duffle bag with a change of clothes.

"Now, you take good care of him." Gran said.

"Course I will." Sylvie replied. She took my Gabardine mac from Gran and tried to put it on me. I wriggled away and did it for myself. I'm eleven, nearly twelve, at the Grammar. I'm not your baby.

The smog had cleared a little. As we walked up the street, she offered her arm. I pulled away. I didn't want to touch her.

We caught the bus towards the city. I stared out the window and said nothing. I hated what was happening. I didn't want to go with her. I was scared of what might happen. But I was also curious – so many questions left. I was determined to find out everything.

She chain-smoked and talked fast, complaining about the smog. I looked at her. She wasn't very old – even younger than Larry's mum. She had blonde hair and blue eyes, like me. Her face was pale, pasty, but quite pretty – when it was still.

I felt bad at the way I'd been treating her. She'd been OK, I suppose – quite nice really. I smiled at her. She was surprised. She smiled back and showed her twisted nicotine-stained teeth.

Her hands darted to and from her mouth as she puffed urgently at her cigarette. Her fingers were stained brown and orange. Her bright red lipstick imprinted the filter tip. Sitting so close to her, I could smell the smoke in her hair, on her clothes, on her breath. She had been drinking – perhaps to build courage for our meeting. She went on about the smog.

I interrupted her monologue. "Where have you been?"

"Well I was in the office. I do typing and secretarial – long hours – pay's crap – boss is a bastard, but the other girls are OK. We get on all right, have a laugh. I try to save up. I gave Mum some money to buy you a coat last month. I went to see her. She said you needed a new coat for the winter, so I saved up and gave her…"

I interrupted. "No. Since I was born."

I wanted to hear her story. I wanted to believe she was a good person.

"Oh." she said, and she was quiet for a few seconds. She puffed at her fag and launched again into a stream of nervous chatter, "I had to go away, America, then I came back, got a job and married Joe. That didn't last. All men are bastards, take all your bloody money, spend it on the horses and other women. I had to get out, got a divorce, cost a bleeding fortune, had to sell the furniture, found a flat, got another job and that was OK. I met Dez, he's from Singapore, you'll see him tonight, we'll go out, meet some mates, have a drink. We'll have a nice time, Tommy."

I stared out the window. We came to Whitechapel.

"Why did you leave… "

"Here we are." She said.

The Blind Beggar

She led me across the main road and we stopped outside a big pub called the Blind Beggar. I'd never been in a pub. I walked past the Wentworth every night on my way home from school. I sometimes heard men inside and the clink of glasses. Sometimes Mr. Kutchinski was sitting by the door and he'd call out, "Hello, Tommy, had a good day at school? Fancy a pint? And the other men would laugh and wave at me. But I'd never been inside.

At the doorway I was hit with a wave of fuggy air smelling of urine, stale beer and cigarettes. The smoke inside seemed thicker than the smog outside.

We crossed a big room heaving with people. They were crammed, six, eight, ten to each small table. Most were men – ugly drunken men with twisted faces and rough voices. They shouted at each other, banging their beer glasses on the tables.

We picked our way through a tangle of chairs. As she walked by, a sweaty-faced man leered, "Hello Sylv, brought something tasty for me tonight?"

He was looking at me!

"I saw him first!" said a man opposite. "He's my little bit of stuff, ain't yer sonny?"

"Filthy poofters!" she hissed. They laughed loud and we pushed by.

A big red-headed man with a face full of freckles and a neck like a tree trunk stood in her path.

"Love of my life!" he crooned, "'How about a little kiss?"

"Piss off, Ginger!" she shouted pushing him back to his seat.

"Fussy now, are we?" he said, "Dez come into some money, then?"

She turned to me and said, "We'll keep out of that one's way – sick bastard. Slashed a girl's face, for doing what I just did!"

We walked past a table with an older lady and a serious-looking man in a suit, who had been watching the exchange. She stopped.

"Reggie. Vi." She said, nodding.

"Don't worry about him, Sylv, he's got it coming."

"Thanks Reg." She smiled sweetly at them both.

"Your boy?" The lady asked. She had a soft voice and a big warm smile.

"Yes, Vi" She said proudly "My Tommy!"

"Got an intelligent face, that one." Reggie said, "Look after him."

He mussed my hair. I pulled away. He had heavy brows and his hair was Brylcreemed and brushed back behind his ears. I recognized him from Mr. Needleman's photo.

"Oh I will. I will." She said, "Tell Ronny I said hello."

"I will, darling, don't you worry." Vi said. She winked and waved to me.

She hustled me on.

"That's Reggie", she whispered.

"Yes." I said, "Mr. Needleman made that suit and I know how he hangs."

She looked puzzled and said, "Oh no, they'll not hang Reggie. He's too clever. Not like Ronny. They put him away Guy Fawkes."

I'd heard about Ronny and Reggie at school. Word was they got people beaten up or murdered. I glanced back to take another look at Reggie. He was laughing with the older lady. I guessed she was his mother. She obviously loved him and enjoyed his company.

My mind was racing. If that lady could love her sons, and stay with them even though they were killers, then why didn't my mother stay with me? Was there something bad in me – was I worse than a murderer? If a murderer's mother could be kind to a boy like me who wasn't even her son, why did my mother go away and leave me?

"Here we are,"

We came to a table with a man and two women and some empty seats.

"Where the fuck have you been?" The man asked. He had a strong Irish accent. He was thin and pale, with a few days' stubble and wild curly black hair.

"This is Jerry," she said. "Jerry, this is my son, Tommy"

Why did she say that? She has no right. I'm not her son. She didn't bring me up and care for me. She left me. Gran and Granddad cared for me. She has no right to be proud of someone she left behind.

"Oh, pleased to meet you, your Lordship." Jerry said.

"Where's Dez?" she asked.

"At the bar with some tart. He got bored with the waitin'."

She took my arm and dragged me to the bar. A sallow faced thin man in a crumpled grey suit was talking to a barmaid. She had blonde hair with dark eyebrows, skin caked in makeup and bright red lipstick.

Sylvie grabbed the man by the shoulders and spun him round on the stool.

"Hello, Darlin'" she said, "Here's my Tommy."

Dez managed a slow smile. He offered his hand. "Welcome to the madhouse." he said. He had an accent I'd never heard before. I didn't touch him. I said nothing.

"Quiet little mouse." He turned back to the bar, took a swig of his drink and carried on talking to the barmaid.

"Get us a drink, while you're chatting up your tart." Sylvie looked the barmaid up and down. Dez spun round irritated and asked what she wanted.

"Gin for me and orange juice for my Tommy."

He slapped a five-pound note on the bar and said to the barmaid, "You heard the old cow."

The big man called Ginger suddenly appeared with two rough-looking mates. He crashed his big fist hard on top of Dez's. "Thank you so much.." he said, "I knew you'd keep your promise."

"Smack 'im, Ginger." said one of his mates.

"Time he got his come-uppance." said the other.

There was evil in their eyes. One of them snatched an empty beer bottle, held it by the neck and cracked it down on the edge of the bar. Glass splintered into the air. Dez might get more than a smack, I thought, and suddenly we were surrounded by a small crowd who gave Ginger more encouragement.

"'Urt 'im, Ginge."

"Teach 'im a lesson for me."

"Hey, that's mine!" Dez protested, trying to slide his hand and the fiver from under Ginger's big fist.

"Not now, it's not. You owe me." Ginger said.

"You fucking tight bastard," Dez said, "You can wait a bit longer, can't you?"

"Well that's just where you're wrong, my friend. Let me explain." He removed his hand from Dez's, and as Dez clutched the fiver, Ginger lifted a beer glass and brought it down like a hammer crushing Dez's fist. Dez yelled, "Fuck you!" and struck out with his other hand, which glanced across Ginger's chest.

"Not in front of the children." The big man picked the fiver from the bar and waved it daintily in the air as he walked away. The man with the broken bottle turned on Dez. He raised the bottle to Dez's throat. Dez pulled back, his eyes wide.

"Enough!" A voice cut through the crowd. Everyone turned to see Reggie standing at his table, waving a finger at the man with the bottle, like he might be telling off a naughty child. The man nodded and dropped the bottle. He turned to Dez and snarled "Next time." and followed Ginger.

Reggie scanned the room. It went quite for a moment. It seemed that everyone in the pub was looking his way. Men paused from their drinking, looked up and gave him the smallest of nods and then carried on talking. He sat down quietly and continued chatting to his mum.

I remembered what Aunt Marlene had said about Uncle Sammy and Uncle Solly running London if it were not for the Krays. I imagined Sammy and Solly in this bar. Sammy would be laughing and clowning, but Solly would bellow with his deep dark voice and people would listen, even these people. But I didn't believe Sammy and Solly would come to a place like this. None of the people here were like my family. My people went AWOL, commandeered army lorries and nicked stuff and smashed a few Italian noses, but they were not murderers. They wouldn't wave a broken bottle in someone's face for a fiver. These people were her people.

"Here have this." Sylvie said, passing Dez a pound note. "Bring it over. When you can tear yourself away"

"Give me another one," he demanded, nursing his hand and his humiliation, "I'm making an investment." and Sylvie handed over another pound.

"Investment, my arse." She said as we walked away, "He's gambling. And he promised never again. Bastard!"

We sat with Jerry. The two women looked rough but they seemed harmless compared to everyone else in the room. Dez joined us with the drinks. He passed me the orange juice. I thanked him, but didn't touch it. They talked, joked, teased and abused each other and cursed the rest of the world. Most of the conversation was a blur. I felt very vulnerable. It was like being in the middle of a picture our art teacher showed us by Hieronymus Bosch, full of ugly people torturing each other.

Later she went up to the stage. There was a piano player in a black suit, with a droopy mustache and cigarette dangling from the corner of his mouth and a skinny drummer in a Teddy-Boy suit. Mrs. Kray had just finished singing. Vi gave Sylvie the microphone. "Here you are Sylv." She stepped on to the stage and she sang.

> *"Bei mir bist du shayn,*
>
> *Please let me explain.*
>
> *Bei mir bist du shayn,*
>
> *Means that you're grand."*

Aunt Marlene sometimes sang that when she got drunk. She said it really means "To me you are beautiful".

I wanted my mother to be beautiful. Up on that stage she looked like Marilyn Monroe on the cover of Vinny's Picture Post. She had blonde hair, blue eyes, pale skin and red lips just like Marilyn. My friends would think she was beautiful. Perhaps she was beautiful.

As she sang, she pouted like Marilyn. She swayed her hips so her dress flared out. Sometimes she bent down towards the drinkers and pushed her bust forward. She made eyes at each of the men close to the stage like she was in love with them. A few people clapped. She followed that song with Sentimental Journey – that's what Aunt Hannah said she'd sang that night at the American base.

She sang really nicely. Her voice sounded soft, sweet and innocent. I just closed my eyes and listened for a while and I imagined her to look like she sounded – like that young girl cycling to the army base for the first time. I saw her pretty face all fresh and excited and I remembered what happened afterwards.

She finished and smiled at the drinkers near the stage. The bright stage lights picked out her yellow teeth. She skipped back to the table like a little girl, flirting with the men as she passed. One of them put his hand up her frock. She laughed loudly and then pushed him away and continued to the table.

"That was for you, Tommy." She blew me a kiss and sat down.

I couldn't help thinking that close-up she looked like the barmaid she had just called a cheap tart. "You sing really nice." I said.

"I am so proud of my Tommy", she announced to the table. "He's very bright you know. He's going to get a good education and leave all this behind."

She has no right to be proud of me. She left me behind. She gave me nothing of what I am. Yes, I will get an education and I won't have to be in places like this, with people like you. "My eyes hurt." I said.

She said my eyes were bloodshot. It must be the smoke. She told Dez we should go. He said he had some business to attend to and he'd follow later. He tossed her a bunch of keys.

She made me link arms with her like I was her boyfriend and she strutted out, beaming like a film star among her fans. She waved and blew kisses to the men on either side as she passed. None of them took any notice, but some of the women said "'Night Sylv."

At the door I pulled away from her. The warm muggy air of the pub gave way to the sharp cold night and the wispy remains of the smog.

We made our way up Cambridge Heath Road. She skipped ahead, pausing to regain her balance a few times and to hold her hand out for me. I stayed a few paces behind. I didn't want to touch her.

We came to a doorway between a fishmonger's and a greengrocer's. After several attempts she inserted the key into the lock, opened the door and pushed me ahead up a dark narrow staircase. At the top of the stairs I stopped on the landing. She passed me and unlocked the flat, tripped inside and beckoned me to follow.

The room smelled of dirty clothes and spicy cooking, like Errol's house. It was lit dimly by the streetlights. I could see a gas cooker and sink to the right of the door, and as it opened further I saw a settee and a low coffee table covered in stuff.

She picked her way to the middle of the room and reached to the light. She groped for the string pull. The curly brown flypaper stuck to her wrist. She flicked it away. The light from the bare bulb didn't seem to make much difference – the room was still gloomy.

There was stuff everywhere, clothes, newspapers and books covering the settee, spilled across the floor. The coffee table was half-buried in newspapers. At one end an ashtray full of fag ends, some with lipstick on the filters, a dirty teacup and saucer, a glass with lipstick on the rim, a plate with a knife and a wrinkled brown slice of apple. Our camp was tidier than this.

The wall behind the settee was piled high with cardboard boxes with names printed over them: *Royal Standard, Remington, Imperial*. In a corner by the window there was a wooden chair and a sewing table, the sewing machine stowed away beneath it and a typewriter taking its place, loaded with a few sheets of paper with carbons between them. It was surrounded by little bottles of correcting fluid, reels of red and black ribbon a scatter of paper clips and piles of typed papers.

"That's what I do." She said. "Secretarial. Touch-typing. Eighty words a minute. And I can spell really well. Don't need too much of that." She waved at the correcting fluid.

She teetered unsteadily to the other side of the room. In the corner opposite the settee, there was a television set, a brand new Decca with a big screen in a modern wooden cabinet on thin round legs. It had doors on the front that opened up and slid back beside the screen. It was the only clean thing in the room.

"Dez got it for me." She said, reaching for the cigarettes and matches on top of the cabinet.

Gran didn't have television but Uncle Solly did – a Bush 22-inch in black Bakelite, with a big magnifier on the front. He sometimes let us kids watch *Take Your Pick* and *I Love Lucy*. I didn't love Lucy at all. I thought she was stupid and had an annoying voice and her husband Rikky, from Cuba, seemed to me a bit... sleazy. In fact, he looked a lot like Dez. He even talked like Dez.

She lit a cigarette. "Filters" She said, waving the cigarette for my inspection. "Good for you. You know he's a nice man really, Dez. When you get to know him."

I didn't want to get to know him. I didn't want to get to know her either, but I had a million questions. "Where is my sis..."

She interrupted "Cup of tea?"

Before I could answer she stumbled over to the kitchen corner.

With the cigarette wiggling up and down in the corner of her mouth, her eyes screwed up against the smoke, she chattered over the clattering of her tea making. I stood near her.

She filled a kettle from the geyser on the wall, popped the whistle on, moved one of the pans from the hob, dropped the kettle in its place and lit the gas. I wanted to know about my sister Carol.

"Dez's gonna get me one of them new electric ones – boil a pint of water in a minute. Dez says nothing's too good for me. He worships me you know, under all that swank. It's all just show, for the boys. Inside he's a good man. Calls me his Princess. Treats me like a queen."

She took a white china teapot from the sink, emptied the dregs, and dropped it on the stainless steel draining board. She reached up and took a tea caddy from the shelf, rattled in the sink for a spoon, flipped three spoons of tea leaves into the pot. I wanted to know what happened to Jacqueline.

"He's getting us a new flat, a nice modern one in Golders Green. Just needs to sell a few more typewriters. Promised me a new electric one – Olivetti – much faster and quieter and better on the fingers. He's been looking out for me."

She fished two cups and saucers from the pile in the sink. She rinsed them quickly under the geyser and slapped them down on the draining board next to the teapot. I wanted to ask her about my real father.

"Dez can get anything you know. Get you a nice little portable if you like." She reached up to the shelves for a milk bottle. She splashed milk into the two cups, some of it spilling into the saucers.

"We're gonna have a real bathroom with a proper shower and everything modern – Formica kitchen, fitted carpets, everything. You'll like it Tommy. We'll have a spare room and you can come and stay. I'll teach you to type, come in handy when you're a professor."

She reached for a jam jar of sugar. She fumbled and dropped it. Sugar spilled in a wide arc as it fell and it crashed onto the draining board making the cups and saucers bounce. "Whoops!" She scooped some of the sugar back into the jar and sprinkled a handful between the two cups. I wanted to ask her why she left me behind.

"We're gonna be alright, you and me, Tommy. You can come over and we can go out for a drink with Jerry and the girls. You can meet some of my friends. They're good for a laugh. Dez'll take you to the dogs if you like, have a little flutter. Dez's OK. Not like other men. Most men are bastards. They use you for a house slave and play around with other women. They gamble your money away, hit you for doing nothing. But I know how to handle men like that.

"I know." I said, remembering what she'd written to Aunt Marlene.

"What do you know," She laughed. "You're just a kid!"

I wanted to tell her I knew more than she could ever guess.

"Not Dez though. He's OK. Wanna biscuit? New ones – Maryland Cookies. They're nice- bits of chocolate."

She dropped a biscuit in each saucer. The kettle began to whistle. She picked up a tea towel wrapped one end of it round the hot handle and lifted it off the gas. With her other hand she wrapped the other end round the whistle and pulled it off. She splashed the boiling water into the teapot and dropped the kettle back on the gas. The tea towel caught alight in one corner and she waved it around above her head trying to put out the flame but it flared up more.

"Oh shit! Oh bloody shit!" She cried breathing heavily, building into a panic.

This was getting dangerous. She could set her hair alight. I stepped towards her to help, but she'd already plunged the burning cloth into the sink, drowning the flames under the washing up water.

"Oh shit! If Dez finds out about this he'll kill me! You won't tell him, will you Tommy? You know what men are like. He's got a wicked temper on him. Anything will set him off. You won't tell?"

I suddenly felt I was in a scene from *I Love Lucy*. Scatterbrained Lucy had got herself into one of her daily disasters and had to sort it out fast before Rikki came home. Only this Lucy and Rikky were for real and they swore and smoked and drank and lived in a horrible mess and had dangerous gangsters for friends.

I shook my head. She turned off the gas. Put the lid on the teapot, lifted it and swirled it round for a few seconds. She found the tea strainer beside the taps, tapped the dregs out into the sink and she poured the tea. She crashed the teapot down and stirred both cups. She didn't notice the snake of ash at the end of her cigarette drop into one cup – the one she handed to me.

"Here you are, Tommy. Nice cuppa tea."

The door burst open. Sylvie froze. Dez stood in the frame for a moment. He said "Hi Honey I'm home!" in a fake Spanish-American accent – just like Rikky Ricardo.

He had a big crooked smile. His hair was tousled, his clothes in a mess. He had a red mark on his left cheek. When he saw me looking at it he wiped it away with the back of his hand. He winked at me and lurched forward between us, knocking the teacup from Sylvie's outstretched hand. I stepped back. The cup and saucer bounced across the lino and the tea splashed against their bedroom door. She stood with her mouth wide open and her dead cigarette dropped to the floor.

"You don't want tea. You want a proper drink." He bustled Sylvie out of the way and reached above the sink for glasses. He took down three tumblers and three bottles – gin, whisky and orange cordial.

"You go and sit down, Princess, and I'll bring you a drink. Orange for you, m'lud?"

Sylvie cleared a space on the settee and sat down at one end, patting the seat for me to sit beside her. I looked around for somewhere else but there was no alternative.

Dez came back with the drinks. He brushed the papers and books from the coffee table and placed the three glasses in front of us – one gin and two orange juices.

"Bloody books everywhere. Reading's all she's fucking good at. Reading and writing – all bloody words. Words, words, words. As if there aren't enough bloody words in the world. Still, suits me. They want more words, they have to buy more typewriters."

He dumped himself on the settee to my left. For a moment the three of us sat there reflected in the blank television screen – looking just like a scene from Lucy.

I was thirsty and reached for the orange juice. I took two or three gulps before I realized it tasted strange. Then I felt a burning in my throat and my head was spinning. I cried out and threw the glass away over the table.

"Your kid's drunk my fucking whisky!" Dez shouted.

"Don't mind, Tommy, it'll keep you warm on a cold night like this." She said.

The room was moving strangely. I felt sick. My face was burning. She fetched a glass of water and told me to drink the lot. I did, as fast as I could. To stop her fussing and breathing in my face, I pretended I was all right, although I felt really bad.

Dez went to the kitchen corner and heated up some curry and rice. I'd never had curry. She said he was from Malaya and he made fabulous curry. He brought back a plate for each of us. It looked and smelled wonderfully strange and tasted great at first but after a few mouthfuls my throat was on fire. I bolted down more water. Dez grinned.

My stomach, full of whisky and orange was not best prepared for spicy food. My head started spinning again and I ran to the kitchen and threw up in the sink full of dirty crockery. I was mortally embarrassed, being sick in front of these people. I pushed her away as she fussed around me. I grabbed a towel from her hand to clean myself up.

I was relieved when she said it was time they went to bed. She told me the toilet was upstairs on the next landing. She offered to go with me. I shouted "No!" and she backed off quickly.

I desperately need a pee, and although there were no lights outside I groped my way up the stairs. There was a door on the next landing. I pushed it open. There was no light. I had to grope around for the toilet. It smelled bad and I was glad I couldn't see anything. I found the bowl and peed in its general direction until I heard the splash and then tried to stay on target as much as I could. I groped around in the air for the chain but couldn't find it, gave up and made my way back downstairs.

Dez brought some blankets for me and they both went into the bedroom. I rolled myself up in a tight tube on the settee. I kept all my clothes on, even my shoes. My head was still strange from the whisky, and when I closed my eyes I felt the bed turning. I took deep breaths to stop being sick. It passed and soon I dropped into a very deep sleep.

I woke in the middle of the night to shouting in their room. I couldn't hear what they were arguing about, just the odd word from him "whore... bitch". I heard a slap and she yelped. Then it went silent. Then I heard low sounds like "ummmm", "Oh Dez", "ohhhh". Sounds like Davy said Mrs. Rosenberg did when she was doing it.

I lay awake, hearing their sounds, going through what had happened that night, trying to take the fear out of it. I thought about her and Frank in the caravan and my sister on the next bed. I didn't want to be there. It was a long night.

Before daylight, I got up to leave. I'd have sneaked out, but I had no bus fare and it was a long walk home in the cold and dark. I had to wait for her to get up.

At about six, she came from their room. There was a bruise over her right eye.

"What happened?" I asked.

"Oh, just a little tap. He was upset about my singing, gets jealous of my fans – shows how much he loves me. He likes you too, Tommy."

"Will he tap me, then?" I asked.

"Don't be daft. He likes you, said you can have a typewriter, for a Christmas present." She swept her arm towards the pile of cardboard boxes. "You can pick one out if you like." She said. I ignored her offer.

"Can I go home now?" I asked.

I couldn't wait to get out. She said it was too early. It was still dark. She offered breakfast. I was starving, but I refused. "Just some toast, eh?" she said, but I refused. She wanted to take me home, but I said I'd rather get the bus. I was adamant, so she gave me the bus fare. I grabbed my duffle bag and I ran from the flat as fast as I could, leaping down the stairs three at a time.

Outside it was raining heavily and I realized I'd left my mac upstairs. I wasn't going back for it, so I kept running. In a few seconds I was wet through. My jumper was soaked. My shirt was soaked.

I got to the main road. There was no bus. I walked through the dark streets for half an hour and then a bus came. I jumped on.

When I got home Gran was making tea for Granddad. "Tommy, you're soaked. Get those wet clothes off."

I told her I never wanted to see that woman again.

"What happened?" she asked.

"Nothing. She's just bad."

"You don't have to see her." Gran said, "I won't let her come here."

"Gran, did she give you money for a coat?" I asked.

"Did she say that?" Gran said, "She always was a liar. Never gave no one nothing. Just took everything. All she cares about is herself... and chasing after men."

"I hate her."

"Here, have some tea – warm you up." Gran said "Oh nearly forgot. Larry called round last night."

"What did he want?"

"He wrote it down."

She handed me a scrap of paper.

Larry had scribbled, "Tunnel tomorrow at 9." It was eight o'clock. I leaped down the stairs and threw off my soaked jumper. My white shirt was stained red and blue from the dye.

I remembered my shirt was dyed red once before – back in the Muller. It was the day after I'd desecrated Aaron's Big Picture Bible. We were on a special outing, down to Broadstairs Harbour. One of the teachers led us – a line of kids holding hands in pairs. We started out in bright sunshine, but got caught in the most terrible storm. The wind was strong enough to knock the smaller kids off their feet. The rain poured down like a river over a waterfall, not in drops, but in sheets. We were all soaked to the skin in seconds.

The sea was wild, with huge waves, higher than a house. They crashed high over the sea walls and flooded the promenade. We had to run away up a hill. I turned back to watch the storm. The huge stone jetty was shaking. "Look, Miss, look!" I shouted and all the kids turned to see the massive jetty detach with an explosive crack. An enormous wave broke it free and twisted it towards the shore. More waves broke over the sea wall, lifting cars and smashing them into the houses beside the promenade.

Despite the cold and wet, it was thrilling to see the fantastic power of the sea smashing what men had built – jetties, cars, and houses.

"Come on, follow me. Quickly now." The teacher made us march up the hill and kept us walking quickly all the way to the Home.

Later, when we stripped off, my shirt was stained bright red from my jumper. It looked like blood and it frightened me. It made me think that people were going to die. In the night I dreamed of people being smashed by flying cars and falling houses and I got sucked out into the sea by a huge wave.

The next day Matron told us the storm was the worst ever known and thousands of people were killed and made homeless all over the South and East of England. We had to say special prayers for the victims and their families. I felt terribly guilty. It was the most thrilling thing I had ever seen. It was marvelous. It was a miracle. But lots of people were dead and perhaps it was my fault because I tore Aaron's bible or because I enjoyed the spectacle. Perhaps I made them die.

I looked at the red and blue dye marks on my shirt and felt the same as I did after the storm. I secretly loved the smog but it killed cows in the market, birds in the air, old people and little babies and lots of people coughed their lungs inside out and died and some of them didn't even say goodbye. Things that made me excited made other people die.

I remembered Larry's message and threw the shirt on to the chair under the window. I changed into dry clothes and ran upstairs.

"See you later Gran." I shouted "Going to Larry's" and I ran off.

The Tunnel of Death

Every year, at the start of the Christmas holidays, we challenged the Ropery kids to a Tunnel Race. It was the culmination of weeks of preparation that usually started just before Guy Fawkes Night.

During the build up to 5th November, we'd try to set fire to each other's bonfires. We'd set guards in the evenings and usually caught the other gang in the act, so most years the fires survived until the big night.

To keep us occupied during guard sessions, we'd build go-carts from bonfire wood.

There were always a few prams on the debris, and the Eric Street Engineers – Ronny and Larry would dismantle the axles and wheels. Ronny would borrow tools from his dad, some pipe brackets and screws to fit the axles. Larry would pick out a good plank for a chassis and burn holes in the wood with a red-hot poker, so we could bolt on the wheels.

We'd nail on an orange box seat and fix some string to steer the front wheels and we'd have a two-man go-cart. I would sneak an oilcan from Vinny's bedroom and we'd grease everything that moved. After hours of discussion, we'd choose a name and paint it on the back. This year we called it the Dan Dare. I painted Dan Dare's face – well, it was a red blob really, but *we* knew it was Dan Dare.

Eric Street and Ropery Street were a few hundred yards apart, but they were like two separate countries. Larry lived in Ropery Street but he played mostly with us, so he was part of the Eric Street gang. We were the cowboys and Ropery Street were the Indians. We were the English and they were the Germans.

When I got to Larry's the rest of the gang was already there. We did some final work on the cart and set off for the tunnel. We had to get there early before the traffic built up.

Viv, Larry and I walked ahead. Errol and Davy followed ten yards behind. "Where were you yesterday," Larry asked. "I called round."

"You won't believe it if I tell you." I said.

The dark happenings of the day before were lurking in a black cloud in my head. Ugly faces I wanted to forget would flash into sight as if lit by lightening. Frightening events rolled over and over like thunder. I was afraid to say anything. I didn't want to make it real by talking about it. I didn't want to disgust my friends or make them think badly of me. I knew I wouldn't be able to forget the experience or dissipate my feelings, but I needed temporary relief. I needed a different story.

"What?" Viv asked.

"Secret." I said, gesturing back towards Davy and Errol.

"Secret." she said.

"I met my mother."

"But she's in America." Viv said.

"No she's not, stupid," Larry said, "she came back on a boat."

"She's here." I said. "And I met Jesus!"

"Liar!" Larry laughed.

"No, really!" I said.

Viv skipped ahead of me walking backwards. "Tell us. Tell us."

I told them about coming home from school and having a laugh with Jesus on the bus, and how Sylvie jumped out of the fog. How she was drunk and smoked, and had this sneer on her face and yellow teeth and bad breath. How she took me to a pub full of gangsters and men who tried to grab me. I told them how she drank loads of gin and went on the stage and sang and the men tried to put their hands up her dress. How her foreign boyfriend got beaten up and robbed at the bar and how we had to escape and ran up the alley to their disgusting flat. How he made me drink a whole glass of whisky and eat red-hot curry and I was sick in the sink. I told them about the screaming in the night and how he beat her up for singing and then they did it right next-door and it was disgusting and how I escaped at dawn and ran all the way home in the freezing rain and told my Gran I never wanted to see her again.

I was lost inside the story. Viv and Larry had listened silent, wide-eyed, and... so had I. I had been listening to the story tell itself from my mouth – a story close to the truth, but like a play about someone else. I suddenly came back and saw two mates staring at me. I felt guilty for exaggerating and I knew they wouldn't believe me.

"What?" I asked, fearing I might have said too much, that they might be disgusted.

"Blimey!" Larry said

"Bli-mey!" Viv said.

Davy and Errol caught up and crashed into us on purpose. We bundled for a while and continued towards the docks.

When we arrived. Larry's cousin Tony Abrahams and three kids I didn't know turned up jeering and cocky at the mouth of the tunnel. Their go-cart was decorated with skull and crossbones and called Black Death. It looked a lot better than ours.

Two boys rode each cart – the heaviest in the back for ballast and the lightest in the front for steering. Larry was a year older than me and big boned with steel hard stringy muscles. He was the most solid person I knew. He punched me in the face once and it felt like walking into a lamppost.

Larry sat behind me. Abrahams steered for his team with Nathan Isaacs – the stamp swapper for ballast. Once we were in our seats and at the start line we shouted in unison,

"Ready, steady, go!"

The first section of the tunnel is a long downhill run. Errol and Davy pushed us, and in a few seconds, the Dan Dare was well up to speed. Ronny gave up first and then both the Ropery Street ground crew. But there was something about Davy that could make him explode with wild energy when he got excited. It was as if he switched on his booster rockets. While the others fell away panting, he just raced us faster and faster and when his feet couldn't keep up, he yelled "Dan Dare, pilot of the future! Into the Tunnel of Death!" and gave one last shove. He jerked us off course a bit but gave us an early lead as we raced downhill into the tunnel. The Dan Dare had bigger wheels and a heavier chassis than Black Death. Gravity and all that grease worked to our advantage and we were soon 10 yards ahead.

We hadn't yet invented the brake, so we relied on Larry dragging his feet to control the speed. This worked fine at lower speeds. Hot shoe leather burned and nails sparked against the asphalt enhancing the illusion of speed. But as we flew faster and faster, the slightest contact between shoe and ground sent his legs flying dangerously, so we pulled in arms and legs and held on tight to the steering ropes.

The Ropery kids had hand brakes on both back wheels – wooden levers bolted to either side of their orange box. The ballast rider could pull one end of the lever and the other rubbed against the wheel. This gave them control at much higher speeds than our crude method and it was beginning to pay off. Black Death was rapidly catching up and about to overtake us. Abrahams made Messerschmitt engine noises. Isaacs shouted, "Bandits at 5 O'clock!" and machine-gunned us, "Uh-uh-uh-uh-uh-uh-uh-uh!"

For a moment they were the enemy. I didn't see Abrahams and Isaacs, I saw Dez slapping my mother's face. I saw Frank beating her by the roadside. I saw Malinski cuffing kids in the playground. I didn't hear the yells of kids, but the screams of women and babies.

We were halfway down the slope and going flat out and they were gaining on us. We had no chance. Our wheels wobbled. Larry and I knew what was next. With equal measure of fear and determination, I pulled hard on the steering rope and I locked my skinny legs against the amplifying wobble, but in a moment I lost control and we were snaking wildly from kerb to kerb.

Just as Ropery Street drew level, we slewed across in front of them. Our back wheels clipped their front wheels and they turned sharply –

too sharply. Their cart veered off to the right and scudded to a halt against the kerb. The two Luftwaffe pilots were flicked off, and rolled for another ten yards to stop in a heap of bloody knees, elbows and curses in the gutter.

We didn't fare much better. We slammed front-on into the kerb, somersaulted over the front wheels and smashed against the tunnel wall bashing our heads together on landing. Dazed and disoriented I saw two policemen towering above me. I heard a baby's cry echoing in the distance. I felt my face swollen like a melon, my body sore and wet with blood. The cops leered down like phantoms, swimming in and out of my tears. They spoke like the Lone Ranger.

"Well look at all this rubbish on our nice clean highway!"

"Trailer trash. Throw him in the car and we'll take him to the dump."

It was Wayne and Earl. When I named them, they disappeared and my mind cleared. Larry's weight crushed me back to gravity and my leg, jammed in the steering mechanism of the cart, brought me back to pain – real pain.

Larry moaned and rolled to the pavement. I rolled the other way and freed my trapped leg. There was a raw weal where it had been pinched between the steering arm and the chassis, but no blood. I was OK, but Larry's head was bloody and he lay still, moaning. Then he went quiet. I crawled over to him and pulled his head around to see if he was OK. He had a gash over his eyebrow and blood covered half his face. His eyes were closed, his mouth dropped loose.

He was dead! I killed him! It was all my fault. I lost control of the cart. I've killed my best mate. Wayne and Earl returned. "We'll take him, Son. He can take a ride with us. In the trunk."

"Larry!" My scream echoed through the tunnel. "Laaaaary!"

He twitched. His eyes flicked open and he sat up.

"Did we win?" His only concern was who was in front. He scanned the accident scene, worked out the slope of the road. Black Death was about ten yards uphill

"Victoreeee!" He whooped, "Dan Dare beats the Black Death!"

It was only on the long walk back, dragging our busted carts that we noticed the blood soaking our jumpers.

Lorries thundered by as we meandered up the road, singing and shouting "Victoreeee!" Larry missed his footing, tripped off the pavement and veered into the road, as a coal lorry clattered up the hill. Without thinking, I reached out and pulled him back and the lorry missed by inches.

"Thanks, mate!" he said with a big grin, and threw his arm over my shoulder. We staggered and tripped our way back to Larry's.

"Hear about the old tramp?" Larry asked.

"What?"

"That smelly Old William bloke. He's dead."

"What!"

"Joan told me. Yesterday. They dragged him out of the cut. Said it was the fog. He couldn't see a blind thing. Walked right into the Grand Union."

Poor William. I didn't say goodbye to him, nobody did. We walked on in silence for a while.

"'ere, Tommy you crying?"

"No – got dust in my eyes."

"Well," Larry said, "You found your mum."

"Yea, and now she can get lost again."

"You can't mean that. She's your mum."

"No, she made her choices. She chose not to be my mum or anybody's mum. She left me and she left my sisters. Now it's my turn to choose."

"What you gonna do?"

"I'm going to leave her. Leave her under the floor."

"What?"

"I'm going to find my sister. That's what."

"Blimey!"

I wanted to get home to see Granddad. When I walked in, I wanted him to say, "My Tommy, you've been in the wars." and then I'd tell him all about the race. And then I'd ask him to help me find my sister.

Granddad Comes Home Late

On Saturdays Granddad usually came home from the park around one o'clock for dinner. I ran home from Larry's in time to meet him. But he didn't turn up.

Gran, Vinny and I waited for an hour and he still didn't come.

Vinny went to the phone box outside the station and called Uncle Solly.

Uncle Solly drove round with Aunt Marlene, Connie and Sarah.

We waited another half hour and then Uncle Solly said, "Better go and find him." and he left in his motor.

It was another hour before Uncle Solly returned with Granddad.

"Found him." Uncle Solly said, "Went all the way to the park and back again and found him sitting on the kerb, corner of Burdett Road. He's been knocked down."

I remembered my own accident with the Austin 7.

Granddad climbed slowly down from the car and brushed away Aunt Marlene and Gran who tried to hold him up. "I'm all right", he said, "Stop bloody fussing. I've still got two bloody legs, ain't I?"

But he let them support him either side until they reached the door and hustled him down the passage to Gran's bedroom. They went in and closed the door. I squatted on the floor in the passage with my back to the wall.

Later the doctor came. He went into Gran's room and came out after fifteen minutes.

"What's wrong with Dad?" I asked.

"Oh, don't you worry, Tommy" the doctor said, "He was knocked down by a motorbike, but he's got a strong constitution. He'll be all right."

A few days later Granddad went back to work. But he wasn't himself. Nothing much – he just didn't smile or joke like usual.

On Christmas Eve the whole family came round and we decorated the basement with coloured paper chains and paper bells and Uncle Sammy brought a Christmas tree that he stood in front of the coal cellar and we covered it with red and silver globes and tinsel. Everyone brought cards and we arranged them on the sideboard and we draped yards and yards of tinsel around the mirrors and family photos.

We had a huge feast with turkey and stuffing and Brussels sprouts and baked potatoes and mashed potatoes and peas and Christmas pudding and custard. Aunt Marlene kept smiling at me across the room

– perhaps to let me know she knew about Sylvie and what happened when I met her – perhaps to assure me everything was all right.

Aunty Hannah took me aside.

"You all right, Tommy?"

"Yes, Aunt Hannah."

"So your mum's back." She said.

"No, she's gone for good." I said.

She raised her eyebrows, then smiled and put her arm round my shoulder. "One day, you might find it in her heart to forgive her." She said.

"What for?"

"For being human." She said.

I shrugged.

"Come on, kids" said Uncle Sammy, "Let's have a sing song." He gathered up all the cousins into an untidy mob and conducted us in Jingle Bells. Everyone joined in and we sang through the easy verses of every Christmas Carol we knew.

The men laughed and drank more than usual and some of the women lifted their skirts and pranced around. But Granddad was quiet. He didn't drink his pale ale and he didn't sing.

At about ten o'clock, Granddad left the front room to go to the toilet . By now the men were well into their game of Klabyash and the women were chattering, when Aunt Hannah suddenly sat bolt upright with her eyes wide, pointing towards the living room door. She mouthed some words, but nothing came out. Her face was white. Those who had noticed looked to the door. Aunt Marlene and Vinny both caught their breaths and their mouths dropped open. I followed their stares but saw just a little cigarette smoke wafting in the draft.

"Oh my God!" Aunt Hannah said, and Aunt Marlene covered her face in her hands. Vinny looked shocked, and turned to Aunt Hannah, as did everyone else.

"It was Katy!" she said, "Did you see her?"

Aunt Marlene nodded quickly.

Vinny said, "She said something."

"What did she say then, Vinny?" Sammy jeered "Put some more coal on the fire, it's bloody cold on the other side!"

The men laughed.

Aunt Hannah and Aunt Marlene both said, "Don't leave me behind."

"That's it." Vinny said.

Granddad stepped back into the momentarily silent room and stood in the doorway, in the cigarette smoke, where Katy had stood. Everyone stared at him. "What's up with you lot?" he joked, "Seen a bloody ghost?"

Aunt Marlene opened her mouth to speak but froze in Uncle Solly's glare. Sammy broke the silence. "Come on Dad, I need some help here. I've got a lousy bloody hand." He swung Granddad's chair around and banged a glass of beer down in his place. Granddad sat and lit a Woodbine, and the evening continued as if nothing had happened.

When I woke on Christmas day, Granddad wasn't there. Vinny said he'd been taken to hospital. For the first time it was just me and Gran and Vinny.

The doctors later told Gran that Granddad had cancer of the bowel. Gran thought it might have been brought on by the shock of the accident. He was very ill. He was in Mile End hospital for a week and I wasn't allowed to see him.

The next Friday was my twelfth birthday but I didn't want to think about birthdays. Nor did anyone else. Gran and Vinny forgot, but I wasn't surprised or upset. On Saturday morning Granddad didn't come to my room as usual to sneak me some extra pocket money and tell me a joke.

On Saturday night, the family came round. The men drove the aunts back and forward to the hospital in shifts. I asked Aunt Hannah if I could see Granddad.

"It's not a good idea." She said.

"But I want to see him. Please!"

The Aunts and Uncles had a consultation.

"He's got as much right to see Dad as we have." Uncle Solly said.

Vinny drove Gran and me to the hospital in the Austin. I took a bunch of Christmas bananas from the sideboard. He liked bananas. The journey there is a blank. All I remember is my Granddad in a white nightshirt, in white sheets, on a high metal bed, surrounded by white screens. My Uncles and Aunts came to the bed two by two and left with sad faces.

I wanted them out of the way. I couldn't wait to see him. I thought if I gave him enough love, I could make him well again. I could save him, like he saved me and my sisters.

"Come on, Tommy," Aunt Hannah put her arm round my shoulder and walked me to the bedside.

Granddad was far away. His body was thin. His face was a shadow – yellow and collapsed. He had no expression. He dribbled a little. His chin trembled. His deep brown eyes were clouded yellow, grey, like the smog. I knew he was going. I was frightened and I wanted to turn away, but I could see that Gran wanted me to say something – for her, not for him. "Here, Dad," I said, "I brought you a banana."

I held it out to him, feeling foolish. He made a tiny moan, hardly more than a breath. Then he turned his head very slowly to me and looked towards my face. From a million miles away his fading eyes searched for me. And then he saw me. His pupils dilated and he stared into me. I fell into his gaze. I was no longer outside him. I was inside, looking out. Like the stag in the forest, like my sister in the photo. From his eyes, I saw Tommy, a small, frightened, curious boy. I heard him singing like he always did,

> *"I leave the sunshine to the flowers. I leave the raindrops to the trees. I leave the moon above, to those in love. When I leave the world behind. When I leave the world behind."*

He was leaving all that to me. But he was leaving me! I screamed out inside and perhaps outside, I don't know.

"Don't leave me, Granddad! Please, don't leave me behind!"

But he drew me back and I felt his love bathe me in sharp sunlight that burned up every dark shadow. I saw through his eyes a boy like Tommy, but different – a boy with Granddad's strength and courage, his intelligence and resourcefulness, his humility and compassion, his kindness and his humour. I knew these were his gifts to me.

I knew then he wasn't leaving a small boy behind, abandoned or rejected. He was leaving me behind like he left the sunshine and the flowers, as his parting gift to the world.

He had saved me, protected me, cared for me through unconscious infancy and curious childhood and now my eyes were open and my mind was awake. His last job in this world was to pass on to me what was good in him, and to tell me I was to be the gift he left behind. I leaned close to his face and whispered, "I love you Granddad. Thank you for looking after me."

His eyes closed.

His breathing stopped.

He was gone.

I panicked. I couldn't let him go. I grabbed his shoulders and buried my face in his chest. I chased after him, down a long dark tunnel, reaching out to drag him back, but as fast as I ran, he floated faster ahead into distance, darkness and silence. I stared at his empty body for minutes.

I didn't know I was crying, until I noticed the banana in my hand was wet with tears. I folded the ridiculous offering into his thin dead hand, feeling foolish and alone. He was the most important person in my life and the first person that died.

"Tommy."

I spun round surprised to see Gran and Vinny. I was suddenly dazzled by the white screens in the white room, my ears battered by the clatter of nurses' heels on polished floors and the smell of disinfectant hit my head like raw ammonia.

This place was nothing to do with my Granddad. I walked quickly away from the bed.

Gran reached out to take my hand. But I pulled away. I wanted to tell her that I knew all the things she had been keeping secret from me. I wanted to shout everything I knew out loud and shame her in front of the family and the nurses and doctors. I wanted to punish her for sending my mother away and for letting her come back, for giving my sisters away and for hiding their existence from me. I wanted to throw all her secrets in her face.

I looked at her face. It was soft. All the years of heartache and pain were erased for a moment. There were tears in her eyes and for the first time I could remember, she was smiling at me and I realized that anything I had to say would only bring the heartache back and I realized that anyway she knew what I knew and it was all right now and there was nothing I needed to say.

She said "Your Grandad loved you." and I said, "I know, Gran." and for the first time I took her hand and felt its soft warmth and for the first time Vinny placed his hand gently on my shoulder.

Aunt Hannah came over. She knelt down in front of me and pulled me to her. She hugged me close for a long time. Then she held my face in both hands and she said, "You know, I love you Tommy. You will come and see me again?"

I nodded.

That night, 1956 finished without a party and 1957 began in the dark.

At midnight I sat on Poor Dead Katy's chair where Granddad used to sit and although I knew I was now entirely on my own in this world, fatherless and motherless, I could feel his ghost inside me.

I held my sister's photo in the light from the street lamp. She looked at me with that big wide smile and I decided. "I'm coming to find you."

And as, I found out later, at that very same moment she promised to find me.

EPILOGUE

Tommy Angel's life includes much of my own and here's what happened next in real life.

My Grandmother died soon after Granddad, and my uncle and I were evicted from the house in Eric Street. The council gave us a prefab where we lived for a few years. I did fine at school, but half-way through sixth form, I caught tuberculosis and spent a year in a sanatorium. I returned to live with my uncle until I secured a place at teacher training college.

I've kept in touch with three of my closest friends from Eric Street, who grew up to be engineers. Most of my cousins got married and had babies in Essex. My aunts and uncles have all died except my lovely Aunt Lillian.

My sister Carol and I searched for each other for years and finally after a series of small miracles, she tracked me down. I was 37 years old, head teacher of a primary school, married with two lovely children. One evening the phone rang. "Hi I'm your sister." Everything changed in that moment. When we met, I saw in her all that was beautiful in my mother – all that had been spoiled or destroyed and I was freed of a fear I'd carried all my life – that I might inherit Sylvie's darkness. Carol is married to the kindest man and they have a loving family. My sister and I have a deep bond of love. Not a love that's chosen, but a love that's a given. No matter how life unfolds, we will belong with each other.

Around the time my sister appeared I met the greatest love of my life who is now my wife and my best friend.

We've tried to track down my younger sister Jacqueline, who was sent to South Africa, but with no luck.

In the sixties, the Victorian terraces of Eric Street were demolished and replaced with flats, and that's where Sylvie returned to live out her last years in a ground floor flat in a high-rise. My sister, my wife and I tried to bring her into our families, but it was difficult. She was full of resentment and blamed her children for ruining her life.

In 2001, at the age of 73, her body gave way and she died in London Hospital. My wife and I were with her at the end, and my sister came to her bedside and, although it was the hardest thing for either of us to say, the last very words Sylvie heard as she left this life were,

"I love you, Mum."

- Robert Hart, 2009

Printed in Great Britain
by Amazon